HISS ME
DEADLY

A Cat in the Stacks Mystery

HISS ME DEADLY

Miranda James

Berkley Prime Crime
New York

BERKLEY PRIME CRIME
Published by Berkley
An imprint of Penguin Random House LLC
penguinrandomhouse.com

Copyright © 2023 by Dean James

Library of Congress Cataloging-in-Publication Data

Names: James, Miranda, author.
Title: Hiss me deadly / Miranda James.
Description: New York: Berkley Prime Crime, [2023] |
Series: Cat in the stacks mysteries
Identifiers: LCCN 2023000961 (print) | LCCN 2023000962 (ebook) |
ISBN 9780593199497 (hardcover) | ISBN 9780593199503 (ebook)
Subjects: LCGFT: Detective and mystery fiction. | Novels.
Classification: LCC PS3610.A43 H57 2023 (print) |
LCC PS3610.A43 (ebook) | DDC 813/.6—dc23/eng/20230113
LC record available at https://lccn.loc.gov/2023000961
LC ebook record available at https://lccn.loc.gov/2023000962

Printed in the United States of America
1st Printing

Book design by Tiffany Estreicher

For Susan Burch Clark,
who gave me a lifeline and put up
with me for eight years,
my profound thanks and deep affection.

HISS ME
DEADLY

ONE

||||||||||||||||||||||

I frowned at Melba Gilley, my coworker and longtime friend. "Sorry, I just don't remember anybody called Wil Threadgill."

Melba returned my frown with a scowl. "Honestly, Charlie, I wonder about your memory sometimes. Maybe you ought to be taking one of those supplements they're always going on about on television."

Diesel, my Maine Coon cat, chirped loudly and moved against my leg. He apparently didn't like Melba's tone.

"I don't have your encyclopedic memory for everyone who has lived and died in Athena, Mississippi, over the past fifty-odd years," I replied, trying to keep my tone even. "Remember, I was gone for twenty-five years." I rubbed Diesel's head to reassure him that I was fine.

"True," Melba said grudgingly. The scowl receded, to be replaced by a thoughtful expression. "Do you remember *Fred* Threadgill?"

I thought for a moment. That name did ring a bell. "Yes, I think so," I said, drawing out the words. "Wasn't he in high school with us? But a little older?"

Melba nodded. "That's Wil."

"So Fred is Wil?" I asked, still puzzled.

I ignored the eye roll.

"His name was Wilfred," Melba said. "He never liked anyone to call him Wilfred, so he went by Fred back in high school."

"When did he become Wil?" I had vague memories of a tall, skinny, redheaded guy who never had much to say to anyone. He'd always seemed to be lost in his own little world.

"When he went to California and became a famous musician," Melba said, a note of triumph in her voice.

"Okay, but why am I supposed to have heard of Wil Threadgill?"

I could see that Melba was again trying to hold on to her temper. I wasn't deliberately trying to aggravate her. My knowledge of the California music scene was fairly limited, despite the fact that my daughter Laura had spent several years there trying to establish her acting career. I knew the famous names, of course, like Meryl Streep, Robert De Niro, and Diane Keaton, as well as the greats from the Golden Age, like Katharine Hepburn, Cary Grant, Bette Davis, and Jimmy Stewart. But musicians? Not so much, unless they were from the sixties and seventies, like the Supremes, the Beatles, ABBA, and the Carpenters.

"He's been nominated for an Oscar and a Golden Globe for film scores," Melba said.

"That's impressive," I replied. "But I never watch those award shows. I guess that's why I didn't recognize his name." I hadn't been to the movies in I didn't know how long. My late wife, Jackie, and I used to go occasionally, but neither of us was a big movie buff. We both preferred Golden Age Hollywood in all its glamour. I reminded Melba of this.

She sniffed. She was an avid moviegoer and knew who all the current stars were, who wrote the movies' scores, and probably even who the best boy was, or other trivia. "I'll let it pass this time," she said, her tone mock severe. She pulled out her phone, tapped on it several times, then thrust it at me. "This is Wil."

I took the phone, and Diesel warbled. Surely he didn't want to look at the phone. I patted his head as I examined the photograph of Wil Threadgill.

The long red hair, streaked liberally with gray, hung well past his shoulders. His thin face and shy smile recalled the high school loner to my memory. "His hair style hasn't changed much, but I remember the face." I gave the phone back to Melba. "I didn't know him well. He always seemed like he wasn't really in the present."

Melba sighed as she gazed at the picture. "I don't like that long hair, but if you block some of it out, you can see Wil almost the way he was back then." She put her phone away suddenly. "Wil has always been a dreamer. A misfit, too, I guess. He never felt like he really belonged here."

"A conservative, small Southern town," I suggested. "When he wanted to rock and roll." Diesel warbled again.

"Something like that," Melba said. "I had such a crush on him. He was a sweet guy, and we were friends, sort of. I think I was as close to him as any other girl was, but all he was really interested in was music."

"Did he have a band?" I asked. "In high school, that is."

Melba nodded. "There were four of them. They got together in the eleventh grade. Called themselves Southern Drawl."

I laughed, and Melba grimaced.

"Yeah, not a great name," Melba said. "It wasn't Wil's choice. The other three outvoted him. They played some gigs around here, but then Wil just up and disappeared one day. It was right after school let out for the year. He never came back for his senior year."

"He went straight to California?" I asked. "What about his family here?"

"There was only his daddy, and they didn't get along," Melba said. "His daddy died about twenty years ago. I thought Wil might come home for the funeral, but he didn't."

"That's sad," I said. "He really had no other ties here."

"No strong ones anyway," Melba said. "He actually wrote to me that fall he went to California and told me where he was," Melba said. "A short note, that was all, but he included his address. Asked me to keep it to myself, and I did." She shrugged. "I wrote him every once in a while, and sometimes he'd answer. He moved a lot, and then finally I stopped getting letters from him."

Having known Melba since we were kids, I knew she had been hurt by this. She was the most loyal person I knew, and I figured she might have been in love with the guy. I heard a trace of pain in her tone as she talked about him. "I'm sorry," I said.

Melba shrugged again. "It was a long time ago, and I got over him. I haven't thought much about him for over twenty years, except hearing him on the radio or seeing his name pop up in the credits at the movies." Diesel moved close to her and rubbed against her legs. She smiled and stroked his head.

"What brought him to your mind again, then?"

My question earned me a trademarked Melba snort of exasperation. "Charlie, don't you *ever* read the campus newsletter? The announcements from the president's office?"

"Sometimes, but since I'm not full time, I don't pay a lot of attention to anything other than library news or the theater department." My son-in-law, Frank Salisbury, served as head of the department, and my daughter Laura, his wife, was a faculty member in it.

"Wil's getting an honorary degree," Melba said, "and he's going to be here in a couple of weeks conducting clinics with students in the music department."

"Not bad for a guy who never finished high school," I said, and I meant it.

Melba narrowed her eyes at me, but evidently satisfied that I wasn't attempting sarcasm, she nodded. "He's done really well. With talent like that, he had to succeed."

"Did he ever get married?"

"Not that I know of," Melba said.

"Is he gay?" I asked.

Melba considered that for a moment. "No, I don't think so. He went out with a few girls that I can remember. I reckon he's just not the settling-down type. I could be wrong. He might arrive with a couple of women in tow. You never know about these Hollywood types."

I wondered if Melba was still carrying a torch for Wil Threadgill after all these years. She had never had much luck with men, and that always surprised me. She was a good, loving, smart woman, but maybe *too* smart and *too* good for the men she encountered in Athena, Mississippi.

Melba was like a sister to me, in many ways, and yet I hesitated to ask her right out, *Are you in love with him still?*

She solved my dilemma by suddenly telling me, "I think I'm still in love with him, Charlie. Otherwise the thought of seeing him again wouldn't have me all discombobulated like a teenager. Isn't that the stupidest thing you ever heard?"

I shook my head. "First loves are always special. I don't know that you ever truly get over them."

Melba shot me a sympathetic glance. She knew my first love was my late wife, Jackie, who died of pancreatic cancer several years ago. We had been devoted to each other, and I still missed her, though I had made my peace with her death. I had even found another woman whom I loved, my dear Helen Louise Brady. We were engaged to be married, if we could ever agree on where to live after the ceremony.

"I kept hoping he'd come back," Melba said, and her wistful tone made my heart ache for her. "But he never did. He would always sign his letters *Love, Fred,* and then later, *Love, Wil,* but I learned not to take that literally."

"I'm sure he did love you, as far as he was capable," I said. Almost as if on cue, Diesel trilled loudly. "Artists who are that driven to succeed can suppress a lot. They also sacrifice a lot. He is the poorer for not ever coming back to you, or inviting you to come to California."

Melba turned away, and I knew she had teared up. She couldn't stand to let anyone see her in what she considered a moment of weakness. I pulled some tissues out of the box on my desk, got up, and took them to her, pushing them into her hand. She didn't look at me, and I returned to my chair. When she faced me again, she had regained her composure.

"Thank you. He wrote me a couple weeks ago." She stopped abruptly.

I waited a moment, but she remained silent.

"What did he have to say?" I asked. Diesel remained by her side, his head on her lap. She stroked him absentmindedly.

Melba frowned. "It was an odd letter. He acted like we hadn't lost touch all those years. Maybe in his mind, we hadn't. He sounded like the same old Wil, for the most part."

"But?" I prompted her when she fell quiet again.

Melba's gaze met mine and held it. "The last bit of the letter has been worrying me. Wil said he thought coming back might be a bad mistake. Stirring up old feelings and causing unhappiness. He said things might get ugly."

"What things?" I asked, rather disturbed by this.

"He didn't say," Melba replied. "He might be talking about the guys in the band. He did leave them in the lurch right as they were getting some decent gigs."

"That's nearly forty years ago," I said. "Surely they're not still angry with him after all this time."

Melba shrugged. "Sounds ridiculous, I know, but some people hold grudges a long time."

"He might have to face them and apologize," I said, "and that wouldn't be pleasant. Surely he's man enough to do that."

"I sure hope so," Melba said. "But I know one of the guys from the band, and he's the one I'm afraid of."

"Why? What do you think he might do?" I asked.

"Kill Wil," Melba said, and her obvious sincerity shook me.

TWO

"You sound awfully sure," I said. "Who is the guy you believe might want to harm Wil Threadgill?"

"John Earl Whitaker," Melba said, her tone flat. "I doubt you know him. He graduated four years ahead of us, and just barely at that. He was in trouble a lot of the time." Her expression grew hard. "His family was about as sorry as they come. Drunk, shiftless, can't hold a job, you name it."

I didn't know this paragon of society, or his family. Didn't sound like I'd ever want to, in fact. Melba could be hard on folks sometimes, but she was truthful. These Whitakers must be a pretty useless lot.

"John Earl is still around?" I asked.

"You may have seen him once in a while at an intersection near the highway." Melba sighed. "He begs, saying he's homeless, all that crap with a pathetic little cardboard sign. Police or sheriff's deputies eventually run him off, but he turns up again at another spot after a week or two. He probably ends up taking money away from real homeless people who really could use the help."

"That's sad," I said.

Melba snorted. "No, it's not, he's just too damn lazy to get jobs and stick to 'em." Her face softened suddenly. "The truly decent one is John Earl's wife, Natalie. She cleans here on campus during the week, and on weekends I think she cleans people's houses. Used to do housekeeping at the Farrington House. She works really hard."

"That's good," I said. "At least they're not starving."

"If it weren't for Natalie, they would be," Melba said darkly. "I swear John Earl'd rather starve than work as long as he can get drunk. He gave up on music sometime after Wil left town. He blamed Wil for every bad thing that happened to him after that." She snorted. "When he's drunk enough, he gets up in the front of whatever bar he's in and starts singing, though. Fancies himself as Elvis, I hear."

"That's stupid," I said. "Wil may have abandoned his friends, but I can't see why that would have ruined their lives."

"That's John Earl all over. Can't accept responsibility for anything. It's always someone else's fault." Melba gave Diesel one last head rub before she stood. "I'd better get back downstairs. I've got work to do."

I watched Diesel amble around my desk and crawl up into the window embrasure behind me. He loved to watch birds and squirrels in the trees nearby.

Melba waved and headed out the door. I heard her footsteps on the stairs as she hurried down to her first-floor office here in the library administration building. An antebellum home that had once belonged to a prominent Athena family, the building had come to Athena College in the late 1800s. Now it housed the library director's office, along with my office, the rare book collection, and the college archives. Several of the downstairs rooms sometimes hosted small meetings or the occasional cocktail party for fund-raising.

I needed to get back to work on the old books I was cataloging, but instead I found my mind stuck on all that Melba had told me about Wil Threadgill and his erstwhile friend, John Earl Whitaker. Melba wasn't prone to exaggeration—at least, most of the time she wasn't—but I had to wonder about her description of Whitaker. He might be every bit as worthless as she said, but to hold a grudge for so long, and over a high school band that fell apart—well, that seemed extreme to me.

I thought her nerves were betraying her. I could tell she was eager to see Wil Threadgill again. She said she was still in love with him, but was she really in love with only the *memory* of him? After all, she hadn't seen him in over forty years. I was inclined to discount her fears about John Earl Whitaker. Other than trying to embarrass Wil Threadgill in a public setting, I doubted he would do anything worse. Perhaps Melba's feelings for Wil made her overly anxious.

On a sudden whim I checked my work email, and I found the message from the president's office about the imminent return of Wil Threadgill to Athena. Though Wil had never been a student at the college, he had nevertheless done his hometown proud with his achievements. The college planned to award him an honorary doctorate in music at the conclusion of his stay as the guest artist in the music department.

I didn't begrudge Wil Threadgill any of this because he had obviously worked hard to survive and thrive in California's vibrant music scene, not to mention Hollywood. My concern focused on Melba and the effect that his return would have on her. I didn't want her to be hurt, but I knew that I couldn't do anything to prevent that. I simply needed to watch and wait and be there, if necessary, to pick up the pieces once Wil Threadgill went back to California.

That decided, I focused on my work at hand. For about three minutes, then my office phone rang.

I identified myself, and a cool voice with a definite Southern drawl spoke in my ear. "Please hold a moment for President Wyatt. He wants to talk to you."

I managed to say I would hold, stunned by the fact that the college president would soon be on the line. I rarely came into contact with him, though I knew he respected me based on past interactions. I had a great deal of respect for him as well, but I couldn't imagine why he would be calling me. I hoped he wasn't about to tell me the college was going to fire me for some reason. I loved this job, but maybe my small bit of notoriety as an amateur crime solver had brought adverse publicity for the college.

"Good morning, Charlie." The president's voice sounded calmly in my ear. "How are you doing this morning?"

"Fine, and you?"

He chuckled. "Doing well. I'm calling you because I need a favor, and I think you're the person for the assignment. I won't insist if you feel you're not ready to take it on, but I'm confident in your abilities."

Oh good lord, what am I about to get into? I cleared my throat. "I'm flattered that you thought of me. What is it you need me to do?"

"The request comes from outside the college, actually. I'm sure you are aware that Wil Threadgill, the musician and Athena native, is coming here for two weeks as a guest artist."

"Yes, I know about it," I said. "It will be interesting to see him again after all these years." I thought that was a diplomatic response. What on earth did the president want me to do with the impending visit?

Wyatt chuckled again. "It seems your fame has spread all the way to California, Charlie. Turns out that Wil Threadgill is a big mystery reader, and he also happens to love cats."

My heart sank, and I had to suppress a couple of expletives that I wanted to utter.

"I didn't know that about him," I managed to say.

"He wants to meet you, and your cat of course," Wyatt went on. "He would like to spend some time with you and talk to you about the incidents that you've been involved in, and I thought you wouldn't mind catching up with an old friend."

I started to protest that I barely remembered Wil Threadgill, but I figured it was a lost cause. "I'll be happy to meet with him, President Wyatt. I'm flattered that he even remembers me."

"He certainly does," Wyatt said. "Now that it's settled, I will make sure you have a copy of his schedule. He arrives on Saturday, and on Sunday there's a reception for him at the Farrington House Hotel that evening. I hope you and Miss Brady will be able to attend. It's up to you whether you bring your cat, of course."

After a few innocuous comments between us, the president ended the call. I thought for a moment, then picked up the phone again. I punched in Melba's extension.

"I just got off the phone with the president," I said.

"Of the United States?" Melba said pertly. "My, fancy that."

"No, the college president," I said, imitating her pert tone. "Apparently I'm to become Wil Threadgill's new best friend, thanks to my cat and my detective exploits. Now, I wonder how Wil found out about all that. I wasn't aware that any California media knew about me and Diesel."

"That *is* amazing, isn't it?" Melba laughed. "Come on, Charlie, you must have realized I told Wil about you and Diesel and your cases."

"I figured you had," I replied, "but I still don't know why he would be interested. Surely you two had other things to write about when you reestablished contact."

"Not so much as you'd think." Melba sounded wistful. "Anyway, he asked about you. He remembered you from high school, and he'd evidently already heard from somebody else about you and Diesel. I still don't know who told him about you two."

"Strange, but I guess I can ask him when he gets to town," I said. "I can't think why he would remember me, of all people."

"Because of Jackie," Melba said. "He told me one time he had a big crush on her, but she wasn't interested in anyone but you. He really envied you."

My late wife and I went through school together, from the first grade on, but it wasn't until we were in the eighth grade that we decided we were perfect for each other. That held up through high school, college, graduate school, and beyond, until the day she passed away. She was the love of my life and mother of our children.

"He certainly had excellent taste," I said. "I never thought of myself as anyone's rival for her affections, though."

"She never looked at anyone but you, Charlie," Melba said tartly, "and you know it."

"I do, but it's nice to hear it from you."

Melba snorted into the telephone. "Don't get a swelled head. Now, listen here, I think I know why Wil wants to get to know you and spend time with you. He kind of hinted at it in his most recent email."

"Okay, I give, why?" I said when the pause grew too long. Melba really liked to milk things way too much sometimes.

"I think he wants you to figure out whether he's in danger from anybody when he gets back to Athena and help protect him from whoever it is."

It was my turn to snort into the phone. "He wants me to be his *bodyguard*? That's insane. I'm too old and not in good enough shape for that kind of job."

Melba laughed. "I know you're not. He doesn't want a physical bodyguard, I don't think. He needs an intellectual one, so to speak, and that's you."

"That's different," I said slowly as I pondered the idea. "I suppose I could at least talk to him about it."

"Good. He gets in on Saturday, before the big shindig on Sunday. Maybe you and Diesel can meet him at the hotel sometime that afternoon or evening."

"Okay." I wondered what I could be getting myself into.

THREE

IIIIIIIIIIIIIIIIIIIIIIIIIIIIIIIII

Over the next several days, I occasionally thought about Melba's statement that Wil Threadgill needed an intellectual bodyguard. Odd, definitely, but I could understand it when I considered it fully, for it reminded me of situations in Golden Age detective stories where a frightened person had called in the aid of a famous detective. I had to laugh at the idea of my being in the role of Hercule Poirot or Sherlock Holmes, but I admitted, at least to myself, that it was intriguing.

Bowing to the inevitable, I decided I might as well do some research on Wil's music career. I wasn't that interested in his rise to fame. I was curious about his music, and I found numerous recordings on the Internet. To my surprise, I found echoes of some of my favorite Baroque composers—Telemann, Bach, and Vivaldi—in his work. I loved the mathematic orderliness of the Baroque, and I found that same kind of structure in Wil's movie scores.

I also found videos of his early rock music, and to me it sounded fairly derivative of late seventies and early eighties harder-edged music. His film scores appealed to me much more with their grace, precision, and maturity. I now began to look forward to meeting him and talking to him about it, my *intellectual guard duty* aside.

Diesel evidently like the film scores, too, because I caught him, head up, staring toward the computer screen. He appeared to be listening intently. I experimented by switching to one of Wil's rock pieces, and Diesel lost interest right away. Perhaps the raucous vocals didn't appeal to him. They certainly didn't appeal to me. He perked up again when I went back to the film score. I chuckled. My cat shared my taste in music. I rubbed his head affectionately, and he purred in his rumbling way.

The president's chief aide sent me Wil's schedule via email. Wil was arriving on Saturday afternoon, and the reception for him and his entourage at the Farrington House was set for seven on Sunday evening.

The next morning at breakfast, while I shared small bites of bacon with Diesel and his younger brother, Ramses, I asked my housekeeper, Azalea Berry, about Wil Threadgill. Azalea, like Melba, knew many people in Athena, or knew about them. She had known the Threadgills, father and son. Azalea could have retired several years ago, but when I hinted at that, she had informed me that she liked to keep busy. She and my late aunt Dottie had been friends for many years, and when my aunt left me this house, Azalea said she had promised to take care of it. I couldn't argue with her on this, so as long as she wanted to, this was her house to take care of.

"His mama died when he was still a baby, I seem to recollect." Azalea set a plate of biscuits on the table, and I reached for one. My cousin, Alissa Hale, currently a boarder in my house, grinned and scooped up two biscuits. I watched as she broke them open and slathered butter on the four halves. Then she added some of Azalea's homemade red plum jam. Alissa was a tiny thing and could pack away the calories without ever gaining an ounce. I switched my gaze to Azalea so I wouldn't be tempted to snatch up more biscuits myself while Alissa enjoyed hers.

"That's sad," I said. "Wil grew up without his mother. Did his father remarry?"

Azalea shook her head. "Story was old Mr. Threadgill wasn't interested in any other woman. Both that poor boy's parents were in their forties when he was born. He raised that boy by himself, even though there were enough women sniffing around who would have taken them both on." She grimaced. "Mr. Threadgill was too smart to let one of them catch him like that."

"Charlie said Wil ran away when he was seventeen." Alissa reached for another biscuit, and I focused on eating my one. It was my third one, after all. "Was Mr. Threadgill mean to his son?"

Azalea sighed. "Not when the boy was young, but at some point, Mr. Threadgill took to drinking. He was a mean drunk. Soon people started saying that he whipped the boy sometimes for no reason at all. Whipped him hard."

"That's horrible," Alissa said with a grimace. "My parents never spanked me."

"Yes, it is horrible." I'd had a few spankings in childhood, nothing really painful, more humiliating than anything. My parents soon learned that sending me to bed and not allowing me to read there was the worst punishment I could receive.

"What happened to his father after Wil Threadgill ran away?" Alissa asked, her attention focused on Azalea rather than on her plate where half a biscuit lay uneaten.

"He didn't live long after the boy ran off. Got drunk, as usual, and fell off the porch and broke his neck."

Alissa scrunched up her face as if she were trying not to cry. Old Mr. Threadgill's death saddened me, too. A tragic situation any way you looked at it.

Diesel, evidently sensing Alissa's distress, went to her and laid his head on her knee. She looked down at him, her eyes bright with tears, and rubbed his head. I knew she must be thinking, if only briefly, of her late grandfather who'd had his own struggles with alcohol.

"Wil didn't come back when his father died?" I asked.

Azalea looked at me, her head cocked to one side, and I felt a touch of scorn when she replied, "Nobody knew where he was or how to find him."

"I'd forgotten that," I muttered.

Diesel came back to my side and meowed at me. Ramses had abandoned me for Alissa who, I pretended not to notice, was feeding him small bites of buttered biscuit. He had grown plumper since Alissa's arrival in the household, and I figured I should probably caution her about giving him too much. He would eat until he got sick and throw it up, I had learned to my dismay. Diesel had done that on occasion when he was still young, but to my great relief he grew out of that behavior.

A glance at my watch reminded me that I needed to leave for work soon. I finished my food, downed the last of my coffee, and pushed back my chair. After I deposited my dishes in the sink, I turned to Alissa. "What's on your agenda for today?"

"Apartment hunting," she said. "I love it here, but I don't want to get too comfortable. I finally have the ability to be independent and live on my own as an adult. I want to know what that feels like."

Alissa had for years been the one to keep her family afloat with her jobs, but now she had enough money to live on her own and get an education. I was proud of her for doing this, but we would miss her presence in the house when she finally moved out.

I put these thoughts into words, and Azalea seconded my sentiments. Alissa ducked her head, and I detected a bit of red in her cheeks. The poor girl wasn't used to this kind of treatment, and that made me dislike her mother—safely in California and out of the way—even more. Alissa's mother placed many burdens on her daughter's shoulders when she could have done much more to take care of Alissa and her late brother.

"Thank you." Her voice quavered, but she looked up at us with pride in her smile. She stood, her plate clean, and took it and her utensils to the sink. "I'll load the dishwasher," she told Azalea.

"Thank you, honey." Azalea nodded.

"Diesel and I are going to work and get out of your way," I said. "You don't mind having Ramses underfoot today, do you?"

Azalea glanced my way, one eyebrow raised. I knew she didn't mind, but I felt I at least had to ask. I smiled and thanked her.

"Come on, Diesel, let's go see our friends at the public library."

My big boy perked up at that because he recognized our destination. After the birth of my first grandchild, Laura and Frank's son, Charlie, I had cut back my volunteer hours at the public library. Instead of working every Friday for several hours, I now worked only two Fridays a month. Diesel loved the attention he received from both library staff and the public. The late September heat had abated after a rainstorm yesterday, and the cooler weather felt invigorating. Relatively cooler, of course, with highs in the upper seventies instead of the low nineties. Diesel tugged at the lead on his harness in his eagerness to get inside the library, and I picked up my pace to keep up with him.

Several of his admirers awaited him on the other side of the door. I allowed them, a group of young children under five with their mothers, a couple of minutes to talk to my cat and to stroke him happily before politely taking Diesel away. We greeted our library coworkers, Bronwyn Forster and Lizzie Hayes, before we headed back into the office area where I cataloged new items for the library.

We paused to wish Teresa Farmer, the library's director, a good morning, and we chatted a few minutes while Diesel got his expected pats and kisses from Teresa.

"Melba came in a couple days ago to pick up some books we had on hold for her," Teresa said, her hand atop Diesel's head, "and we got to talking about Wil Threadgill." She chuckled suddenly. "I can't believe I knew something about him that Melba didn't know."

I had to laugh at that. Melba was the font of all knowledge about the people of Athena. "What on earth was it?"

"His father and my maternal grandmother were siblings," Teresa said. "That makes him my cousin, of course, and the minute I told

Melba, she said she had known that but it had slipped her mind." She grinned.

"She probably did know it at some point," I said with a chuckle. "Even Melba can't hold on to every fact these days the way she used to."

"I thought you'd get a kick out of it," Teresa said. "I'm looking forward to meeting him."

I made a quick mental calculation. Teresa was in her mid- to late thirties. "He ran off to California before you were born."

"He did, so I never had the chance to meet him." She frowned. "My grandmother, I was told, refused to have anything to do with her brother because of his drinking. She wouldn't even go to his funeral."

"How sad," I said. Diesel meowed, and Teresa rubbed his head.

"My grandmother was a hard woman," Teresa replied. "She died when I was ten. She scared me."

"That's unfortunate." I remembered my own paternal grand-mother, who had been a loving and affectionate person.

"My mother fortunately didn't take after her mother," Teresa said.

"I'm glad to hear that," I replied. "Your cousin wants to meet me and Diesel. Melba has stayed in touch with him, off and on, all these years, and she evidently told him about us."

Teresa grinned. "I did, too."

"I thought you didn't know him."

"I haven't met him," Teresa said, "but I found his website several years ago and wrote to him through it. It took him a while, but he wrote back to me. He was curious about what Athena is like now, so he and I started corresponding on a fairly regular basis. Of course, I had to tell him all about you and my favorite cat."

"Mystery solved, then," I said. "Between you and Melba, you must have really impressed him. Melba is concerned that someone he knew before he left might want to harm him. She says he wants me to spend time with him and keep an eye out for such a person."

Teresa cocked her head to one side and regarded me for a moment. "Wil did say that he'd heard from some of his former bandmates after his website went up and he won a few awards." She frowned. "He never mentioned anything about threats, though. It's been nearly forty years. Surely no one is going to harm him now. That's crazy."

"I'm inclined to agree."

Diesel warbled loudly, and both Teresa and I smiled.

"You never know, however," I said. "There's one man in particular that Melba thinks could be a risk."

"John Earl Whitaker." Teresa grimaced. "He's a complete waste of space. I know his wife, Natalie, slightly. She's a saint for putting up with him."

"So I've heard," I said. "I don't know that I've ever met her, but I might have seen her on campus. Melba said she is part of the cleaning crew."

"She's pretty self-effacing," Teresa replied. "I think she's embarrassed about John Earl and tries to stay in the background as much as possible."

"I don't understand why women stay with men like that," I said. "But then none of us really know what goes on between a husband and wife behind closed doors, do we?"

Teresa shrugged. "Love is unpredictable. Maybe she loves him so much she can't leave him."

"Maybe." I wondered how love could survive that long, given such circumstances. I realized how lucky I had been, first with Jackie and now with Helen Louise.

"Are you going to be at the reception at the Farrington House Sunday night?" Teresa asked. "Wil made sure I was invited."

"Yes, Helen Louise and I will be there. Diesel is invited, too, but I'm not sure he's going."

The cat meowed and then settled into the rumbling purr that earned him his name.

"You're not going to take him?" Teresa asked.

"I haven't decided. I'm not sure it would be wise to take him with all those people there."

The purr abruptly ceased, and Diesel stared up at me and warbled.

Teresa laughed. "Diesel obviously disagrees."

"You're too smart for your own good," I told the cat. He blinked at me. "We'll see."

With that he stretched out on the carpet by my desk.

"I don't have any idea how many people will be there," I said.

"Why don't you ask Melba?" Teresa said. "She's bound to know. She always finds these things out."

"Good idea." I pulled out my cell phone and called Melba. When she answered, I asked her about the reception.

"Only about thirty people," Melba replied. "Wil particularly asked the president to keep the numbers down. He's not fond of crowds."

"I'm with Wil," I said. "I might go ahead and bring Diesel, then."

"Wil's surely going to be disappointed if you don't," Melba said.

"Well, we can't have that," I said wryly. "See you there." I put my phone back in my shirt pocket.

Teresa and I chatted a couple of minutes more before I settled down to cataloging. She left the office for a meeting with the mayor, so Diesel and I had the space to ourselves.

As I worked, I thought about Sunday's main event. I was curious to meet Wil, naturally, but I wasn't fond of affairs like the reception. I hoped it would all pass without incident and that Helen Louise, Diesel, and I could get away fairly early.

Nothing was ever that simple, of course.

FOUR

Melba called me Saturday morning to say that she'd had a message from Wil Threadgill about meeting me and Diesel. He should be settled in the Farrington House Hotel around four, and he suggested five o'clock. I told her that was fine, and she agreed to let Wil know.

Thus on Saturday afternoon Diesel and I piled into my car at a quarter of five and headed for the Athena town square, site of the Farrington House for over a century. I found a parking space in the lot behind the hotel, and Diesel and I entered the lobby about three minutes of five. I inquired at the reception desk, and the clerk on duty consulted a list. He gave me the suite number after he had assured himself I was expected. Diesel and I took the elevator to the top floor.

Suites at the Farrington House offered the luxuries of prime hotels in cities like New York and elsewhere, or so I had been told. I had experienced them only briefly, having never resided in one my-self, though I had attended an occasional party in one. Arriving at the appropriate door, I knocked, and moments later the door opened.

"Right on time," Wil Threadgill said with a shy smile. He stood back and waved Diesel and me in, closing the door softly behind us.

Wil's appearance surprised me. His long hair was gone, replaced by a short cut that revealed the bony structure of his head. He topped me by a couple of inches, but where I was verging on portly, he was whipcord thin. He wore faded jeans and a polo shirt, and I noticed that intricate tattoos covered both arms down to the wrist.

Wil bent to rub Diesel's head, and the way my cat responded told me that he liked Wil. He pushed against Wil's hand and purred loudly in happiness at the attention. "You're a handsome boy, Die-sel," Wil said, and Diesel chirped in agreement.

Wil laughed as he stood and motioned for us to precede him far-ther into the living room of the suite. "Can I offer you something to drink?"

"A bottle of water, if you have it," I said.

"I have plenty," Wil said as he strode over to one wall to open a refrigerator. "I gave up liquor years ago, except for the occasional glass of wine." He extracted two bottles and brought them back to where I stood. Wil motioned toward the sitting area, and I chose the sofa. Diesel remained on the floor by my leg, but he kept his gaze focused on Wil as our host seated himself across from us in an over-stuffed armchair.

"I sure do appreciate you taking the time to come meet with me like this," Wil said, hints of a Southern drawl in his voice. All those years in California had eroded most of it, but the ghost of it remained.

"I'm flattered that you think I might be able to assist you in some way," I said.

Wil nodded. "I'm also glad to meet Diesel here."

Hearing his name, Diesel decided to go over to Wil and accept more attention. Wil chuckled at the cat's obvious ploy as he began to stroke Diesel's head. "I have four cats myself back in California. All rescues of various kinds. None of them is a Maine Coon, though. This guy is the largest one I've ever seen."

"He's larger than the average Maine Coon male," I said. "When I found him in the public library parking lot, I thought he was full grown. When I took him to the vet, I found out he was only a kitten. I'd never even seen a Maine Coon at that point, and Diesel just kept growing. He's fully grown now, though."

"Melba's told me how smart he is, and how sensitive he is to people when they're upset," Wil said.

"He's remarkable in that way," I said. "I think he's unusual, more like a dog in some ways."

I wondered when Wil would get closer to the point of his inviting me here. Perhaps I should introduce the subject. Before I could speak, however, Wil did it for me.

"The reason I wanted to talk to you," Wil said, his tone turned serious, "is nothing concrete." He shot me a look full of doubt. "I might be seeing problems where they don't actually exist, but I just can't help feeling something is off."

"Off how? And with whom?" I asked.

Wil took a long swig of his water before he responded. He set the bottle on the table beside his chair and leaned forward. "That's what I'm not totally sure of," he said. "Lately there's been this odd tension in the air when I'm with the guys in my band back in California. Usually my agent is there, along with my personal assistant."

"Do you think one of them is unhappy about something?"

Wil shrugged. "That could be, but I don't have a clue what anyone could be unhappy about. We're still working and making money. We don't do as many gigs as we used to because I spend a lot of time these days working on movie scores. But they still get paid well, and they all have side gigs, too. So it's not like I'm keeping them on a leash working only for me."

I considered this. Sounded reasonable to me that there shouldn't be any reason for hard feelings, but people weren't always reasonable. An idea came to me. "Maybe it's the composing. I assume that's a solo thing, and perhaps somebody in the group is jealous of your success with it."

Again, Wil shrugged. "The composing is solo, yes, but I always ask for their input before I turn in a finished score. They're really good with critiquing my work." He paused. "I thought by including them in the process I was doing the right thing, but maybe they resent it. I just don't know."

Jealousy took strange forms sometimes, and it wasn't always straightforward or even reasonable.

"You don't have any idea who it is who's unhappy?"

Wil shook his head. "No, it's all so vague. I just get this feeling when we're all together that something isn't quite right." He paused for a moment. "Melba says you're really good at picking up on things that others might miss. I think having a complete outsider's perspective on things could be helpful."

"I'll give it my best shot," I said, "though I can't promise anything." I glanced at my cat, still at Wil's side. "Diesel can be an indicator by the way he behaves around new people. He took to you right away, and that's always a good sign."

Wil grinned. "Cats always know when they meet a cat lover."

"And when they meet someone who doesn't like them or is afraid of them," I said. "He can be a litmus test sometimes, although not liking cats doesn't make someone a villain."

"My cats are always around when the guys are at my place," Wil said, "and the only one who doesn't like them is my manager. Vance Tolliver. One of those no-nonsense, let's-focus-on-business types. He's a good manager, though, and I've worked with him for over twenty years. I don't think he's the problem. It must be one of the guys in the band who's nursing a grudge, I guess."

"Will they all be at the reception tomorrow night?" I asked.

"Yes, they'll all be there," Wil said. "I'll make sure you get a chance to meet them, if possible. After the reception there's going to be a private party here in the suite, and they'll all be here, in case there's no chance to meet them during the reception. I'm sure you know how those things go."

I nodded. "I do. I don't think I'm going to bring Diesel with me. He doesn't do well with a lot of strangers around. He tends to hide. I think he gets overwhelmed." I laughed. "I do, too, sometimes."

Wil had a pained expression. "I know exactly what you mean. I'd just as soon not have to deal with so many people, but I've had to learn to cope over the years. I'm always wrung out afterward."

"I can only imagine," I said. "I couldn't do it." I decided to change the subject. "Melba also told me that you're concerned about how your old bandmates and other people you knew might react at your return. Anyone in particular who concerns you?"

Wil sighed heavily. "They had every right to resent me back then, because I just up and left without a word to anybody." He shot me a look. "I imagine Melba or somebody probably told you about my father."

I nodded. "I'm really sorry that you had to go through all that."

"He was never a happy man, and he couldn't handle a son who was more interested in music than anything, even girls. He wanted me to stay and run the farm, but there was no way in hell I was going to be a farmer." He sounded bitter, and I could understand. My own father had left the farm he grew up on, and it had disappointed my grandfather, though not to the extent that he became abusive. I mentioned this to Wil.

"Your dad was lucky, then," he said. "My dad couldn't handle it, and finally the only way out I had was to get as far away from here as possible. I made it to California, eventually."

"Your dad is out of the picture," I said. "What about your bandmates? Are you concerned one of them is still harboring a grudge?"

"There's only one of them who's probably still pissed off at me." Wil gave a half smile that looked more like a grimace. "John Earl Whitaker. Do you know him?"

"Not personally, though I've heard about him from Melba and my housekeeper, Azalea Berry."

Wil sighed. "It breaks my heart that he turned out like he did. I hate thinking I'm responsible for it."

I shook my head. "No, don't go down that road. He made his own choices. You didn't force him into anything."

"I know you're right, but I can't help remembering him the way he was," Wil said. "He loved being in the band, always thought we were going to be the Next Big Thing. He had talent himself, but he needed the band to put it all together."

"That's a shame," I said.

"One of the problems was that he got Natalie pregnant when she was a senior in high school, and her dad took a shotgun after John Earl. Marched the two of them to a justice of the peace and made them get married." He snorted. "Natalie's family was Catholic, and John Earl started talking about getting out of the marriage. Natalie's father wouldn't hear of a divorce or even an annulment. She was soiled goods. He actually used those words about his own daughter, can you imagine?" He shook his head in disgust.

"So John Earl felt trapped," I said. "I wonder why he didn't run off himself. He must have been tempted if music was his passion. But perhaps he really loved Natalie and wouldn't abandon her."

"I don't know," Wil said. "I've wondered that myself. I wrote to him about a year after I'd landed in California to let him know where I was, even hinted he could come out if he wanted to, Natalie too, but he never replied."

"Do you think Natalie could have been responsible for that? She might have been afraid to leave her family and strike out for California, where the only person she and her husband knew was you."

Wil laughed suddenly. "Natalie never seemed to like me all that much. I imagine she did what she could to rein John Earl in. In fact, if she got to my letter before he did, John Earl probably never saw it."

"That's likely," I said. "You never wrote again?"

"No, I didn't, and I probably should have." Wil sighed. "Like I probably should have come back here when my old man fell off the porch and died from the fall. I just didn't want to face people, especially my aunt, who was the most self-righteous, sanctimonious old biddy the good Lord ever created."

"I've heard from your cousin Teresa that her grandmother was a hard woman."

"I'm looking forward to meeting Teresa. Sounds like she's a relative I'll be happy to know. And she's right about my dear aunt Dahlia. If she made it to heaven, which to me is highly doubtful, she's probably been telling God what to do every minute." He grinned.

I couldn't help but laugh. "She does sounds pretty awful. But you're going to love Teresa, I have no doubt. She's great."

"Thank you, Charlie," Wil said, making a move to stand. "I'm sorry I can't talk longer just now, but the band and I need to get together and rehearse." He grimaced. "Vance promised we'd play a few songs tomorrow night at the reception, and I can't back out." On his feet now, he bent to rub Diesel's head. "Looking forward to seeing you both tomorrow night. If you don't want Diesel to be overwhelmed by the crowd, he could stay here in my suite until after the reception."

Diesel looked up at him and warbled loudly. Wil grinned. "Sounds like he approves."

I shook my head at both of them. "Don't encourage him. I'll see if my cousin Alissa will come stay with him while we're at the reception if you don't mind. She'd like to meet you, I think."

"That's fine," Wil said. "Happy to meet any family of yours." He moved closer to shake my hand, then he escorted Diesel and me to the door.

"See you tomorrow evening," I said, and Wil closed the door. "Come on, boy, let's go home. It's time for our dinner."

Diesel chirped approvingly, and we headed down the corridor to the elevator, both thinking happily of food.

FIVE

||||||||||||||||||||

When we arrived at the Farrington House Hotel, Helen Louise and I were a couple minutes late and so missed some of the opening remarks made by Athena College's president. We entered the midsized reception room, and as I gazed around from our vantage point at the rear, I estimated there were at least fifty people present. Definitely more than Wil had estimated, and several more people entered the room after Helen Louise and I did.

We began to move to one side of the room to escape the crush in the center. I spotted Melba near the back standing a few feet away from the dais where President Wyatt continued his speech of welcome. On the dais with the president stood two people, Wil and a woman I recognized as the head of the music department at Athena, though I couldn't remember her name at the moment.

Will looked quite distinguished. Gone were the worn jeans and polo shirt. Instead, he wore an expensive, well-cut suit with cowboy boots. His extensive tattoos were not visible, and to my mind he looked more like a record company executive than the popular idea of a music celebrity.

President Wyatt gestured in Wil's direction. The honoree stepped forward. He thanked the president for his introduction.

"I'm delighted to be back home again," Wil said. "I never meant to stay away so long." I thought he looked right at Melba as he said these words, but I might have been imagining it. She shifted but didn't take her eyes off of Wil. "But I found a new life out in California, and eventually, success. The longer I stayed away, the harder it was to think about coming back to Athena again." His expression turned somber. "I have a lot of great memories of growing up here, but I also have more than a few sad ones. When I left here all those years ago, I was trying to run away from my past. All I could think about was my future, and I was determined to have the kind of future I wanted. Nothing meant more to me than music, and I sacrificed so much over the years because the music was everything."

He paused and glanced around the room. "I'm deeply appreciative of the honor the college wishes to bestow on me. I do regret I never made it to college here, but it just wasn't going to happen." He smiled suddenly. "Enough of the past, however. Time to celebrate the present and to appreciate this wonderful welcome you've given me." He stepped back from the microphone.

The responding applause lasted at least a minute, if not slightly longer. The head of the music department stepped forward to the microphone but had to wait until the applause ended.

"We're delighted to have Wil Threadgill here for the next two weeks. Our students are anxious to meet him and learn from him, not only as a composer but as a consummate musician. I am sure you're all familiar with his wonderful film scores and his own recordings with his band." Here applause broke out again, and she waited politely until it died down. "This is an amazing opportunity for the students at Athena, and I must congratulate the college's board of trustees for their decision to award him the honorary Doctor of Music degree."

She stepped back to yet more clapping, and President Wyatt took the microphone again. "Thank you all for being here tonight. Now, in a little while, after we've all had an opportunity to refresh ourselves with the fine food and drink provided by the hotel's catering staff, we are going to have some music, courtesy of our honored guest and his band." He escorted the head of the music department off the dais, and Wil followed them down, to even more enthusiastic applause.

Melba had found her way through the crowd to stand by Helen Louise and me. After a quick greeting, she urged us to follow her toward Wil. She moved quickly to intercept him before he made it even two feet away from the dais. Helen Louise and I shared an amused glance, but we did as Melba commanded.

The moment Wil spotted Melba, he grinned, and his eyes seemed to glow. He swept her up into an embrace and swung her around. Melba giggled like a teenager until Wil set her down again. They stood staring at each other for a moment before Melba tugged on his arm and drew him nearer to Helen Louise and me.

"This is Wil," Melba said to Helen Louise as she slipped her arm through his and hugged it tight. "Wil, I know you've met Charlie already, and this is Helen Louise Brady. She and Charlie are engaged."

Wil tried to extend his right hand, but Melba didn't loosen her grip on his arm. He laughed, his expression apologetic. "I remember you," he said to Helen Louise. "It's wonderful to see you again. Melba tells me you got tired of being a lawyer and went off to Paris to become a French chef."

Helen Louise smiled. "It's great to see you again, Wil, although I still think of you as Fred, I have to admit."

Wil grimaced. "Poor ole Fred."

"Fred was a thoroughly nice guy," Helen Louise said warmly. "I hope you'll have time while you're here to stop by my bistro and have a meal, or at least a dessert or two."

"I can vouch for the pastries and the cakes." I patted my midriff.

"It's actually kind of surreal to be back here. So much has changed since I left all those years ago." Wil shook his head.

"Most of it for the better, I hope," I said.

"I sure hope so, too," Wil said. "I'm looking forward to spending time with y'all in my suite after the performance." He grimaced. "Not my idea, but always give the people what they want."

"Everyone's excited to hear you and your band play," Melba said. "It's going to be such a treat after all these years."

"If you say so." Wil grinned.

"After tonight things will be pretty hectic, especially when I start meeting with the music students." His face lit up. "I'm really looking forward to that. I love doing this kind of thing."

A young woman of about thirty, I estimated, approached Wil and laid a diffident hand on his arm. "Sorry to interrupt, Wil, but I think the president wants to introduce you to some of the board members now."

Wil frowned. "Thanks, Chelsea. This is my right hand, the woman who keeps me organized. Chelsea Bremmer." He quickly introduced us to her. I noticed Melba regarding the younger woman with narrowed eyes.

Chelsea smiled at us, but I could tell she was more focused on getting Wil away from us than talking right now. She tugged at Wil's arm.

"See y'all later," Wil said and turned to follow his assistant.

"Wil brought several people with him from California," Melba said. "I thought they were all musicians, though."

She didn't sound happy, but I thought she needed to be careful. Chelsea probably was nothing more than assistant, although an attractive one.

"She's young enough to be his daughter," Helen Louise said. "I imagine a man as busy as Wil needs someone to help him stay organized," she said. "I'm sure it's a purely professional relationship."

"Probably it is," I said. "Look, here she comes."

"Hello again," Chelsea said, her tone friendlier. She turned to Melba, phone in hand. "Wil would like to have dinner with you tomorrow evening, Miss Gilley, if you're available. Would seven work for you?"

"That'll be fine," Melba said, brightening. "Tell him I'm looking forward to it, if I don't get a chance to speak to him again tonight." Her tone held much less frost now.

Chelsea tapped on her phone. Once she finished, she looked at Melba for a moment. "Don't worry," she said. "He's not my type."

Before Melba could respond, Chelsea hurried away. Helen Louise and I exchanged a glance. I knew we both were struggling not to laugh.

"Well, of all the nerve," Melba said. Suddenly she laughed. "I guess I deserved that."

Wisely, neither Helen Louise nor I commented. We instead began to move in the general direction of the food and drink. I had eaten a light supper so that I could afford to snack tonight. The food at the Farrington House never failed to be delicious and inviting, and I was looking forward to grazing the tables. I glanced around, hoping to spot Teresa Farmer, but I couldn't find her in the milling crowd.

Melba trailed along with us. I expected her to talk more about Wil, now that she'd had a chance to talk to him and, most important, receive a dinner invitation from him, but she remained uncharacteristically silent. As the three of us chose from among the finger foods on offer and filled our plates, I speculated more about the depth of Melba's feelings for Wil Threadgill.

Had she been in love with Wil all these years, as I had thought earlier? She had one bad marriage and a couple of failed relationships that I knew about. Did Wil have any part in that? I wondered. I found it hard to believe that Melba had carried the proverbial torch for Wil for forty years. That was a long time to carry on hoping, and I had never considered Melba the hopeless romantic type. She had always impressed me as far too pragmatic.

I knew, however, that the heart wants what it wants. That wanting wasn't always logical or practical. Maybe Melba really had held on to that girlish, romantic picture of Wil all those years. Considering how happy I was these days with Helen Louise, my children, and grandchildren around me, I wanted my dear friend to find happiness as well. Melba was, in many ways, the sister I never had. We had grown close since my return to Athena, and I didn't want to think about her potentially getting hurt by Wil Threadgill. When, and if, Melba wanted to talk about it with me, I would be ready to listen. Until that happened, there was little point in my repining over the situation.

Our plates filled, we moved away from the buffet station and headed for an unoccupied area against one wall. There was a crowd toward the center of the room, surrounding Wil Threadgill and President Wyatt and the college board members. The Ducote sisters, Miss An'gel and Miss Dickce, must have had a more pressing engagement, I mused, or they would certainly be there with the rest of the board members. I hadn't heard from either of them in over a week, and given that they were both over eighty, I hoped that they were well.

One of the delicacies at the buffet was spanakopita, my favorite Greek bit of deliciousness. I had taken four of them, and I was about to sample the first one when I noticed a small man coming straight toward me. His gazed appeared fixed on me, and I put the spanakopita back on my plate and waited for him to reach me.

The man's head was nearly round, with fringes of hair at the sides and back, and he wore a suit straight out of a 1970s movie. I hadn't seen anything like it in years. Lime green paints, a plaid blazer of mixed purple, yellow, and gold, with a purple shirt and yellow tie. I exchanged a quick, amused glance with Helen Louise, and turned back to see the man halt about two steps in front of me.

"You're the guy with the cat, right?" His voice had a low, gravelly timbre to it.

After I nodded, he stuck out his hand, and I took it. His grip was strong, and he shook vigorously. I retracted my hand, trying not to wince.

"Vance Tolliver." He nodded at Helen Louise and Melba, but then he focused on me as if they had walked away.

"Charlie Harris, Mr. Tolliver. Yes, I do have a cat. Are you connected with Wil Threadgill?"

"Yeah, I'm Wil's manager, business and personal," Tolliver replied. "Look, I think you ought to know something. Wil might tell you, but he might not."

"Tell me what?" I asked, feeling a bit alarmed.

"Wil's letting his imagination run away with him. Nobody's going to hurt him. He needs to focus on what he's got to do here without any distractions. He's got major work lined up back home in California with a deadline coming up soon. So we'd all appreciate it if you and your cat would mind your own business, and let us get on with ours."

Before I could reply, he turned and hurried away.

SIX

"Did he say what I think he said?" Helen Louise asked me, a note of outrage in her voice.

"I didn't catch it," Melba said from on the other side of Helen Louise. "His voice was too low."

"He was warning me not to get involved with Wil," I said. "Said Wil's not in any danger, and he had too much to do to be distracted by me and Diesel."

"Who the hell is he to say something like that?" Melba asked hotly.

"Wil's manager," Helen Louise replied. "Charlie, what is going on here? I thought Wil just wanted to meet Diesel because of what Melba has told him in her letters."

"Yes, that's mainly true," I began, but Melba cut me off.

"Wil's worried about something, no matter what his manager says. I don't think Wil's imagining it, either," Melba said, moving to face me and Helen Louise. "He won't tell me precisely what, but I've told him about Charlie's experiences with, well, you know, murders, and he said he wanted to consult Charlie." She paused, and her expression revealed her unease. "I think maybe he's worried someone will try to harm him."

"If that's the case," Helen Louise said sharply, "then he needs to be talking to the police, not Charlie. What is Charlie supposed to do about it?"

"I think he wants me to observe the people he interacts with, both the people he brought with him and people from his past he's expecting to meet here. I told you about my conversation with Wil. Don't let that guy alarm you." I finally took a bite of spanakopita. It was as delicious as I expected.

Helen Louise frowned. "I wasn't worried until now. You told me Wil just had a feeling something was off, not that he was in physical danger."

"I think it might be his anxiety over coming back to Athena that has made him feel overly sensitive," I said. "There's probably nothing seriously wrong, like his manager said, and I'm sure when nothing happens, he'll relax and forget about these vague feelings he's been having."

"What if something does happen?" Melba's tone betrayed her concern.

I replied after swallowing more spanakopita. "I will advise him to go to Kanesha Berry. If he needs protection, she's the one to provide it, or the police department, one or the other. Certainly not me and Diesel."

"Amen to that." Helen Louise expelled a breath. "You'd better not let Sean and Laura get wind of this."

My son and daughter tended to take a dim view these days of my involvement in murder cases, and I certainly understood their concerns. I wouldn't go out of my way to worry them, but I had no intention of locking myself inside my house for the rest of my life and never experiencing any kind of adventure. If, I supposed, you could call solving murders an adventure.

"I haven't committed to anything beyond observing Wil and his band members. And his manager and assistant," I said, keeping my tone mild.

"I'm sure Wil wouldn't do anything to put Charlie or Diesel in danger," Melba said, looking troubled. "I wish he would have told me more in his letters, but he was pretty vague. I think he's more worried about the guys who were in the band with him here. When he disappeared, he left them high and dry. He was the one with the most talent, and without him, they couldn't keep the band going."

"Surely after forty years and more, they've gotten over that," Helen Louise said.

Melba shrugged. "You'd think so, but John Earl Whitaker has been bad-mouthing Wil all this time. He's drunk most of the time, and he's an ugly drunk. No telling what he might take it in his head to do if he gets close enough to Wil."

"That's definitely a problem for law enforcement." Helen Louise shot a pointed glance at me. "Not for Charlie."

"I appreciate your concern for my welfare," I said in slight irritation, "but I am able to work these things out for myself. I'm too old and not fit enough to be a bodyguard, and I don't doubt that Wil is perfectly aware of that."

Helen Louise patted my arm. "I know, love, and I'm sorry if I was patronizing in any way. I worry about you, too, you know."

I leaned toward her and kissed her cheek. "I know you do, and I wouldn't worry you intentionally for anything. But things just happen sometimes, and I can't help that."

Melba snorted. "I don't know about that. You seem to have a knack for getting yourself into situations."

"I always get out of them, in case you don't remember," I said.

"So far," Melba said darkly. "Just watch and listen, but don't get into anything that could get you and Diesel hurt."

"I won't." Time for more spanakopita. I was tired of this thread of conversation.

"Howdy, y'all," a cheerful voice called out.

All three of us turned to see a tall, rail-thin man in jeans, Western shirt, and bolo tie clumping toward us in worn cowboy boots. He had to be a member of Wil's entourage.

"Howdy yourself," Melba said, staring up at the stranger. He appeared to be around our age. He doffed his cowboy hat to Melba and Helen Louise, and I could see his thick, grizzled hair. He held the hat in front of him, properly having removed it in the presence of ladies. His voice had more of a Western twang than a Southern one, I thought.

"I reckon you must be Miss Melba Gilley," the stranger said. "I'm Zeb, short for Zebulon, Jones. Pleased to meet you, ma'am."

"Nice to meet you, too, Zeb." Melba shook his proffered hand. "This here's Helen Louise Brady, and that's Charlie Harris."

Zeb Jones shook our hands in turn, smiling shyly. "Nice to meet y'all. I'm with Wil Threadgill. I play the guitar and the banjo. Ever' once in a while the mandolin."

"I've probably heard you then on Wil's records," Melba said.

Zeb nodded. "Yeah, I been with Wil for over thirty years now." He glanced at Helen Louise and me. "I hear y'all went to school with Wil."

"We did," Helen Louise said, "although he was, I think, a couple of years ahead of us."

"You look way younger than that, Miss Brady. You too, Miss Gilley."

Melba preened slightly, but Helen Louise only smiled and thanked him for the compliment.

"Wil don't ever talk much about growing up here." Zeb frowned. "He let loose a few things when he told us all about coming here for him to get his honorary degree, and for us to be working with some of the college kids. He was real excited about it when he first told us."

I sensed concern in his tone on the last few words. "Do you think he's not still excited about being here?"

Zeb shrugged. "I don't rightly know. Wil's my best friend, but he don't like to let on if something's bothering him. I can usually tell, though, and I think there's something bothering him about coming back here."

"I wouldn't worry too much about that," Helen Louise said. "I'd be a little nervous myself, coming home to a place I haven't seen for forty years. That's a long time to be away."

"I reckon you're right," Zeb replied. "Seems like people here are real glad to have him back."

"We are," Melba said firmly. "You can come home again, no matter what some people might say." She glanced at me. "Who was that writer? You know the one I mean, Charlie."

"Thomas Wolfe," I said.

"Yeah, Wolfe," Melba said. "I had to read that book in high school, and I hated it. I guess that's why I can't ever remember the man's name."

"In the book," Helen Louise said, "the main character wasn't happy when he went home again. The people drove him away."

"Because he wrote about them, and they didn't like it. They thought he made them look bad," Melba said. "Wil never did that to people here."

"He'll be all right, I reckon," Zeb said in a placatory tone. "Wil doesn't like being the center of attention. He likes to hang back, out of the spotlight. Once he's been here a day or two, he'll be fine."

Zeb didn't sound totally confident in his assertions, but I hoped he was right. I could understand Wil's discomfort with being in the spotlight. I didn't care for it myself, which was why I was more than happy to keep my name out of the newspaper when I was involved in the sheriff's department's investigations. Chief Deputy Kanesha Berry didn't like my getting involved, but she did appreciate it when I was able to help sometimes.

"He's going to get a lot of attention while he's here," Melba said. "But I think Wil really wants to make peace with the past."

"How so?" Zeb asked.

"He ran off when he was seventeen," Melba said. "Left all his friends and family without a word. No one knew where he was or what happened to him. He wasn't happy here. I can't blame him for running away, though. Sometimes you have to if you want to have a decent life."

"I know Wil told me once his daddy was a bad man," Zeb said. "Treated Wil pretty awful. After that one time, though, he's never spoken about him again."

"Mr. Threadgill was a nasty, abusive man," Melba said simply.

"I ain't never been able to understand a daddy who mistreated a child of his," Zeb said. "Wil did right to get away from him in that case."

"I think Wil is trying to get your attention, Zeb." I nodded toward the center of the room where Wil stood with his hand raised in a beckoning gesture.

Zeb turned to look, and Wil waggled his hand. "I guess he wants me to talk to somebody," Zeb said, sounding glum. "It's been nice talking to y'all, but I guess I'd better get on over there." He smiled in turn at Melba and Helen Louise before he walked away to obey Wil's summons.

"He seems like a nice guy," Melba said. "He acts like he's really fond of Wil, too."

"Yes, he does," Helen Louise said. "They must have been through a lot together."

"Probably so," I replied. "It's good that he has a friend like Zeb with him on this trip."

"He's going to need his friends," Melba said, staring hard toward the doorway. "Look who just walked in the door."

Helen Louise and I turned to see the person Melba indicated, and I figured she was talking about a stocky man around our age in an ill-fitting suit. He looked uncomfortable as he stared at the crowd.

He hesitated for a moment before he half turned toward the door, as if he were debating whether to leave.

"Who is he?" I asked. "I don't know him."

"Mickey Lindsay," Helen Louise and Melba said in unison.

The name sounded vaguely familiar.

"We went to school with him," Helen Louise explained.

"He was in Wil's band." Melba spoke over her shoulder as she walked away from us in the direction of the doorway. She managed to catch Lindsay before he bolted from the room. He flashed Melba an awkward smile when she greeted him. After a brief conversation, with Melba's arm looped through his, he let her guide him over to Helen Louise and me.

I still didn't remember him, and the fact that he was one of Wil's bandmates back in high school didn't mean much, either. He was Melba's height, but she was wearing six-inch heels. That meant he was about half a foot shorter than either Helen Louise or me. As they drew close, I could make out his face better, and I was shocked to see that he looked considerably older than I expected. Life had not treated him kindly, I reckoned.

"He looks rough," I murmured to Helen Louise.

"He's been pretty ill," she said, sotto voce, right before Melba and Mickey reached us.

"Mickey, you remember Helen Louise Brady," Melba said brightly.

"I sure do." Mickey gazed up into Helen Louise's face as she smiled and extended a hand for him to take. He had that soft Mississippi drawl, evident in only three syllables.

"It's good to see you, Mickey," Helen Louise said. "How have you been doing?"

"Better, thank the good Lord." Mickey turned to me. "I bet you don't remember me, Charlie," he said. "I remember you, though. I had a big crush on Jackie, but she wouldn't even look at me." He smiled.

I had never realized that several other guys had crushes on Jackie, but I supposed I shouldn't have been surprised. She was truly special. "I was a very lucky guy."

"You were," Mickey said. "I was sure sorry to hear about her passing."

"Thank you," I said, touched by the obvious sincerity of his words.

He turned to look toward the center of the room. "Fred sure is a big star now," he said. "I always figured he'd be the one of us to make it."

"You were in the band with him in high school," I said.

Mickey turned back to face me and nodded. "Yeah, I was the bass player. I wasn't that good, but I got by. Fred . . ." He stopped. "I got to remember to call him Wil now. Anyway, Wil was always encouraging me, but I wasn't nowhere near as good as him and the others."

"I'm sure he'll be glad to see you," Helen Louise said.

"Maybe." Mickey shrugged. "I just want to thank him."

"For what?" Melba asked.

"I don't know for sure," Mickey said slowly, "but I think he was the anonymous donor who paid for my heart surgery six months ago."

"That was kind of him, if indeed it was him," Helen Louise said.

"He's the only friend I have who ever made anything of himself," Mickey said. "He was my best friend back then. Even though I haven't seen him since high school, I still think he's a good guy, no matter what other fools have said."

"What other fools are you talking about?" I asked.

"John Earl Whitaker, for one," Mickey said, his tone dark. "Somebody should have knocked his lights out years ago and saved everybody the misery of putting up with his crap. Natalie and his kid would be better off with him six feet under."

SEVEN

I shot a swift glance at Melba. She didn't appear in the least surprised by Mickey's words, or the feelings that prompted them.

"He's hardly a model citizen," Helen Louise said in a mild tone.
"But is he really that bad?"

Mickey snorted. "He damn sure is. You don't know him like I do,
and you'd better thank the good Lord for that. John Earl has always
thought the world owes him a living without him ever having to lift
his little finger."

"I agree with you," Melba said. "He bad-mouths Wil whenever
I have the misfortune to run into him. Thankfully, it's not that
often."

"Last time he bad-mouthed Wil to me," Mickey said, grinning,
"I knocked him flat on the ground. I'll do it again if I have to, as
many times as it takes."

Mickey obviously felt a great loyalty to Wil, even if Wil hadn't been the anonymous donor. I suspected that the Ducote sisters might have had a hand in that. I knew they regularly donated money to the hospital to cover medical bills for the medically indigent, but they didn't ever want publicity for their kindness in doing so.

"He hasn't shown up here, has he?" Mickey cast a glance around the room.

"Not so far," Melba said. "I'm hoping he won't have the gall to do it, even if he knows Wil is here."

"He probably knows," Mickey said. "Natalie sure does. I ran into her the other day when I dropped my granddaughter off." He addressed Helen Louise and me. "My granddaughter Jordan is a music student at the college."

"She has a beautiful voice," Melba said.

"I know," Helen Louise said. "I've heard her sing at our church during our Christmas pageant. She is amazingly good."

Mickey beamed. "Thank you. I'm hoping Wil can hear her sing. Her mama, my daughter-in-law, wants her to be a nurse like her, but Jordan lives for singing and performing."

I wondered if my daughter Laura knew Jordan Lindsay. Laura was in the theater department, but they often worked with the music school to put on musicals. Chances were, Laura did know the young woman. I'd have to remember to ask her what she thought of the girl's abilities.

"I'm sure Wil would be happy to listen to her sing," Melba said. "That's one of the reasons he's here, after all. He *wants* to work with students and help them with their music."

"And if he discovers someone who's really talented that he thinks has a chance to make it professionally," Helen Louise said, "I'm sure he'll say so and may be willing to help."

Mickey smiled. "I sure do hope so. I love that girl so much. She got all the talent in the family. She deserves to have her dreams come true."

"I hope for both your sakes that they do."

Mickey soon excused himself and moved off into the crowd.

I felt my phone vibrating in my jacket pocket. I pulled it out to see a text message from Teresa Farmer. I scanned it before replying quickly. As I put my phone away, I shared the message with Melba and Helen Louise.

"Teresa isn't going to make it. There's a bad leak at the library, and she's got to deal with it."

"That's a shame," Melba said.

"I hope the damage won't be extensive," Helen Louise said. "It's too bad she can't meet Wil tonight."

"She's going to miss the music, too," Melba said. "Apparently Wil and his band are going to play for us a little later. I'm not exactly sure where, because this room isn't all that big."

I glanced around, and I realized that Melba was right. People filled the room without a lot of space to spare, unless everyone packed themselves tightly in a corner. Then I noticed that this was one of the function rooms that had a movable wall. I surmised that the band's equipment must be set up on the other side of it. I was proved right about ten minutes later when hotel staff began moving the partition.

A couple of minutes before the staff moved the partition, I noticed Wil leave the room, accompanied by Zeb Jones, Vance Tolliver, and Chelsea Bremmer. Three other people followed, two men and a woman, who I presumed were part of the band.

The opened wall revealed a larger chamber with chairs set in front of a raised platform where the band's equipment awaited them. President Wyatt took the microphone again to ask everyone to find a seat and get ready to enjoy a brief musical interlude, courtesy of Wil Threadgill and his friends.

I was amused to note that a number of women immediately began pushing themselves through the crush in order to get to the seats closest to the stage. Helen Louise, Melba, and I found seats in one of the middle rows, but we had perfectly good visibility for watching the band perform. I sent up a silent prayer that the music wouldn't be terribly loud. I had stopped going to concerts a few years ago because I always came home with a raging headache and impaired hearing for at least two days afterward.

Good grief, I thought. *Could I sound any more like an old fogey?* I had to suppress a surge of laughter. I could remember my father commenting rather acidly upon my own choices of music as a teenager. Which, I remembered, I tended to play too loudly on my record player while I bopped around my bedroom to the Beatles and the Supremes and other artists from the sixties and seventies. I felt a sudden pang of loss for those days when I was young and my parents were still alive. They had been gone for many years now, but I still missed them.

There was a lull while we in the audience waited for Wil and his bandmates to get their instruments and equipment ready for their performance. Desultory conversations continued around us, and Melba chatted with the person next to her, someone I didn't know. Helen Louise turned to me and asked a question, her voice low.

"Have you picked up on anything that Wil is worried about yet?"

I shrugged. "Not really. I haven't seen or heard anything tonight, though, that makes me worry about his safety. Other than his squirrely manager," I added as an afterthought.

"That's good," Helen Louise said. "I can't imagine someone would be carrying a grudge for forty years. How twisted would you have to be to do that?"

"I don't know," I said, "but think of families that have carried on feuds for generations. How crazy is that?"

"True," Helen said. "The Hatfields and the McCoys."

"So far all I've heard is about John Earl Whitaker," I said. "He's apparently been bad-mouthing Wil for years."

"He would," Helen Louise said. "I'd feel sorry for him if he hadn't brought it all on himself. I know Natalie managed to get him into treatment programs a couple of times, and he came out each time swearing he was cured. But in less than a month he was back drinking and being a good-for-nothing jerk."

"Why has she stayed with him all these years?" I asked. "How can you keep loving someone so set on self-destruction? It's hard for anyone on the outside of a relationship like that to understand it, I know, and I shouldn't sound so self-righteous about it. I do feel bad for her."

Helen Louise shifted uncomfortably in her seat. "She's a devout Christian, so all I can think is that she believes it's her duty to stick with him. Her preacher is really conservative, I've heard, and I imagine that if he has had anything to say about it, he's told her she has no other option." Helen Louise's tone indicated how little she appreciated the preacher's views.

A burgeoning noise from somewhere behind us caught our attention, and we both turned in our seats to see what was going on. We weren't the only ones. It looked like the entire audience was doing the same thing.

A couple of hotel staff were grappling with a tall, disheveled man who was not happy being manhandled. He managed to loosen his right arm and landed a blow to one man's jaw, knocking him to the floor. The other employee, seemingly shocked by this, suddenly let go of the man, who stumbled forward.

"John Earl Whitaker," Helen Louise hissed. "I can't believe he had the nerve to show up here."

"And obviously smashed out of his gourd," I said in disgust.

Whitaker, now unimpeded by anyone, continued his stumbling path toward the front of the room where Wil Threadgill and his bandmates stood frozen. When Whitaker was perhaps ten feet away, Wil shook himself out of his paralysis and put his guitar down on the stage. He stepped down and came forward to meet his former friend.

"John Earl," Wil said, his voice sounding strained but still friendly. "How are you doing, buddy?" He held out a hand, but Whitaker brushed it aside.

"How's it look like I'm doing, Freddy boy?" Whitaker swayed slightly as he confronted Wil. "Drunk as a skunk." He laughed uproariously, and Wil responded with a weak smile.

"I think we'd better find you a seat and some coffee." Wil glanced around for a member of the hotel staff, but they had all retreated to the back of the room as far as I could tell.

"Don't need no stinking coffee." Whitaker sneered at Wil and let loose a string of obscenities that cast many aspersions against Wil's birth and parentage. Wil simply stood there and took it.

A couple of men sitting near the front row started to rise, but Wil saw them and waved them back. They sat.

"I hope someone has called the cops," I said. "Although it looks like Wil wants to handle this himself."

"President Wyatt is probably calling right now." Helen Louise pointed toward the front row where Wyatt sat, his phone to his ear.

"Good," I muttered. "I wonder where hotel security is right now. Wil is going to need help."

Suddenly Whitaker pushed Wil out of the way. He had to have pushed pretty hard because Wil stumbled and sat down hard on the edge of the stage.

Whitaker reached up to grab the microphone off its stand, and the moment his hand closed around the stand, he screamed. There was a horrible buzzing sound, and Whitaker's body jerked in a macabre dance. There was a smell of burning flesh, and Whitaker dropped to the floor, his hand still closed on the metal.

EIGHT

There were screams as people ran from their seats, away from the horrible sight of John Earl Whitaker's body twitching on the floor. I rose from my seat, thinking I ought to go to him, but Helen Louise grabbed my arm.

"You can't touch him," she said loud enough for me to hear over all the confusion near us, "or you'll get electrocuted, too."

Stunned, I dropped back into my seat. Beside Helen Louise, Melba sobbed into her hands.

As I watched, Vance Tolliver rushed forward to keep Wil Threadgill from making the same mistake I had attempted to make. He screamed at Wil to step away from the now still body.

Wil urged his bandmates away from the stage while Tolliver looked around to find the source of the electricity. After a few moments, he crouched to peer under the stage. Then, on his hands and knees, he crawled under it. The hubbub in the room had quieted as we all watched. Seconds later, Tolliver emerged, rose to his feet, and looked down at his now dusty trousers.

"It's okay now. I've unplugged it." He turned to the crowd. "I'm sorry, ladies and gentlemen, but under the circumstances, the show cannot go on. Please move back into the other room for the moment until the authorities arrive to take over."

Helen Louise had wrapped an arm around Melba's shoulders and led her, still sobbing into her hands, back into the other room. I followed closely behind. I didn't think I would ever get that horrible smell out of my nostrils. My stomach heaved, and I had to concentrate hard not to throw up.

Hotel staff were already at work to close us off from the horror near the stage. As soon as they finished, I felt somewhat better. I didn't want to see or hear what was happening next door. I glanced toward one of the doors that opened to the corridor outside, and I saw a team of EMS workers pass by. Right after them came a couple of city police officers. I wondered if anyone had alerted the sheriff's department. As my mind cleared, I realized that John Earl Whitaker's death was probably not an accident. Something about Vance Tolliver's expression after he disconnected the electric current had made me think that the electrocution was planned.

Not for John Earl Whitaker, that was certain. He had showed up without warning and inserted himself into the proceedings. He grabbed the mic stand before anyone else could. I had little doubt that Wil Threadgill had been the intended target.

If murder had been the object, then the sheriff's department would take over the investigation. Our city police did not have homicide detectives. Chief Deputy Kanesha Berry served as the primary homicide detective in our county. The daughter of my housekeeper, Azalea Berry, Kanesha had the experience and the intelligence to sort out this whole horrible mess.

Hotel staff brought in more chairs since the room originally had held only a few, and many people needed to sit and recover from the ordeal. Helen Louise quickly found a chair for Melba and called me over. "Find her something to drink," she said. Melba had stopped sobbing, but she looked as if she might burst into tears again at any moment.

I went to the bar and joined the short line. A couple of minutes later, I returned to Helen Louise and Melba with brandy and soda for all of us. I was not normally a drinker of spirituous liquors, preferring wine most of the time, but in view of what had happened only about ten minutes ago, I thought brandy the best choice.

Melba tossed hers back, gasped, and set the glass down on the floor beside her chair. Already I could see the color returning to her unnaturally pale face. "Thank you, Charlie." She gazed up at me. "That was like a nightmare."

Helen Louise sipped at her drink, but I knocked mine back the way Melba had done. I felt the warmth spreading through me, and my stomach steadied itself. "Yes, it was." I wasn't going to voice my thoughts to them about Wil's being the target of the electrified mic stand. I knew both women were capable of figuring it out, and I was in no hurry to discuss the implications with them.

"I wonder how long it will be until we can leave," Helen Louise said, just loud enough to be heard over the buzz of conversation in the room.

"Not soon enough," I said. "At least they got the other room closed off. How about another round?" I held up my glass.

"I'm in," Melba said. Helen Louise declined. I went back to the bar for refills for Melba and me. This time, Melba sipped at her drink, as did I.

"I'm terrified for Wil," Melba said, staring into her glass.

"Because you think he was the intended target," Helen Louise stated flatly.

Melba nodded. "Who else?"

"I agree with you," Helen Louise replied. "I'm sure Charlie does, too."

"I do, but John Earl Whitaker saved Wil's life, unintentionally, of course," I said. "He muscled in where he wasn't wanted, and he paid the price."

"I didn't like him," Melba said, her eyes closed. "But I wouldn't wish that on anyone. It's a horrible way to die."

"Yes, it is," Helen Louise said. "I'm going to get another drink after all." She headed for the bar.

Melba looked up at me. "You've got to find out who's behind this, Charlie. I'm scared to death for Wil's safety."

"I'll talk to Wil tomorrow when I can," I said. "He may have some inkling as to who hates him enough to want him dead. But I can't give him the kind of protection he's going to need if someone is really determined to kill him. That'll be up to the police or the sheriff's department."

"The person who probably hated him the most is dead," Melba said. "I have to wonder who else might want to murder Wil." She shook her head. "I just don't know."

"Wil could have brought the killer with him from California," I said.

Melba looked startled. "I hadn't thought about that, but you could be right."

"We don't know anything about Wil's life in California, other than the usual stuff you can read on the Internet. I looked around earlier, and I couldn't find anything really negative about him, so whatever it is, it has to be deeply hidden."

"What's deeply hidden?" Helen Louise appeared next to me, her glass refilled with brandy and soda.

I explained what I meant, and she nodded. "It seems to me far more likely that whatever enmity is directed at him has a more recent source. Perhaps Wil's imagination isn't off. Something could be badly wrong with his bandmates."

"I don't know," Melba said. "All I want is for Wil to be safe. I'm sorry that John Earl died that way, but he saved Wil's life. I doubt his family will agree, and I guess it's horrible of me to put it that way, but so be it."

I understood Melba's feelings on the matter. Callously I thought that John Earl Whitaker's family might be better off without him. I had heard nothing to his credit, frankly, and while I deplored the manner of his death, the fact of it was perhaps a relief for his long-suffering wife and child.

I was watching the door now for signs of more arrivals, but thus far I hadn't seen anyone from the sheriff's department. President

Wyatt, looking a bit less than his usual cool and professional self, walked into the room and asked for everyone's attention.

The crowd grew quiet as Wyatt glanced around. Then, satisfied that everyone was listening, he spoke. "I know we are all saddened by the terrible incident we witnessed a few minutes ago. A man has died, and his death must be explained. The authorities are dealing with all aspects of the situation, and they ask you all to cooperate with them by remaining here until the scene next door is cleared. The police and the sheriff's department will want to talk to each and every one of us to find out anything we might have observed tonight that could help shed light on the situation." A brief expression of pain flashed across his features at the infelicitous choice of words, but he moved on. "I assured them that we would all be happy to cooperate and would wait here until we are released."

There was a murmur of protest at this, but that quickly died down when Chief Deputy Kanesha Berry strode into the room.

"I know you're all exhausted and shocked with the recent events," Kanesha said without preamble. "Sudden death is not pleasant, but we owe it to the deceased to find out everything we can. I'm asking you all to be patient, and we will get to you as quickly as we can so you can all go home."

Kanesha let her gaze roam across the room, and I had to admire the way she had taken command of the scene. In her uniform, with her best professional manner firmly in place, she was an imposing presence. No one dared to complain now. Helen Louise and I exchanged wry smiles. Kanesha turned and walked out.

"I never want to see anything like this ever again," Melba said suddenly.

Helen Louise patted Melba's arm. "I wish none of us had to see that, either." She closed her eyes briefly. "I just hope I don't have nightmares about it."

"Amen to that." A commotion at the door caught my attention.

"I'm sorry, ma'am, but you'll have to wait here with everyone else." A young police officer stood there with a woman who was obviously distraught. "Someone will be with you in a few minutes."

The woman grabbed his arm. "Why won't you tell me what's going on? Where is my husband? He's got to be here somewhere."

Melba gazed at the woman in horror. "Oh my lord, that's Natalie Whitaker."

NINE

||||||||||||||||||||||||||||||

The poor woman, I thought. She had no idea yet that her husband was dead. I wondered if the young officer even knew who she was.

Melba got to her feet and made her way to Natalie Whitaker and the policeman. "Natalie, why don't you come with me?" She looked over the newly widowed woman's head to the cop. "I'll look after her."

The cop's expression was almost comic. He'd obviously had little experience handling a distraught person, and he appeared happy to give her over into Melba's care. He dipped his head in a gesture of thanks and stepped out of the way.

Melba led Natalie Whitaker back to where Helen Louise and I waited. When I got a closer look at her, I realized I had seen Natalie Whitaker somewhere before. Her dark hair was liberally streaked with gray, and she had a general air of defeat about her. The dress she wore was old and ill-fitting, its dark gray color not in the least flattering to her weathered face and skin. She looked at least a decade older than Helen Louise and Melba, but she couldn't have been more than two or three years their senior. I supposed that being married to a man like her late husband had worn her down badly over the years.

Melba got Natalie Whitaker seated, then mouthed the word *drink* to me. I went at once to the bar and got straight brandy and brought it back.

"Drink this," Melba said, shushing the woman when she tried to speak. "Then we'll talk."

Natalie obeyed and took a healthy sip of the brandy. She shuddered. "What is this stuff?" she croaked.

"What you need at the moment," Melba said. "Now tell us, what are you doing here?"

Natalie glanced at Helen Louise and me, then back at Melba. "These are my good friends," Melba said. "You know Helen Louise Brady. You may not remember Charlie Harris, but he was in the same class in high school with Helen Louise and me. It's okay to talk in front of them."

Natalie glanced at me uncertainly, and I gave her an encouraging smile. "We only want to help you."

Natalie fixed her gaze on Melba. "Have you seen John Earl? When I got home from work about thirty minutes ago, he was gone. My daughter said he mumbled something about a party at this hotel, so I came here." She paused to take another sip of the brandy, making a face as she did so. "How can he drink this stuff? It tastes awful. Anyway, when I got here I saw the police were here, and the first thing I thought was that John Earl got into a fight. Shaylene said he was drunk when he left the house, and he had a bottle of beer in his hand." She looked at each of us in turn. "Is that what happened? Did he start a fight? That young cop wouldn't tell me anything. He just kept insisting I'd have to wait in here." Her words had come faster and faster until it was getting hard to understand her.

Melba held up a hand to Natalie to halt the flow of words when the poor woman seemed poised to speak again. She stared at Melba.

"Natalie, honey, I'm real sorry about this, but I'm afraid the news isn't good," Melba said, her tone quiet and soothing. "John Earl was here. He crashed the party right before Wil Threadgill and his band were about to perform."

"I should've figured he'd try a stunt like that," Natalie said, her tone turned bitter. "The kind of damfool thing he'd do. Did the cops arrest him? Did he cause a lot of damage?"

"He wasn't arrested," Melba said, and Natalie looked hopeful. "He grabbed the microphone stand, and it, well, it electrocuted him."

Natalie's eyes narrowed. "How could that happen? That's dangerous."

"Yes, it is, extremely," Melba said. "Natalie, John Earl is dead. The shock killed him."

To my surprise, Natalie started laughing, but as I listened I realized I heard hysteria rather than amusement. Melba grabbed her by the arms and shook her until the woman's head bobbed back and forth. "Natalie, get ahold of yourself right this second."

The laughter ceased, and Natalie looked dully at Melba. "He really is dead?" She whispered the words, and at Melba's nod, she drew in a deep breath. "He had a weak heart from all those years of drinking. I guess it wouldn't take much to kill him." Then she burst into tears, and Melba gathered her into her arms and began to rock her gently.

Helen Louise and I stepped away from them. There was nothing we could do at the moment, and I didn't want to intrude on the woman's grief at a time like this. Melba would take care of her. She knew her better than either of us, after all.

"This is all so horrible," Helen Louise said to me when we found two empty chairs about ten feet from Melba and Natalie Whitaker. "That was a vicious thing to do to anybody."

"Yes, it was," I said. "Someone must really hate Wil with a passion to set that up. Anyone could have been electrocuted." I didn't know much about electricity and wiring, but surely it was dangerous to leave a live wire like that. That was truly heinous. Maybe the person who arranged it was simply crazy and didn't care who got hurt or killed.

I realized it was unlikely that a member of the public—other than the unfortunate John Earl Whitaker—would have grabbed the mic stand like that. Was it a fluke of some sort? I wondered. Maybe it truly was an accident, some oversight by the person who had set up the wiring for the band's equipment.

Surely a member of the band had checked everything thoroughly, though. They were professionals, and professionals checked their equipment. The investigation would reveal how it all happened, and I was extremely curious to find out what had really occurred.

I checked my watch. We had been here well over two hours now, inching ever nearer to three. If everyone else here was as exhausted as I suddenly felt, I knew they'd be as happy to be released to go home as I would. I hoped we would be able to leave before much longer. Even as I expressed these thoughts to Helen Louise, I saw two young policemen and a couple of sheriff's deputies enter the room. One of the two latter men was my good friend and boarder Haskell Bates. He shared an apartment on the third floor of my house with his partner Stewart Delacorte, a chemistry professor at Athena College. I was glad to see him. He might be able to tell us a little about what was currently happening in the next room.

The officers seemed to be checking names against a list, presumably the guest list for the party. Haskell spotted Helen Louise and me. He came over after he finished talking to a couple who looked to be in their late seventies and indicating that they could leave. The room was gradually emptying while Helen Louise and I waited.

"Good evening," Haskell said. "I'm sorry to find y'all here. It couldn't have been pleasant to witness that."

"It wasn't," Helen Louise said.

"Has he been taken away yet?" I asked.

"Not yet, but soon," Haskell said. "They want to get everyone out of here before they do it. They have to pass this room to get to the back door."

"Good," I said. "Are y'all aware that the dead man's widow is here?" I pointed to where Melba sat, still with her arms around Natalie Whitaker.

"No, we weren't." Haskell turned to look over at the two women. "One of the rookie cops said something about a woman carrying on about finding her husband, but he didn't make the connection." He turned back to us. "Look, y'all can go home. Kanesha will want to talk to you later, but there's no need to stay here."

"We're ready to go," I said. "But I do have a question. This wasn't a freak accident, was it?"

Haskell hesitated briefly. "No, it wasn't. Someone had assembled a powerful battery capable of delivering a couple thousand volts and connected it to the mic stand. The battery was underneath the stage. Looks like it had some kind of remote-control device to turn it on. That's all we know at the moment."

I felt sick to my stomach again, and Helen Louise's complexion had gone ashen. "How horrible," I said. Then a thought struck me. "Why aren't y'all searching everyone to find the device that set it off?"

Haskell smiled grimly. "Because we already have it. That's all I can tell you at the moment. Y'all go on home and get some rest. I'm going to talk to Mrs. Whitaker and Melba."

After a quick nod, he left us.

"Shall we?" Helen Louise asked.

"I want to, but I really hate to leave without talking to Melba first. I'm worried about her."

Helen Louise hugged me. "I am, too, but she's going to be fine. Taking care of Natalie distracted her. She'll call one of us if she needs to talk."

We headed toward the door, making sure to pass close by Melba and Natalie. Haskell had his back to us, but I caught Melba's eye. I put my hand up to my ear to indicate a phone, and she gave me a quick nod before focusing on Haskell again.

Somewhat relieved, I escorted Helen Louise out of the room.

We made our way out of the hotel to my car. In silence I drove us to Helen Louise's house. I escorted her to the door. "Are you going to be all right?"

She smiled. "Yes, I'm going to have some wine and maybe a snack, and then I'm going to bed. You go on home and don't worry about me."

We exchanged a kiss. I waited until I heard her lock the door behind her before I walked back to the car.

To my surprise, Stewart met me at the back door when I walked into the kitchen. Ramses immediately crowded around my legs begging for attention. I bent to scratch his head.

"I wasn't expecting to see you," I told Stewart.

"Haskell texted me," Stewart said, his tone grim. "Sounds like it must have been really awful for everyone."

"Awful?" Alissa said. "Charlie, what happened? What aren't you telling me?" She shot an accusatory glance at Stewart, including him in that last question.

"Let's have a seat, and I'll tell you," I said.

Alissa did as I asked, and Diesel sat on the floor beside her chair, while Ramses climbed into my lap for more attention. Tersely I explained what had happened tonight, and Alissa's expression grew horrified as I talked. When I finished, I turned to Stewart.

"Did Haskell give you any details?"

"Only that someone was electrocuted at the hotel during the party. Nothing more than you've told us," Stewart said. "Can I get either of you anything? A stiff drink? A glass of wine?"

"Nothing for me." I smiled my thanks for his concern.

Alissa suddenly stood. "I think I'm going to bed. I just hope I don't have nightmares."

"I hope you don't, either," I said. "Read for a while. That will help."

She flashed me a smile, and Diesel followed her from the room. Ramses leaped out of my lap and accompanied them.

"Now give me the details you were holding back on while Alissa was in the room," Stewart said.

I complied with his request, but I kept the grisly details to a minimum. When I finished, Stewart shook his head. "That's a horrible way to go. He probably died almost instantly, though. I doubt his heart was in good shape. He's been an alcoholic for decades. A really nasty drunk the times I encountered him."

"That's what I've been told," I said. "It was his bad luck that he grabbed that mic stand before anyone else did."

"You said he was standing on the floor and not on the stage," Stewart said.

I nodded.

"Then he had nothing to ground him on that carpet," Stewart said. "Did you happen to notice if there was a rubber mat on the stage with the mic stand?"

"I really didn't notice," I said. "Anyone who stood on the mat, if there was one, would have been safe from the shock, is that what you're saying?"

"Yes, the mat would ground anyone standing on it who came into contact with the electrified stand," Stewart said. "Maybe it was simply a terrible accident."

"No, it was deliberate." I shared what Haskell had said about the battery with its remote-control switch that turned it on. "Someone meant to hurt or kill."

Stewart pulled out his phone and tapped away on it. "I texted Haskell and asked him about the mat." He stared at his phone. He had to wait over a minute for a response. After he scanned the words, he looked up at me. "There was supposed to be a mat, but it's not there."

TEN

||||||||||||||||||

"The killer wasn't taking any chances." I pushed back from the table and went to the cabinet where we kept the wineglasses and extracted two. Then I pulled a bottle of Chardonnay from the fridge. I poured us each three-quarters of a glass and drank about half of mine.

"Whom do you think was supposed to be the target?" Stewart asked.

"Most likely Wil Threadgill," I said. "He was apparently uneasy about coming back to Athena." I told Stewart about the conversation I'd had with Wil.

"I imagine Wil is a sensitive person, the kind who picks up on emotions and undercurrents," Stewart said thoughtfully as he stared at his wineglass. "There's obviously something badly wrong if a member of his entourage tried to kill him tonight."

I agreed.

"I have to wonder why someone would hate him, though. From

everything I've read about him, he seems to be a really nice guy. Not one of those Hollywood types who are so impressed with themselves they think the rest of us are garbage," Stewart said after a sip of his wine.

"He is nice, based on my brief acquaintance with him," I said. "Either someone in Athena has been nursing a grudge for forty years, or someone in his entourage really hates him. Only the good Lord knows why in either case."

"Are you going to try to help him figure it out?" Stewart asked.

"I'm hoping I'll get to talk to him again before long, but now that the authorities are involved, I might not have the opportunity. I'm sure Kanesha won't be happy to see me lurking around Wil, even if it's at Wil's invitation."

"No, she won't," Stewart said. "Although you have given her some helpful insights on a number of occasions."

"She has expressed appreciation for that in the past, but not in glowing terms." I grinned briefly. "I know she'd just as soon I didn't try to help. She's like her mother in that way." Azalea liked things her way. She had made it clear that she was in charge of the house, and I wasn't going to argue. Frankly, she had frightened me in the early days before I got to know her better. She had a way of looking at me that reminded me of the scariest teacher I'd had in elementary school, a woman who terrified all of us into behaving like angels. I had blocked her name from my memory years ago. But as Azalea and I had come to know each other better, I no longer found her scary, though she was still formidable. I had grown really fond of her.

Stewart set his wineglass on the table. "Let me play devil's advocate for the moment and look at the situation from the other angle."

"How so?" I asked.

"Let's say that Wil Threadgill is the one who's held the grudge all these years, and he wants revenge for whatever slights, perceived or otherwise, he's brooded over for more than four decades. He comes back the conquering hero, so to speak. He thinks no one would suspect him of wanting to pay people back. He knows who his targets are, and I imagine John Earl Whitaker would be number one on the hit list. Threadgill has had his sources of information in Athena over the years, and he knows what Whitaker turned into. He might easily predict what would happen at a public performance. Whitaker shows up, makes an ass of himself trying to steal the spotlight. But, bam! He's electrocuted, and it looks like someone was out to harm Wil instead. All along Wil is the one who set it up, and Whitaker is dead."

I sipped the rest of my wine while I mulled over what Stewart suggested with this take on the situation. Finally, I spoke.

"Honestly, I can't say you're not right. Wil could be playing a very deep game here. I barely knew him forty years ago, and all I have to go on is what Melba has told me. She's obviously biased in Wil's favor because I think she might be in love with him."

"Or with who she thinks he is," Stewart said.

"Yes, with who she thinks he is. Excellent point," I replied. "All she's had from him are letters, and we both know how easy it is to fake a personality or feelings in a letter. To be completely cynical, you could say that Melba could be a victim as much as anyone else, because she's let Wil build up a false picture of himself over the years. Melba would scratch my eyes out if I suggested any of this to her, though. She's fiercely loyal to her friends."

"That's why we all love her so much," Stewart said. "I wouldn't want to see her get hurt over this. I was only playing devil's advocate, but you have to admit the scenario I sketched could very well be true."

"I do admit it," I said. "I'm going to have to be wary whenever I'm around Wil. He has a charming, low-key manner, but that's how sociopaths operate." I had dealt with a sociopath not that long ago, and I didn't care to repeat the experience. I couldn't allow myself to be won over unless I was absolutely certain Wil was innocent.

"I hope the killer is done," Stewart said. "But if he or she isn't, I'd be nervous if I were anyone closely connected to Wil Threadgill."

"And that includes Melba," I said, suddenly heartsick. "I wish I could get her to keep her distance from him until this is resolved, but I don't hold out much hope of that."

"It can't hurt to try," Stewart said. "She loves you like a brother, and she might listen if you put it to her in terms of cold logic."

"Maybe," I said. "I just don't know."

I pushed back my chair and rose from the table. I carried my empty wineglass to the sink and rinsed it out. "Would you like more wine?"

"No, thanks," Stewart said. "I'd better get back upstairs and see what Dante has destroyed while I've been down here." Dante was Stewart's mischievous toy poodle. He had a taste for shoes and had ruined numerous pairs since Stewart had adopted him.

"I'm ready for bed," I said.

Stewart turned off most of the downstairs lights. He left the light in the entrance hall on for Haskell and came up the stairs after me, headed to the third floor.

Diesel and Ramses appeared a few minutes after I reached my room. They stretched out on the bed while I disrobed and put on my nighttime attire of shorts and T-shirt. I got into the bed with the cats, turned off the light, and tried to get comfortable in the room allotted to me on the bed. Diesel took up a fair amount of space and insisted on being close to me, while Ramses often climbed on my side or lay on my stomach, depending on my position in bed.

My brain was still full of the horrible events of the evening, and I was having trouble getting it all out of my mind so that I could relax and go to sleep. I kept seeing the startling picture of John Earl Whitaker shuddering as he clasped the electrified mic stand.

I had to get that out of my mind, or I was going to have to get out of bed to throw up. Or take some kind of remedy that would help me avoid it. I decided on the latter option. I dislodged Ramses from my stomach and went into the bathroom. Delving into the cabinet, I found the bottle I needed, opened it, and took a healthy swig of the chalky-tasting pink liquid. For good measure, I drank more before I recapped the bottle and put it back in the cabinet.

Ramses climbed into my lap when I sat on the side of the bed, instead of lying down. Diesel stuck his head under one arm and meowed, a plaintive sound. He could tell something was bothering me, and he expressed his concern in his way. I petted both the cats and assured them I was okay. Diesel withdrew his head and went back to his place on the bed. Ramses, however, stayed firmly in my lap, and I didn't have the heart to move him off it.

I must have sat there a good ten minutes, forcing myself to think of other things, when my phone rang, startling me.

I glanced at the caller ID. Melba. My heart rate increased. What could be wrong? I wondered.

"I'm sorry for calling so late, Charlie," she said as soon as she heard my voice. "I hope I didn't wake you up."

"You didn't. I'm sitting here on the side of the bed with Ramses in my lap. What's up? Has something else happened?"

Melba appeared not to have heard my questions. "Natalie is a complete mess," she said. "The police offered to take her home, but I said I would do it. She wasn't in any shape to go home to her kid like she was. We sat in my car for a while before I drove her to her house. She was having a hard time believing that John Earl was really dead, even though she admitted his heart was bad. She kept asking me what she was going to tell the daughter. What was she going to do without him? On and on. I didn't have the heart to tell her she was way better off without him. He made her and the daughter's lives hell the way he carried on."

"Her place was beside her husband," I said. "That's what so many women are told from cradle to grave."

"Exactly. The Lord I follow has better sense than that," Melba said. "No woman should have to put up with a man like that."

"I agree with you," I said. "I assume you finally got her home."

"I did, and I stayed with her while she told her daughter. Shaylene didn't seem too fazed by the news. He wasn't much of a father. I doubt if he could have picked his daughter out of a lineup. He never spent much time at home from what I heard."

"That's really sad," I said.

"It's pathetic." Melba's tone was savage. "The Lord may strike me down for saying this, but John Earl Whitaker was a completely useless man. Everyone's better off with him out of the way."

I couldn't think of anything to say to that. I mostly agreed with her. The tragedy was that Whitaker had never had the courage or the stamina, or perhaps even the support, to redeem himself and be the man he needed to be.

Melba's tone changed. "Charlie, I'm really scared for Wil. That could have been him instead of John Earl. Somebody really is trying to kill him. You've got to help him figure out who it is and stop them. I don't know what I'd do if anything happens to Wil."

"I'm sure Wil is going to be all right," I said. "The police and the sheriff's department are not going to let anyone harm him. I'll be happy to talk to him if he still wants to, but I can't be with him twenty-four hours a day until this is solved."

"I know," Melba said, now sounding defeated. "He is so dear to me, Charlie, in ways I can't really put into words."

"He will be okay. Kanesha will figure out what's going on, and the responsible person will be arrested. You know how thorough she is. She's not going to let you, or Wil, down."

We chatted for a couple more minutes, until Melba confessed she was completely exhausted. She planned to take a sleeping pill and climb into bed.

The conversation over, I moved Ramses out of my lap onto the bed and got comfortable. I thought about taking a sleep aid myself but decided against it. At some point I fell asleep. The next morning when I woke up, it was to the news that there had been another attempt at murder.

ELEVEN

I woke early the next morning not long after six. I had surprisingly had some decent sleep, but I would have been happy to stay in bed another couple of hours. I felt restless upon waking, however, and got up and took a shower.

When I came out of the shower to dress, I saw that my bed was empty. Diesel and Ramses had decamped downstairs to wait for their breakfast. The overnight famine had set in, and they desperately needed nourishment before they fainted from malnutrition.

In the kitchen I found Haskell at the table, nursing a large mug of coffee. Stewart was at the stove fixing breakfast. I bade them both good morning before I poured myself a cup of coffee.

"What time did you get in?" I asked Haskell.

"Not early enough," he replied. "Around three." He downed the rest of his coffee and got up to rinse out the mug in the sink. He went over to Stewart and rested a hand on his partner's shoulder. "Sorry, babe, but I can't stay for breakfast. I'll pick up something later."

"Why the hurry?" Stewart frowned as he turned away from the stove, spatula in hand.

"Got to get to the hotel." Haskell hesitated. "You might as well know. There's been another murder attempt. Kanesha texted me before you came into the kitchen, Charlie."

"Oh, no," I said, horror-struck. "Wil again?"

"One of Wil Threadgill's band members, Zebulon Jones," Haskell said.

The coffee soured in my stomach. "I was just talking to him last night. Really nice guy. What happened?"

"I don't have the details yet, except that Mr. Jones is okay, just shaken up," Haskell said. "Look, I've got to get going." He gave Stewart a quick kiss on the lips and headed out the back door to the garage.

"Oh my lord," I said. "I can't believe this."

Stewart had turned back to the stove. "Truly a nightmare situation," he said. "I'm going to finish cooking breakfast. I know you're upset, but doing without food isn't going to help anyone."

"Where are the cats?" I asked.

"Like sensible creatures, they're having *their* breakfast," Stewart said. "I'm sure they'll be back in the kitchen any moment now begging for bacon."

He was right. Both my cats like people food, especially bacon. By the time Stewart was setting plates of scrambled eggs and bacon on the table, along with whole wheat toast, butter, and jam, Diesel and Ramses sat on either side of me, ready for treats.

Suddenly I found I was hungry. Stewart was right. This promised to be a long, stressful day, and I was going to need all the energy I could muster to face it. I felt bad for Wil, having a friend of so many years coming close to death. I imagined that Kanesha would want to keep a close watch on him and the rest of his entourage now. I might not get another chance to talk to Wil. I hadn't been any help at all so far.

I wondered exactly what had happened, and how Zeb Jones had survived the attempt at murder. I wished I could go over to the hotel, but Kanesha would probably send me home with the proverbial flea in my ear. The last thing she would want was my presence during her investigation. I couldn't really blame her, but my overlarge bump of curiosity wanted satisfaction. I needed to find something to distract me in the meantime so that I didn't end up going to the hotel after all.

I had an idea about that, but it was too early to act on it. I'd wait until seven before I made the call to my son, Sean. With my granddaughter Rosie barely a year old, I knew her parents were probably already up with her. Sean was usually an early riser anyway, even on weekends, but I thought waiting until seven was only polite.

As sometimes happens, Sean must have sensed that I wanted to talk to him. A few minutes before seven, my cell phone rang. Sean was calling me.

"Good morning," I said. "How did you know that I was planning to call you?"

"I'm psychic," Sean replied lightly. "What's up, Dad? I was planning to call you this morning anyway. Thought you might want to go out to the farm with me and see the progress on the house."

"That was exactly what I wanted," I said.

The farm to which Sean referred had belonged to my paternal grandfather. I thought it had been lost to my family when my grandfather died when I was about seven years old, but by an odd twist of fate, I had inherited it after all. Most of the farmland was now leased to a worthy farmer and his son since neither Sean nor I had any desire to farm. We did, however, want to keep the house that had been in the family for several generations. Sean had bought it from me with the idea of making it the home for him, his wife, and his daughter. I heartily approved.

The house needed renovation, however, after not being properly cared for during the previous tenant's lifetime. Sean wanted to update the house while keeping much of its original charm, and he had discussed the planned renovation with me. I thought his and his wife Alex's ideas suitable, and work had commenced a month ago. Alex's father had given her a number of beautiful family heirlooms, including a couple of rooms of antique furniture. I was convinced the old Harris homestead would be a showplace once the work was complete.

"I'll come by and pick you up in about twenty minutes, Dad, if that works for you," Sean said.

"That's fine," I replied. "See you then."

"You'd better finish your breakfast if you're expecting company," Stewart said.

"You're right." I applied myself to my plate, and in between bits of egg, bacon, and toast, I told Stewart what my plan was for the first part of the morning.

Stewart grinned at me. "That ought to keep you out of Kanesha's way for a couple of hours."

I shot him a glance, and he laughed and threw his hands up. "All right, Charlie, that's all I'll say on that subject. How long has it been since you've seen the farmhouse?"

I thought for a moment. "About three weeks, I reckon. I'm sure they must have made good progress by now."

"You never can tell with contractors," Stewart said. "I've heard some horror stories from friends."

"Sean checked out several different contractors pretty thoroughly, and I think his reputation as a lawyer serves him well in these things."

Stewart nodded. "That's true. He seems to be busy all the time."

I frowned. "Alex still hasn't returned to the office full time," I said. "I'm not sure what's going on. Sean doesn't talk about it to me, and Alex doesn't, either. They have a wonderful nanny for Rosie, so I'm not sure what the problem is."

"Do you think Alex maybe just isn't keen on going back to work full time?" Stewart asked. "I don't see her except at Sunday dinners here, and there's always so much going on, it's hard to have a private conversation with anyone. Particularly on such a personal subject."

"I'm worried something is wrong between her and Sean, but neither of them has confided in me. One or both of them might have talked to Laura, but Laura won't break a confidence, even to me. It could be about work, or it might have something to do with the farmhouse. I'm not sure Sean talked it over thoroughly before he decided to buy it and renovate it. It's costing a lot of money, after all."

Sean and his sister Laura were close, as were Laura and Alex. If there were a serious problem between my son and his wife, I knew they probably wanted to keep it from me so I wouldn't worry. The exact thing they fussed at me about when I didn't share something important with them right away. The irony hadn't escaped me.

"Until one of them is ready to talk, I don't think you should try to pry it out of them," Stewart said.

"You're right, and I'm going to do my best not to," I said. "But patience isn't my strong suit, especially when it comes to family problems."

I finished my breakfast and filled a travel mug with coffee. Stewart insisted that he would clean the kitchen, and I left him gratefully to it while I went upstairs to brush my teeth. By the time I returned downstairs, Sean was in the kitchen, chatting with Stewart.

"Good morning, Dad," Sean said. "Ready to go?"

"I am. Okay if Diesel comes, too?"

"Of course." Sean smiled. "I've been giving him and Ramses the last shreds of bacon. You want to bring Ramses, too?"

I shook my head. "No, I can't trust him not to run off, and he hates the leash. Maybe when he's older."

"All right then. See you later, Stewart." I knew Stewart would keep an eye on Ramses until I returned. Sean led the way to the front door, and Diesel and I followed him down the sidewalk to his car, a spacious SUV.

"How have you been?" I asked once we were settled in the front seat. Diesel sat behind us, looking out a window as the car moved down the street.

"Busy as always," Sean said, his tone light. "Business is good, and that's going to help pay for the renovations. I'm fine. So are Rosie and Alex."

There was an air of finality to that last statement, and I knew Sean didn't want me to inquire further. "I hope y'all can come for dinner on Sunday as usual."

"We'll be there." Sean remained focused on the road ahead of us and didn't glance my way. His demeanor did nothing to alleviate my concern for him and Alex. It actually had the opposite effect, and I was going to have to keep myself under tight rein to keep from opening my big mouth and questioning him directly.

"They've made good progress on the house," Sean said. "They got the demo done in a couple of days, and they've finished the Sheetrock. It looks like a house again inside. All the plumbing and electrical work is done, too."

"And no stray bones turned up, I trust," I said jokingly, referring to the bones Diesel and I had found in the attic not all that long ago.

"Not a single one," Sean said. "All we saw were the bones of the house, and they're in surprisingly good shape for a house this old."

"I'm glad to hear that," I said. "I didn't want to think I'd sold you a ramshackle place."

"Not at all," Sean said. "It means a lot to me to have this house that has been such a part of our history back in the family. I'm looking forward to living in it and bringing up my daughter there."

I had a sudden lump in my throat as I remembered my grandparents, particularly my grandmother Harris, who had been such a loving presence in my life. I always looked forward to visiting them, but sadly they both died when I was still a child. I wished they had lived long enough to see their great-grandchildren, but I was happy to know that Sean, Alex, and Rosie would make the farmhouse a home again.

"Rosie's going to be a country girl," I said. "I hope you'll all be really happy in that house."

"Me, too," Sean said. "I'm thinking we might need to do some landscaping as well, but I think that can wait. Nothing major, maybe adding some plants to the existing beds."

"That would add some color," I said. We weren't far from the house now, and I was eager to see it. But I wished Sean would confide in me. I could tell something was wrong, but I could only speculate as to what it was.

Sean turned off the road and into the driveway leading to the house. I could see that the exterior had been freshly painted a pristine white. The roof had been replaced with gray shingles. When we stepped onto the porch, I noticed the boards had been painted as well, a soft gray to match the roof. Sean had had all the windows replaced with energy-efficient ones, a decision I heartily approved.

He unlocked the front door and stood aside for me and Diesel to enter. The cat immediately started wandering around and sniffing. Furniture sat shrouded in drop cloths, and Diesel disappeared underneath one. I left him to his explorations, knowing that he would be unhappy to be called away from them.

Two walls had been knocked down in order to enlarge a few of the rooms on either side of the long hallway that stretched from the front door to the back of the house. We walked through the house, and Sean pointed out some of the renovations. The kitchen showed the evidence of the most change. Gone were the elderly appliances and old, worn cabinets, replaced by sleek Shaker-style ones. There was an island now also. The kitchen was roomy enough for one.

A door on the far wall of the kitchen opened onto the stairway leading to the attic. "Have you done anything to the attic?" I asked.

"Improved the ventilation," Sean said. "I thought it might make a fun playroom for Rosie when she's older."

"That's a nice idea," I said. "Children need places where their imaginations can have scope. I was afraid of the attic here when I was a child, but it was a spooky place back then."

"This one isn't spooky any longer. Why don't you go up and have a look," Sean said.

"Maybe later," I said. "You had the old root cellar cleaned out, too, didn't you?"

"Yes, and also checked to make sure it wasn't going to collapse. I doubt we'll use it as a root cellar, but I'm thinking it will be good as a storm cellar in case of tornadoes."

"That's a great idea," I said. Tornadoes terrified me, and knowing that Sean, Alex, and Rosie would have a safe refuge from them made me happy. I expressed the thought aloud to Sean.

Suddenly he turned to me. I was stunned to see tears in his eyes. "Dad, Alex is really unhappy right now because of me, and I'm not sure what to do to make things right."

TWELVE

||||||||||||||||||||||||||||||||||||||

My heart nearly broke then. Sean had kept this to himself for I had no idea how long, but finally it had been more than he could handle on his own. I opened my arms and gathered him in a fierce hug. He clung to me so hard I thought I wasn't going to be able to breathe, but I would bear whatever I had to. He cried like he hadn't since he was a little boy and his beloved dog had died, run over by a neighbor's car.

The storm of tears began to abate after perhaps a couple of minutes, and when Sean released me I suggested we find somewhere to sit and talk. He pulled out a handkerchief to wipe his face and blow his nose.

"Front parlor," he said.

I led the way, and he walked silently beside me. When we reached the parlor he helped me pull away the drop cloths, and we uncovered the sofa where Diesel was napping. When we sat on either side of him, he immediately climbed into Sean's lap and bumped Sean's chin with his head. Sean stroked the cat and smiled.

Diesel always knew when someone was upset and wanted to comfort that person. I knew he would help Sean feel calmer. I waited until I could see Sean's breathing had returned completely to normal before I spoke.

"What's going on with Alex?" I asked gently.

"Several things," Sean said. "The big thing is that she's not sure she wants to go back to work. She likes being at home with Rosie, and she wants to let the nanny go. I completely understand that."

"Is there a financial impact because of this?" I asked.

Sean sighed. "That's the second thing. Even though you sold me this house for a negligible amount, the renovations are costing a lot more than I'd anticipated."

"How much more?" I asked, feeling suddenly alarmed.

"About two hundred thousand," he said, glancing at me sideways, then glancing quickly away. "Could be another ten to twenty thousand."

"Is this going to put you in a financial strain if Alex doesn't go back to work?" I asked, rather stunned by the amount.

"It might," Sean said. "I fully understand the reasons Alex wants to stay home with Rosie, and I don't mind the work involved for me in the practice. Thankfully, I have Anne Kimbol to pick up some of Alex's work. She's great."

"Maybe you can add a junior to the firm," I said. "That would help, wouldn't it?"

Sean nodded. "I've been considering that, and Alex is on board with it. So is Anne."

"Then I'm not sure I see the full issue with the financial angle," I said. There must be something Sean had yet to tell me.

"Alex isn't sure she wants to live in this house," Sean said. "I mean, she thinks it's a beautiful house, but she's not thrilled with living in the country."

I could understand that. Alex had grown up in town. For that matter, so had Sean. I think he was so wrapped up in the idea of the history of the family associated with this house he might not have considered all the implications that living in the country might have for him and his family. I expressed these thoughts as tactfully as I could.

Sean grimaced. "You're right, of course. It's a lot to expect Alex to move out here, even though it's really only a few miles from Athena. There aren't any neighbors close by, but that's one of the selling points to me. After growing up in Houston where people practically lived on top of one another, I like the idea of having space, the kind of space this house and the land offer." He grimaced again. "Alex has never lived in a huge city, so she doesn't really understand why this is so important to me."

I understood what he meant. Houston had often been overwhelming because of the sheer amount of people and cars, and neighborhoods with houses only a few feet apart. I myself found this house attractive because of its separateness, the open space around it. I loved the quiet of it, as well as its history as part of my family's legacy.

"Perhaps you can keep the house in town for a while, so Alex doesn't feel like you're forcing her into such a big change," I said.

"I hadn't thought about that," Sean said slowly. "That house is paid for, but selling it would help ease the strain here and help pay for the renovations. I guess I was counting on that."

"Why don't you talk it over with Alex?" I said. "That would show her that you're not trying to force her into making such a huge change. Give her some time to live in this house and see its potential advantages."

"Thanks, Dad," Sean said. "I know what I need to do now." He released Diesel from an embrace. "Thank you, buddy. I feel better thanks to you and Dad."

"You know that I'll do whatever you need to help," I said. "The whole family will be there for you."

Sean rose from the couch. "I know you will, and that means the world to me. Family is important, and I want to restore this house for the family. Our roots are here, and I want us to be connected. I want my daughter to grow up here. I think eventually Alex will come to understand that and agree with me."

"I'm glad you feel that way," I said. "Roots are important. Now you'd better get me and Diesel back to the house. I may have an appointment later this morning, and I don't want to miss it."

"What kind of appointment?" Sean asked. "It isn't something medical, is it?"

"No, nothing like that," I assured him as Diesel and I followed him out of the house. We waited while he locked the door and then headed for the car.

Sean paused in the act of opening his car door and looked across at me, his eyes narrowed. "Hold on, now, does this have anything to do with what happened at the Farrington Hotel last night?"

"How did you hear about that?" I asked, surprised. "Surely it hasn't made the news yet?"

"I have contacts in the police department and the sheriff's office," he said.

"In other words, Haskell told you about it," I said in tones of semi-resignation. I opened the back door and Diesel hopped up onto the seat.

"No, not Haskell," Sean said as he got in the car.

"Kanesha?" I asked when I was seated beside him.

"No, not Kanesha," Sean said. "Our new next-door neighbor is a policeman. We both went out to retrieve our papers at the same time, and when that happens, we usually chat for a bit. He and his wife have a toddler, and we swap stories. This morning, though, he was telling me all about what happened last night."

"Did he mention that I was there with Helen Louise?" I asked.

"No, I don't think he knows you," Sean said. "He wasn't involved in it, but he was on duty last night and heard about it. I should have known you were there. I didn't realize you know Wil Threadgill."

"I don't, really," I said. "We did go to high school together, but he was two years ahead of me. He dropped out during his senior year and ran off to Hollywood. Melba knew him better than I did and managed to keep in touch with him sporadically over the years."

"It must have been awful to see that guy electrocuted," Sean said, cutting a sideways glance at me. Then he focused his gaze on entering the highway.

"It was," I said. "It wasn't an accident, either. Did your neighbor tell you there was a second murder attempt?"

Sean's hands jerked slightly on the wheel. He steadied them before he replied. "No, he didn't. I guess he didn't know about it. Did someone try to kill Wil Threadgill again?"

"It might have been aimed at Wil, but it was one of Wil's band members, a man named Zeb Jones, who was hurt," I said. "We met him last night at the reception. He seemed like a nice, really down-to-earth guy."

"Are they sure it wasn't an accident, rather than a deliberate attempt to kill someone?"

"I don't know," I said. "But an accident would certainly be a strange coincidence if it were." I decided I might as well confess to Sean about my conversation with Wil the other day, and about Wil's concerns about his entourage.

Sean didn't respond immediately when I finished. "Dad, I hope you won't get too involved in this situation. From what my neighbor told me, the person behind this is pretty ruthless. Anyone could have been killed last night."

"It wasn't completely random," I said. "I believe Wil was the target. He was the most likely person to use that microphone and the mic stand. The poor man who got electrocuted wasn't even supposed to be there."

"Who was he? My neighbor mentioned a name, but I don't remember it. I didn't know whoever it was."

I explained about John Earl Whitaker and his connection to Wil. "A tragic end to a truly sad life," I concluded.

"Horrible way to die," Sean said. "Death by electrocution is barbaric anyway."

"I don't plan to get any more involved in this than having another conversation with Wil if he still wants to talk to me. I'm more than happy to leave things to the law enforcement agencies here to handle things. Besides, Kanesha might ride me out of town on a rail if I don't."

I had hoped to elicit a smile with that last remark, but Sean didn't rise to the bait. I appreciated his concern, in the same way I hoped that he appreciated my concern for him and his wife and child. Like other men his age, Sean thought his father wasn't as capable as he was and that I needed someone to look after me. Laura tended to side with him on this issue, whenever a murder investigation was concerned.

"I hope you really mean that," Sean said. "You have a habit of getting sucked into these things, based on past history. You have to admit that's true, Dad."

"Yes, I guess it is," I said. "I don't seek these things out. They simply seem to happen somewhere in my vicinity, and I can't always ignore the pleas for help. Especially in this case, since Melba is involved."

"Melba involved? How?" Sean asked as he turned down my street. He pulled the car into my driveway and parked.

"I suspect that she's in love with Wil Threadgill," I said.

"How does that involve you?" Sean asked. "Isn't that her business?"

"It is, but you know that she's my very dear friend, probably my best friend besides Helen Louise," I said, feeling defensive. "When she asks me for help, I can't just say, *No, sorry, I'm not going to get involved.*"

Sean sighed heavily as he regarded me, looking suddenly very tired. "I love how you're loyal to the people you love," he said. "But the people who love you want you to be safe and not put yourself in danger. We've been through all this before, and I suppose I should have learned by now that you're going to follow your conscience in these things. We can't stop you."

"I never mean to cause you or your sister any worry on my part," I said. "When I do, I regret it, the same way you in the past have regretted causing me worry or pain. This is part of life, and we can't go through life without taking risks for the people we love. Melba is like family to me, the sister I never had. I won't let her down, and she would never ask me to do something I wasn't willing and happy to do for her."

Diesel started warbling loudly, and I knew he sensed the emotions running high in the car. I reached back to rub his head.

Sean turned to look at him. "It's okay, boy. We're fine, but I'm going to expect you to keep a close eye on Dad here. Keep him out of trouble."

Diesel answered him with a loud meow, and both Sean and I laughed, breaking the tension. I opened the door and got out. Diesel hopped into my former seat and then onto the driveway.

"Thanks, Dad. Love you," Sean said.

"I love you, too, son."

Diesel and I stood and watched Sean back out of the driveway, then head on his way home. My heart hurt for him and Alex, and I had never felt so helpless in my life.

THIRTEEN

IIIIIIIIIIIIIIIIIIIIIIIIIIIIIIIIIIIIIIIIIIIIIIIIIIII

I watched Sean's SUV until it disappeared down the street before I turned toward the house. I couldn't allow myself to brood over Sean's domestic situation. I loved my daughter-in-law, and I wanted her to feel happy. I would do what I could to support them in any way I could, and I knew the rest of the family would feel the same. Between them, Sean and Alex would be able to work it all out.

Diesel and I entered the house through the garage. The kitchen was unoccupied when we stepped into it. Diesel ambled off to the utility room to take care of his basic needs, and I went to the refrigerator to do the same. I needed a boost, and I pulled out a diet drink with caffeine. As my hand reached for the can, I also spotted the remains of the lemon icebox pie Azalea had made a couple of days ago. Azalea's version of this pie was the best I'd ever had, and I decided it wouldn't hurt if I had the final piece.

I settled at the table with my drink, a fork, and the pie. As I ate, savoring the taste and texture, I checked my watch. Coming up on nine-thirty. I wondered if I should call Wil and tell him I ought to stay away from the investigation completely under the situation. I didn't think there was anything right now I could do for him that the authorities couldn't do better. As I forked the last bit of pie into my mouth, I decided that I would head to the Farrington Hotel with Diesel. My curiosity trumped caution, as usual.

My phone pinged to let me know I had a new text message before I could pull it out and unlock the screen. When I tapped on the message app, I saw that Melba was communicating with me. I scanned the words, then responded simply *OK*. I set the phone down on the table and pondered the cryptic message.

Stay home. I'll be there soon.

Why was Melba coming to my house? She must know something important, otherwise she wouldn't be headed here or have sent such a peremptory text.

"Melba is coming to see us," I informed Diesel, who had taken up position by my chair and stretched out on the floor. He sat up at Melba's name and chirped. He adored Melba. She spoiled him rotten.

Suddenly I realized I hadn't seen Ramses, and I suspected he might be upstairs with Alissa. To be certain, however, I texted her. Ramses was quite the little scamp and had been known to dart outside before anyone realized he was anywhere near an open door. I hated to think of him wandering around outside, perhaps in danger of getting into the street.

Alissa texted back almost immediately to assure me that he was with her, and I thanked her for keeping an eye on him. I put the phone away and decided I should clean away the empty pie tin and my fork. I wondered whether I should make a fresh pot of coffee. Melba drank it throughout the day, and she might want it.

I had barely finished with the coffeepot and turned it on when I heard the front doorbell. Diesel trotted ahead of me, no doubt eager to greet his buddy Melba.

The first person I saw when I opened the door, however, was Wil Threadgill dressed in worn jeans and a denim shirt that had seen better days. He wore sunglasses and had a baseball cap pulled down over his forehead. He gave me a wan smile as he greeted me.

"I hope you don't mind, Charlie," he said as I waved him inside. Melba came in right behind him. She watched him anxiously. When I got a good look at Wil's face, I understood why Melba was in her hovering caregiver mood. Wil's eyes were red-rimmed, and his posture was that of a worn, defeated man. He looked like he hadn't slept at all last night. Melba took his arm and led him into the kitchen.

Diesel walked alongside Wil, warbling at him. He had quickly picked up on the man's obvious distress and wanted to comfort him.

Melba pushed Wil gently into a chair. He pulled off his cap and laid it on the table. He looked down at Diesel and reached a tentative hand out to him.

"Go ahead and stroke his head," Melba said quietly. "He loves it."

Diesel placed a large front paw on Wil's leg and looked up at him, warbling loudly. Wil stroked the cat's head tenderly. "What a beautiful creature you are." Wil's tone was soft, caressing, and Diesel pushed his head against the hand.

Wil glanced at me. He repeated his earlier words. "I hope you don't mind, Charlie. I was desperate to get out of the hotel, away from the horror and the hubbub of the investigation." He smiled briefly. "I doubt your friend the chief deputy is going to be happy with me for doing it, or with Melba for helping me."

"We'll deal with Kanesha when we have to," I said. "Trust me, I have plenty of experience being on her bad side. She'll probably blame me anyway once she finds out you came to me."

I glanced at the coffeepot. The coffee would be ready in a couple of minutes. "How about a cup of hot fresh coffee?"

"Sounds good," Wil said. "Caffeine is about the only thing keeping me going right now." He continued to stroke Diesel's head, and the cat chirped and occasionally trilled for him. I could see that some of the tension had drained away from Wil's posture. Diesel often had that calming effect on people who were troubled.

Melba didn't wait for me to retrieve mugs from the cabinet. She pulled two off the shelf and set them by the pot. Then she went to the fridge and brought out the half-and-half. The moment the coffeemaker finished gurgling, she pulled the pot out and poured coffee for herself and Wil. She added a dollop of the cream to both mugs before handing one to Wil. She added a couple of spoons of sugar to hers and then took a chair across the table from Wil.

I resumed my seat and waited for Wil to speak. I didn't want to hurry him. I burned with curiosity about Zeb Jones's brush with death, but I didn't want to distress Wil with questions right this minute.

After several sips of his coffee, Wil leaned back in his chair, hands cradled around his mug. He looked at me, and I could see the pain in his gaze.

"Zeb could have died," he said. "He's my best friend, and I am gutted that he was in danger because of me. I'm finding it hard to take in because I can't imagine who'd want to hurt Zeb, of all people. The awful way that John Earl died right in front of me, and there was nothing I could do to stop it. Then Zeb was targeted. This is my worst nightmare come true."

"Can you tell me what happened with Zeb?" I asked.

Wil took a sip of his coffee and set the mug on the table. "It was really cold-blooded," he said. "It was the ice bucket in the bedroom. Zeb has this bad habit of scooping ice out with his hand instead of using the scoop they provide. For once it was a good thing he did."

"I'm afraid I don't understand," I said.

"There were small shards of glass in the bucket along with the ice," Melba said grimly. "If anyone had swallowed it he might have died in agony."

"Oh my lord," I said. "How horrible." Though a clever, ruthless way to kill someone, I thought. "Was Zeb injured at all?"

"He had some small cuts on his hand from the glass shards," Wil said. "Thank the Lord he saw that before he tried to drink anything with all that glass in it."

"Yes, thank goodness he realized something was wrong," Melba said.

"It was diabolical," Wil said. "John Earl was in the wrong place at the wrong time. I believe I was the one who was supposed to be electrocuted, but he got it instead." He shook his head. "I thought there might be another attempt to take me out at some point, but I can't believe this maniac targeted Zeb. Why would someone want to hurt him?"

"Were you with him when it happened?" I asked.

"No," Wil replied. "He's sharing my suite, but I was in another room at the time. He called out to me, and I went to see what happened. He showed me his bleeding hand, then told me about the glass in the ice bucket."

"Did everyone in your band and your management know about his habit of scooping ice out with his hand?" I hated to distress him further, but it would help figure out whether any one of them had made this attempt on Zeb's life.

"Yes, they all know." Wil looked puzzled, but Melba shot me a sharp glance. I raised my eyebrows at her, and she frowned. I think she had picked up on the reason for my question.

Wil took a moment longer to get the point. His eyes widened as he stared at me. "Oh my god, you mean you think it had to be someone who knows him. Or else I was the target all along."

"A stranger wouldn't know about this odd habit. If a stranger was responsible, the intent was no doubt to cause maximum harm from swallowing shards of glass, which is far more serious," I said. "Did strangers have access to your band equipment?"

Wil slowly shook his head. "The room was locked until they began setting up for the reception, and that half of the room was shut off by the partition. No one could get in there, as far as I know." *Except a band member.* Wil left the words unsaid, but they hung there, nevertheless.

I waited for him to consider the implications further. He knew his people, but they were all strangers to me.

"I can't believe someone I have worked with for years is behind this," Wil said, obviously badly disturbed by the thought. "How could I not know someone hated me so much? To try to kill me? And to try to harm my best friend. It makes no sense."

I thought that was perhaps a bit disingenuous on Wil's part. The music business was highly competitive, and someone in the group might resent Wil for any number of reasons. His manager, Vance Tolliver, might want a bigger slice of the pie, for example. Or maybe Tolliver had been cheating Wil for years and was afraid Wil was about to find out. There were any number of possibilities. That person might also be jealous of the close friendship between Wil and Zeb.

The fact that I knew nothing about these people hindered me from coming up with plausible suspects. As far as I was concerned, they were all suspect. I imagined that Kanesha had already set in motion background checks on all of them. It was the smart thing to do. She didn't have the advantage of local knowledge in this case, as the source of trouble probably lay in California rather than in Mississippi.

"Time to dig a little deeper into this," I said. "Is there anything you haven't told me, other than these feelings you've had that something is off with your group?"

Wil sipped some coffee before he responded. He sighed heavily. "Yes, there were a few letters. I should have told you the other day. I'm sorry."

I brushed his apology aside. "Threatening ones? Anonymous?"

He nodded. "Like something out of an old detective story. Letters cut out of a newspaper, pasted on a page. Warning me to stay in California, otherwise God might strike me down for the wickedness of my dissolute life." He snorted in derision. "I live the least dissolute life of anyone I know. Most of the time I'm like a medieval monk, holed up in my monastery. I don't go to wild parties, I don't throw them, and I'm about as celibate as they come. All I really care about is music."

I shot a quick glance at Melba to gauge her reaction to these statements, particularly the latter one. She had her head down, ostensibly fascinated by the contents of her mug, so I couldn't really tell whether she was reacting to Wil's words.

Wil continued. "I spend most of my time in my home studio. I have to turn down commissions for movie soundtracks. It's a crazy way to live, I guess, to some people. But I love it." He shrugged. "Maybe I should be paying more attention to what goes on around me, to *who's* around me."

"Whoever it is must be deranged," Melba said flatly.

"Possibly," I said. "But Wil, you have to think hard about this. Is there anyone in your group who might be nursing a grudge against you? A lost opportunity to strike out on their own, perhaps? Or someone who feels they're not getting the acknowledgment they deserve for their contributions to your success?"

"What were the postmarks on those letters?" Melba asked suddenly before Wil could reply to my questions. "Surely that's an important clue."

"They were postmarked in Los Angeles," Wil said.

FOURTEEN

||||||||||||||||||||||||||||||||||||||||||||||||||||||

"That settles it," I said. "Somebody in your group must be behind the killing and the attempted one." I was both relieved and disappointed with the knowledge. Relieved because I could step back from the situation and leave it in Kanesha's hands. Disappointed because I didn't think I could be helpful. The answers obviously lay in Wil's life and relationships in California, not with his life and old friendships here in Mississippi.

I glanced at Melba and saw that she appeared puzzled. "What is it?" I asked.

"That doesn't make a lot of sense," Melba said. "Why would someone in Los Angeles want to keep you from coming back to Mississippi? Seems to me those letters should have come from here if the person who sent them wanted to frighten you away from Athena."

Wil shrugged. "That's what I thought, and that's why I was

inclined not to take them too seriously. I even thought they might be some kind of silly practical joke. Everybody knows I love reading mysteries and watching old-time cop shows when I'm between projects." He glanced at me. "That's how I decompress, because I get so intense when I'm composing."

"I understand," I said. "Reading helps me unwind, too. But I think Melba has a point, though I'm not sure I agree with you that they were a silly practical joke. Do you still have the letters?"

"Yeah, but they're in my house back in California," Wil said. "I didn't think about bringing them here, but I guess I should have."

"Do you have anyone, like a housekeeper, who could get them and send them here? I think Chief Deputy Berry ought to see them."

Wil shook his head. "They're locked in my safe, and though I trust my housekeeper, who's also my cat sitter, I don't want anyone getting access to my safe."

That frustrated me, though I could understand Wil's wish to protect the contents of his safe from an employee, no matter how loyal. If Wil engaged this person to look after his cats, there must be considerable trust involved.

"At least tell Deputy Berry about them," I said. "They could be important in the long run."

"I will." Wil drained his coffee and got up to pour himself another cup. Melba took it from him and pushed him back toward his chair. With a quick smile, Wil did as he was bid, and Melba returned to the table with his refilled mug.

"I have another question," Melba said. "I've been thinking about that ice bucket. Wil, what time did this happen? It must have been pretty late last night."

"Around eleven, I guess," Wil said after a moment's reflection. "Why do you ask?"

"How long had the ice been in the bucket?" Melba said. "If it had been in there several hours, the ice would have melted down quite a bit, wouldn't it? In that case, why wouldn't you just dump it and ask for fresh ice?"

"That's a good point," I said.

Wil thought about it. "I didn't pay much attention to it, frankly. I was drinking cold bottled water from the fridge, but Zeb likes decaffeinated soda with ice. I was more concerned at the time with wrapping up Zeb's hand and stopping the bleeding. Then I called the manager's office, and they found the deputies and sent them in. They took the bucket away before I could look in it."

"Maybe they'll be able to figure out something from it," Melba said.

Melba glanced at Wil. "Kanesha's really focused, and I'm sure she'll get to the bottom of all this mess."

"I don't doubt it after meeting her," Wil said with a brief smile. "I knew her mother slightly years ago, and if she's anything like Miss Azalea, I'm sure she'll get to the bottom of it all."

Melba and I laughed. "Don't dare say that to either one of them," I said. "They'll bristle up at you, especially Kanesha. They think they're really different from each other."

"Thanks for the warning," Wil replied. "I didn't have the chance to mention Miss Azalea when I talked to the deputy last night. I guess I'll hold off on that completely just to be safe."

The front doorbell rang. I wasn't expecting anyone, but I really wasn't surprised when I found Kanesha Berry on the doorstep.

"We were just talking about you," I said lightly. Diesel meowed at her and rubbed against her leg. In times past he never did that, but Kanesha had thawed toward him, the way her mother had, and now she would actually pat his head. She did so now before she entered the house.

"In the kitchen?" she asked. "I saw Miss Gilley's car out front, and I figure she brought Mr. Threadgill here."

"Yes, in the kitchen." I waved for her to precede me. Diesel and I came along behind.

Kanesha had her usual poker face in place, and I couldn't tell whether she was annoyed or resigned to the fact that Melba and Wil had involved me in the situation. I would no doubt find out soon enough. Sooner or later Kanesha would let me know exactly where I stood in no uncertain terms.

"Good morning, Miss Gilley, Mr. Threadgill." Kanesha nodded to each of them in turn. "I'm surprised that you left the hotel, Mr. Threadgill. I'm pretty sure I asked you to stay put."

Kanesha sounded matter-of-fact, but I figured she was actually annoyed by the situation. More because they had come to my house than because Wil had left the hotel.

"You did," Wil said in a calm tone. "But I really needed to get out of there, and Melba offered me a ride here. I wanted to talk to Charlie and visit with Diesel again. I need to get my mind off what happened." He shook his head. "I live a quiet life. Last night was too much."

Kanesha regarded him fixedly. She should be able to see, as I did, the exhaustion in his eyes and hear the weariness in his voice. The electrocution of John Earl Whitaker right in front of him and the attack on his best friend had taken a toll, as they would on anyone. Kanesha didn't lack compassion, I knew, but as a professional, she was dedicated to the task at hand and had laser focus. To those who didn't know her, she often seemed hard and unfeeling.

Diesel had moved to stand by Wil's chair. Wil reached down to stroke the cat's head while he waited for Kanesha to respond.

Finally she spoke. "I understand that, Mr. Threadgill. I know it was a horrible thing to have to witness. I know Mr. Whitaker was once a close friend of yours, as we discussed last night. The injuries Mr. Jones suffered are worrisome also. I promise you that we'll get to the bottom of all this and catch the person who's responsible."

"Thank you, Deputy," Wil said. "I have no doubt you will. Charlie and Melba have been singing your praises."

"I appreciate that," Kanesha said without a glance at either Melba or me. "I'd like you to accompany me back to the hotel, Mr. Threadgill. I have more questions for you and your bandmates about last night."

Wil stood, and Diesel chirped. Wil had stopped stroking his head. He looked up at Wil, who smiled down at him. "He really is a treasure."

"Thank you," I said. "He's well aware of that, unfortunately."

"Thank you for the coffee and the conversation, Charlie," Wil said as he moved to follow Kanesha out of the kitchen. "I needed a break, and you provided that. Melba, I'll catch up with you later. Thanks for bringing me."

Melba nodded. "Anytime."

With a final smile at us, Wil walked out of the kitchen. Kanesha probably already had the door open. I heard it close a moment later.

"I feel like the principal just caught us playing hooky," I joked.

"It's not funny," Melba said shortly.

"No, I suppose not." I saw this response as a measure of how intensely focused her feelings were. Ordinarily she would have at least smiled at my little sally. Evidently her concern for Wil trumped everything else.

"Do you have time for more coffee and a chat?" I asked.

Melba shook her head. "No, I've got a lot to do at home. Laundry, cleaning, and so on. I'll do better if I stay busy."

"Okay, you do what you need to do. It's probably useless to tell you not to worry. Kanesha will see that Wil is safe."

"She damn well better," Melba said darkly as Diesel and I escorted her to the front door. Diesel warbled loudly, a bit alarmed by Melba's intensity. She softened her tone, however, and bent to give him a hug. "It's okay, sweet boy."

Diesel and I stood in the doorway and watched as Melba made her way down the walk to the street. She looked up when she opened the car door. She waved and then got in and drove off.

"Come on, boy," I said, and Diesel followed me back to the kitchen.

Alissa and Ramses entered the kitchen while Diesel supervised my clearing the table and washing, rinsing, and drying the coffee mugs Wil and Melba had used. I made sure the coffeemaker was off as I greeted Alissa and Ramses.

"I saw Melba driving away out of my window," Alissa said. "Ramses and I were reading in the window seat. I thought I'd come down and find out what was going on. I also saw the deputy taking Mr. Threadgill away. Is there something wrong?"

She took a chair at the table, and Ramses climbed into her lap. He sat and put his front paws on the table, as if he were waiting to be served. I looked at him askance. He was incorrigible. "No," I told him, "you're not getting anything to eat." He mewed plaintively.

Alissa rubbed his head to console him while I explained what had happened at the hotel last night. She shuddered when I told her about the glass slivers in the ice bucket. "That's terrifying. Poor Mr. Jones. Thank goodness he didn't drink any of it."

"I know. It doesn't bear thinking about," I said, trying not to imagine the outcome of that.

"Whoever is behind all this must really hate Wil Threadgill," Alissa said. "Or else they ought to be in the insane asylum."

Since the one person who might have had the biggest grudge against Wil Threadgill, and who had actually been heard to threaten him, had been murdered, I couldn't imagine who the culprit was.

Then I was struck by the recurrence of a truly horrifying thought. What if Wil was behind it all? What if he had set up the microphone as a way to put John Earl Whitaker out of the picture?

FIFTEEN

|||||||||||||||||||||||||||||||||||||||||||||

My expression must have alarmed Alissa, because she spoke sharply. "Charlie, what's the matter?"

Startled out of my thoughts, I stared at her. I didn't feel that I could share my suspicions with her, so I hastily said, "Oh, nothing, guess I was thinking about what you said."

"About somebody being insane?" Alissa said, and I nodded. Perhaps Wil was insane, in some way, if he was behind John Earl's death and the glass in the ice bucket.

Setting Ramses on the floor, Alissa pushed back from the table and went to the fridge. She extracted a bottle of juice. "I guess I'll go back upstairs and finish my book. Are you coming with me, Ramses?"

Ramses meowed loudly. He knew Alissa kept treats in her room for him, and if there was a possibility of food being handed out, he was all for it.

They left the kitchen, and Diesel remained with me. He rubbed his body against my leg, and I patted him to reassure him I was okay. My thoughts disturbed me. I hated to think that Wil was some kind of psychopath who would do these things. But, really, what did I know about him? I had only vague memories of him from high school forty years ago. Melba thought he was a wonderful person, but where men were concerned, Melba sometimes overlooked the obvious.

I couldn't imagine the motive for Wil wanting to kill John Earl Whitaker, unless the dead man knew something to Wil's discredit, as Stewart had suggested. The more I thought about it, the more unrealistic the whole idea became. I thought about the threatening letters Wil said he received in Los Angeles, but no one else had seen them. If they existed at all, that is. He could have sent them to himself, but why?

For now, I decided, I had to give Wil the benefit of the doubt, waiting to see what happened next. I would have to weigh carefully whatever he told me and observe his reactions. He had seemed really upset about his friend Zeb, though.

I decided I had spent enough time for the moment thinking about Wil Threadgill and the debacle of last night. I was hungry, and I went to the fridge to rummage for lunch. I found some leftover salad and chicken, and I decided a small salad and a chicken sandwich would be fine for lunch. Diesel eyed the chicken longingly while I pulled enough from the carcass to make my sandwich. I pulled a few extra pieces for him, but he would have to wait until I was seated at the table again before he got any.

I ate my salad first and doled out bits of chicken to the cat. I even pulled a small piece from my sandwich for him, but I finally held up my hand to let him know that was the end of the chicken for him. He meowed loudly before trotting off to the utility room where he would no doubt have some dry food and a drink of water.

I had pushed the situation with Sean and Alex to the back of my mind while I dealt with Melba and Wil, but now the worries came flooding back. I put down the last bite of sandwich and sighed. My heart ached so much for both of them, and for my beautiful little granddaughter. There was so much uncertainty for all of them at the moment, though I hoped Rosie wasn't aware of it. She was barely a year old, and I prayed she couldn't sense her parents' turmoil. I had to cling to the hope that Sean and Alex would work things out soon before the strain affected Rosie as well.

My cell phone interrupted my thoughts, and with some relief I saw that Helen Louise was calling.

"Hello, love," she said. "I would have called earlier, but Henry came over to discuss some changes to the menu, and he left only about five minutes ago." Henry was the manager of Helen Louise's bistro. He had also begun buying an interest in the business, toward the time when Helen Louise would sell it completely and retire. That was still rather far down the road, according to Helen Louise. She had too much energy to step back completely, though she had managed to turn over a good bit of the decision-making and actual cooking to Henry.

"How are things with Henry?" I asked.

"Fine," Helen Louise said. "I'm lucky to have him, and he is much happier now that he is part owner of the bistro."

"I'm glad for both your sakes that you did this," I said.

Helen Louise laughed. "Yes, I know you are. Now, what about dinner this evening? I'm cooking the roast and a couple of the sides. Do I need to bring a dessert? How about wine?"

"The roast and sides are plenty," I said. "Stewart is providing the dessert. He hasn't told me what it is, but I expect he'll be down here in the kitchen before long to make it. As for wine, I think you have my wine supply in good shape, so we can choose from it."

Helen Louise knew far more about wine than I did, thanks to her cordon bleu training in Paris. I was learning, but I had a long way to go to reach her level of knowledge. She also had a more refined and better-educated palate than I did. I was a happy pupil, though.

"I'll be there around the usual time," she said. "Unless you'd like me to come earlier."

"If you could, I'd like that," I said. "We haven't had much time to talk since last night, and I need to tell you a few things. Not only about what we witnessed last night, but also about some family matters."

"Do you mean about Alex and Sean?" Helen Louise asked. "If so, Alex told me this morning while you and Sean were out at the old homestead."

"I'm glad." Alex's mother had passed away many years ago, and she had developed a strong bond with Helen Louise. "She needs someone strong like you to confide in."

"Thank you, love," Helen Louise said, a slight hitch in her voice. "I feel so bad for her because she's really torn over wanting to stay at home full time with Rosie but thinking Sean really needs her at work."

"I talked to Sean about it, and he doesn't seem as worried about losing Alex's contributions at work. He's more concerned about her reluctance to live in the country."

"Alex didn't mention that," Helen Louise said. "I can't say I'm surprised, though. She's never lived outside Athena."

"I suggested to Sean that they keep the house in town, since it's paid for," I said. "I know they could use the money from selling it to offset the cost of the renovations, but I think it will make Alex feel better if she has a safety valve."

"I agree," Helen Louise said. "Once she's had some time to experience living in the country, she might see its appeal."

"I hope so," I said. "The house is going to be stunning when the renovations are complete. But Alex's happiness is important. So is Sean's."

"We'll all do our best for them," Helen Louise said. "We won't let them down. Now, what else was it you wanted to tell me?"

"It's about Wil Threadgill," I said. "Melba brought him over this morning after I got back from the farm." I hesitated to go into further detail, but Helen Louise urged me to.

I told her about the incident with the ice bucket, and she was duly horrified at the potential injury, even death, that could have ensued from that. I told her my conclusion that the threat came from within Wil Threadgill's entourage, and she agreed with me.

"I don't see how anyone from Athena could be involved," Helen

Louise said. "Especially since the one person who potentially meant Wil harm was killed instead of Wil."

"That's what I think," I said. "But there are a lot of unknown factors in this situation. I'm sure Kanesha will sort it all out."

"I'm sure she will, too," Helen Louise said. "There's someone vicious behind all this, and I hope you'll stay out of it."

"I'm going to do my best," I said, and I do believe I meant it. Events might change my mind, however, but I hoped they wouldn't. I didn't want to worry my loved ones as I had on occasion in the past. Especially now, with our concerns for Alex, Rosie, and Sean.

After the call, I decided I needed a distraction, and for me that almost always meant reading. I headed upstairs to my bedroom to retrieve my current book. Diesel came with me. He hopped on the bed while I picked up my book from the nightstand. He stretched out, his head on his pillow, and meowed softly. I chuckled. He was ready for a nap, and I decided I would read in bed, rather than going down to my den as I had intended.

Shoes off, I made myself comfortable beside Diesel and opened my book. I had recently discovered a delightful series set in Aix-en-Provence, and I was entranced by the setting and fascinated by the main characters. The author, M. L. Longworth, was an expatriate American who actually lived in the town. Her descriptions of the town, along with mouthwatering mentions of the local cuisine, had me wanting to board a plane for Provence. I thought it would be the ideal place for a honeymoon, and I realized I ought to mention that to Helen Louise. Perhaps it would encourage her to set a date for the wedding. She kept putting it off, but I was trying to be patient. She'd never been married, and it would mean another big change in her life after her decision to step back from her business a bit.

I soon lost myself in the pages of my book, and I didn't realize how much time had passed until Stewart knocked on my door.

"Earth to Charlie," he said, laughing from the doorway. "That must be a great book. I've been standing here coughing for at least a minute or two."

I shot him a sheepish grin as I stuck in my bookmark and laid the book aside. Regretfully, as I had only a chapter or two left. "You'd love it, if you ever took time to read fiction."

Stewart shrugged. "Maybe so."

I told him a little about the series, and his eyes sparkled at the mention of Provençal cuisine. "Let me borrow it when you're done," he said.

"No, you need to start with the first one," I said. "It's a series."

"Okay," he said. "Now about dinner. The dessert is ready and I've also made a salad. The family should be arriving soon. Time for you to come downstairs." He grinned at my yawning cat. "You, too, Diesel. Ramses and Alissa are downstairs, and you wouldn't want Ramses to get more treats than you."

Diesel warbled loudly, then leaped across to the floor beside the bed.

I swung my legs off the bed and pushed myself up. "I'll be downstairs in a few. I need to freshen up before I face the crowd."

Stewart nodded, and Diesel followed him out of the room.

After washing my face and combing my hair, along with other necessary activities, I headed to the kitchen. In addition to Stewart,

Alissa, and the cats, I also found Helen Louise, whom I greeted with a kiss and a hug.

Within minutes the rest of the family arrived, all except Haskell. I queried Stewart about his absence, and Stewart explained that his partner was tied up at work. "He'll be home as soon as he can," Stewart said, "but I'll probably have to make up a plate for him to eat later. Apparently there's a lot going on with the investigation."

That naturally piqued my curiosity, but there was nothing I could do at the moment to satisfy it. Instead, I focused on my family, giving the most attention to my darling grandchildren. Charlie was busy running around, chasing Ramses, chattering all the while. Rosie was content to sit in my lap and gabble at me. I understood about every third word. She was making progress, but she had a way to go to catch up with Chatterbox Charlie.

Frank asked Sean about the progress on the farmhouse, and Sean, after a sideways glance at Alex, obliged. Alex's expression remained neutral, and no one brought up the subject of Alex's becoming a stay-at-home mom.

"I think I'm going to wait to see it until everything is done," Laura said after Sean concluded his anecdotes about the builders and the renovations. "I saw it before the reno started, and I want to see it when it's done, like the homeowners do on some of those reno shows on TV."

"Don't be getting any ideas about renovating our house," Frank said in a mock-serious tone. "I don't think I'd survive the chaos."

Laura grinned at him. "Don't worry, I'll wait until we buy a bigger house." She patted her belly. "We're going to need one soon."

"We'll see," Frank said.

While we were enjoying Stewart's marvelous dessert, apple pie a la mode, my cell phone rang. I pulled it out to discover that Melba was calling. I excused myself and stepped out of the dining room to take the call. I had a strange foreboding, as they said in the old mystery novels, that something was wrong.

Melba barely heard my *hello* before she launched into speech. "Somebody attacked one of Wil's band members with a knife!"

SIXTEEN

|||||||||||||||||||||||||||||||||||||||

"Oh my lord," I said. "Was he killed?"

"No, thank heavens," Melba said, her voice shaky. "He's gone to the ER now. I don't think his injuries are life-threatening, but they're pretty bad."

"Who is the band member?"

"Jackrabbit Colson," Melba replied.

"Jackrabbit?" I hadn't met anyone of that name so far.

"It's a nickname," Melba said, "because he's real high-energy, always on the move."

Probably hyperactive, I thought. "Where was he attacked?"

"Outside the hotel. He's a smoker, and he went out to the back parking lot to smoke. It had begun to get dark, and whoever it was came out of the bushes from behind him and stabbed him."

"Did he get a look at whoever stabbed him?"

"No, he didn't. By the time he could turn around, the stabber had disappeared, and he was in no condition to chase them. He staggered back into the lobby and collapsed there."

"Were you at the hotel when it happened?" I asked.

"I was talking with Wil in his suite when he got the call. By the time we got down to the lobby, the police were there, and the EMS team arrived about two minutes later."

"I hope he's going to be okay," I said. "I'm sure Wil is really shook up."

"He's practically catatonic now," Melba said. "We're back in his suite, and he's just sitting in a chair staring at the good Lord knows what."

One thing I knew now. If Melba was with Wil when the attack on Jackrabbit Colson occurred, then Wil couldn't possibly have done it.

Unless, the little nagging voice in my head said, the person who did it was an accomplice of Wil's, but that might be pushing things too far.

"What about the other members of Wil's entourage?" I asked. "Could they all account for where they were when it happened?"

"I don't know. They're still being interviewed," Melba said. "I sure hate to think one of them did it, but it has to be one of them, don't you think?"

"Most likely," I said. "This whole thing is so screwy, though. Kanesha'd better get this thing resolved soon, because none of them are safe. And that includes you, Melba. I think you've made yourself a potential target by hanging around Wil. Have you considered that?"

Silence on the other end. I waited and was about to repeat my question when she spoke. "I've thought about it, Charlie." She had lowered her voice. "But I can't leave Wil to face this by himself. I just can't."

I suppressed a sigh. Her feelings for Wil were as seriously engaged as I had thought they might be. I knew that arguing with her would do no good and could possibly cause an estrangement between us. I didn't want that, so I would have to do what I could to protect her.

"I understand," I said in a soothing tone. "I'm sure Wil appreciates your friendship and loyalty to him. You have to promise me, though, that you'll be careful around those people."

"I will, believe me," Melba said. "You've got to help us, Charlie. I trust Kanesha, of course, but I'll feel better if you're working on this, too. People are more likely to talk to you. She intimidates the heck out of people, she's so intense, and they clam up around her."

I thought Kanesha used her intensity to good effect a lot of the time. I understood what Melba meant, though. That technique of Kanesha's wouldn't work on everyone. It mostly didn't work on me anymore, for one.

"What do you want me to do?" I asked.

"Could you come over to talk to Wil and me? And bring Diesel. I think he'll help," Melba said.

"I can't right now. We're just finishing family dinner," I said. "Once they leave, if it's not too late, I'll come. With Diesel. Text me when the coast is clear," I added.

"Thank you," Melba said.

"Okay." I ended the call and put my phone away as I headed back into the dining room.

"What was all that about?" Helen Louise asked as I resumed my seat.

"Just Melba calling about something," I said. "Go on with what you were talking about."

Sean rose and pushed back his chair, Rosie in his arms. "Alex and I were waiting for you to come back before we said good night, Dad." Sean patted his daughter's back. Her head lay against his shoulder. "Our princess needs to be at home in her own bed."

I smiled at my sleeping granddaughter. "I'll walk you to the door," I said.

"We need to be going, too," Laura said. She motioned for Frank to waylay Charlie as my grandson wandered around the table. "Charlie needs to be in bed, and so do I." She did look tired, I thought.

"All right," I said. "Wagons ho."

I escorted them all to the front door and watched as they headed down the walk to their respective cars. Helen Louise and Diesel joined me. Alissa had thoughtfully kept Ramses with her and Stewart.

When I closed the door, Helen Louise said, "Okay, give, Charlie, my love. What did Melba want?"

"I'll tell you in a moment. Let's go back to the dining room and start clearing the table." I knew Stewart would already be at work, and he might as well hear this, too, along with Alissa.

Stewart was stacking plates, and Alissa held Ramses under one arm while she gathered up the linen napkins to take to the laundry room. "Hang on a minute," I said, and they both stopped what they were doing. "There's been a development at the hotel."

Alissa dropped down in a chair when I told them about the knife attack on Wil's band member. "Horrible," she said.

Stewart looked down at the plates he held. "At this rate, Haskell won't be home for hours yet." He sighed. "I'm sorry for this Jack-rabbit guy. I hope they catch the lunatic soon." He left the dining room with his burden. Alissa rose and followed.

Helen Louise and I began gathering the food dishes to remove to the kitchen. None of us spoke until the dining room was clear and we were all together in the kitchen.

Stewart was loading the dishwasher while Helen Louise took care of the leftovers. That was when I announced that Melba wanted Diesel and me to come to the hotel to talk to her and Wil.

Helen Louise stopped in the middle of scraping leftover mashed potatoes into a container and stared at me. "You're not going, surely."

I shrugged.

"I don't think it's a good idea," Stewart said after a swift glance at Helen Louise's expression. "It's bad enough Melba is stuck like a leech to Wil Threadgill, putting herself in danger. I don't think you need to add yourself to the mix."

"I know," I said. "But it's hard to resist Melba when she's fright-ened like this. I think she's really in love with Wil, and she's not the most reasonable person in these situations."

"No, she's not," Helen Louise said, snapping the lid on the pota-toes. "But that doesn't mean you have to cater to her. This is one time when I think you'll simply have to tell her no."

I really didn't want to go to the hotel tonight. I was tired, and I couldn't see that my presence, or that of my cat, would accomplish anything. Melba and Wil ought to be safe enough locked in that suite, along with Zeb Jones. There would be police or sheriff's deputies around.

"I'll let Melba know." I pulled out my phone and texted her, telling her I was exhausted and couldn't come. I was sorry, but I would see her tomorrow. I almost added that Helen Louise and Stewart had insisted that I stay home, but that would have been cowardly. I hated to disappoint a friend, but sometimes you had to. I had to hope Melba would forgive me.

Once the kitchen was done, Stewart headed upstairs. Alissa soon followed, taking Ramses and Diesel with her. Helen Louise planned to spend the night here, and I appreciated Alissa's thoughtfulness. Helen Louise poured glasses of wine for us, and we sat at the kitchen table to talk for a while before heading upstairs.

"I'm glad you decided to stay home," Helen Louise said. "Has Melba responded to your text yet?"

I checked my phone. "No, not yet." I sighed and put my phone on the table.

"She'll be okay, Charlie," Helen Louise said.

"I know." I had a sip of wine. "I think I'm using this whole thing with Wil Threadgill to distract me from thinking about Alex and Sean," I said in a sudden burst.

Helen Louise didn't look surprised. She simply nodded. "It's hard to think about your children going through such a situation. I feel so bad for Alex, and Sean, too, of course. Financial pressures can be really rough on a marriage, or any kind of relationship."

"I know," I said. "I could lend them the money for the renovations, but Sean would not be happy with me for offering. He's really independent. He even squabbled with me over the sale of the house, but I wouldn't budge." I sighed. "All I can do is pray that it all works out for the best."

Helen Louise nodded. "And we will." She paused a moment. "I need to change the subject for a minute to Laura, Frank, and Charlie."

That surprised me. "How so?"

"With the baby on the way, they're going to need more room than Frank's two-bedroom house," Helen Louise said. "They need a larger house, and I have one."

My stomach did a flip or two. Did this mean what I thought it did?

"Yes, they do, and you do have a larger house." Helen Louise lived in her family home, which had four bedrooms and three and a half bathrooms. Rather large for a single person, but it had been in her family for three generations. "What are you thinking about doing?"

"I think of them as family," Helen Louise said, glancing away for a moment. "And it's time that a family with children brought the house to life again." She paused to take a slow, measured breath. "I'm going to give them the house and move in here with you." She smiled at me now, and I could see the glint of tears in her eyes.

I felt too choked up to respond right then. I hoped my expression told her everything she needed to know. I got up from my chair and went to her. I pulled her up and into my arms. "God bless you," I said. Then we kissed.

Finally Helen Louise pulled away and gave me a mischievous

grin. "How about we finish our wine and then head upstairs to talk wedding dates?"

I gave a shaky laugh. "Sounds wonderful." The moment had finally come, and I was feeling giddy and excited at the same time.

Upstairs, we lay in bed and talked dates. Helen Louise wanted a church wedding, since this would be her first, and I was happy to agree. She wanted to keep the wedding itself small, limited to family and close friends. The reception, however, would be a larger affair. I agreed with that, though I quailed at the thought of hundreds of people turning up. We would have to limit that guest list, too, but we could work that out later. I knew she didn't want a circus, either.

After a surprisingly brief discussion, we settled on the first Saturday in February for our wedding day. That gave us plenty of time to plan everything, and with that done, we decided to call it a night. I got up and opened the bedroom door slightly. I knew if I didn't, either Diesel or Ramses—if not both of them—would eventually be scratching to be let in.

I fell asleep feeling really happy, despite the lingering worry over Alex and Sean, and concern for Melba and the miasma of fear and uncertainty surrounding her and Wil. I prayed for good outcomes in both situations.

SEVENTEEN

|||||||||||||||||||||||||||||||||||||||||||||||||||||||||||||||

Helen Louise didn't stay for breakfast the next morning. We were up early, because she liked to be out of the house before Azalea arrived. I understood why, but I felt sure Azalea wouldn't condemn her for spending the night with me. Nor did I think Azalea looked askance at me on the occasions when I came home in the morning from having spent the night with Helen Louise.

Come February, once we were married, no one could look askance at anything. I smiled to myself. After discussing it briefly this morning before she left, Helen Louise and I decided to wait to share the news about the wedding date with family until we were all together again at family dinner.

Azalea must have detected something in my manner as she served my breakfast, however, because she stood, one hand on her right hip, examining me closely while I picked up my fork.

"You sure are in a good mood," she said. "With all this mess going on at the hotel, I didn't think you'd be happy 'bout much."

Ramses prodded her leg with a paw, eager for a bite of bacon. Azalea looked down at him. "You hold on a minute, mister. You've had enough bacon." She turned her gaze back to me. "So what's got you so happy?"

I sighed and put down my fork. I had to answer, otherwise she'd keep prodding me until her curiosity was satisfied. "I'll tell you, but you can't tell anyone else. Absolutely anyone, all right?"

Azalea frowned. "You know I can keep a secret. So did you and Helen Louise finally set a date?"

I grinned. "You're a witch, Azalea. How you figure things out before I can tell you defeats me. Yes, we've set the date for the first Saturday of February. We decided last night after all the family left, and we're going to wait to tell them this coming Sunday when we're all together again."

Azalea beamed at me. "I'm happy for y'all," she said. "You let me know whatever you want me to do for the wedding."

"I promise we will," I said as I picked up my fork. Diesel placed a large paw on my thigh and nudged me none too gently. "All right, boy, I know you've been patient." I gave him about a third of a slice of bacon, and he meowed his thanks. I knew that paw would return to my thigh ere long, and I was prepared to dole out the other two-thirds of the bacon slice.

Azalea left the kitchen, humming, with Ramses trailing in her wake. Diesel remained by my side, waiting for bacon. I had consumed perhaps half my breakfast when Stewart appeared, looking rather bleary-eyed. He mumbled good morning and went straight to the coffeepot. I waited until he seated himself and had a couple of sips of coffee before I spoke again.

"Haskell get in late?" I asked.

Stewart nodded. "Yeah, there was a bad wreck out on the highway, and he was stuck with that for a couple of hours. No fatalities, thank the Lord." He drank more coffee.

"Is he still in bed?"

"No, he was out the door around five-thirty," Stewart said. "The hotel murder. They're following up possible leads on whoever it was that stabbed the band member last night."

"Was there a witness?" I asked, surprised.

Stewart shrugged. "I'm not sure. Haskell didn't say much. He was in a hurry to bathe and shave, and honestly I was too sleepy to ask questions." He yawned before he drained his cup. "Now I have to go get the demon child and take him out to use the bathroom before he tinkles all over the bed." He grimaced. "He's such a spiteful baby sometimes." He pushed himself up and ambled out of the room.

Stewart grumbled frequently about Dante, his toy poodle, but I knew my friend was devoted to the dog, despite Dante's quirks, like chewing on shoes he found left lying within reach. I suspected Stewart of occasionally letting Dante have old shoes to chew up, though he always fussed.

What we do for our four-legged children, I mused. People who didn't have pets didn't understand and often thought we were soft-headed as well as soft-hearted, but I pitied them because they didn't experience the love and companionship that we pet lovers did.

I had finished my breakfast and poured myself a second cup of coffee by the time Stewart reappeared. He was now fully awake. He had another cup before he glanced at the eggs and bacon Azalea had left warming in the oven for him. He helped himself, and while he ate, we discussed the hotel murder case.

Diesel finally gave up begging for bacon and left the kitchen, probably in search of Azalea and Ramses.

"So who do you think is behind this?" Stewart asked. "One of the California group or someone here in Athena?"

I told Stewart about the threatening letters, postmarked in Los Angeles, that Wil had told us about. "To me, if those letters really exist, that means somebody in the entourage is behind it."

"If they really exist?" Stewart arched his brows in surprise. "Do you think Wil might have made them up?"

"I don't know," I said, "but it's a possibility we can't overlook. You were the one who suggested he's behind all this, remember." I paused for a moment. "None of us knows Wil at all, and despite Melba's belief in him, I have to look at him as a potential suspect. Maybe he's the one who has harbored a grudge for forty years and set up that death by microphone himself."

"That's stone cold," Stewart said. "You're right, though. Even Melba doesn't know him that well, but I guess she believes she does."

"She does," I said. "I think she's in love with him. I wonder if Wil knows that, and if he does, how he feels about it." I sighed heavily. "I hope she's not setting herself up for heartbreak."

"If he's not behind all this himself, maybe once the case is settled, well, who knows?" Stewart said. "Melba certainly deserves some happiness."

"She does, but can you see her living in California?" I asked. I had trouble envisioning Athena—and my life—without Melba in it.

Stewart shook his head. "Honestly, no, I can't, but love makes you do crazy things sometimes."

I felt a sudden urge to tell him that Helen Louise and I had finally set the date, but I resisted. Bad enough that I caved and told Azalea. I would have to confess that to Helen Louise.

I pushed back from the table and set my dishes in the sink. "Time for me to be thinking about work," I said. "Will you be in for lunch or dinner?"

"Dinner," Stewart said. "I'm hoping Haskell will be able to join us, too."

I left him with his coffee and headed upstairs to brush my teeth. Diesel joined me when I was ready to leave for work. I swore he could tell time, because wherever he was in the house, he never failed to appear when it was time to go to work at the college archive.

The day promised to be cool enough, so we walked the few blocks to the building that housed the archive. I braced myself when we went inside because I would have to stop and say hello to Melba. I hadn't heard from her since I texted last night to say I couldn't come to the hotel. She might be angry with me over that. She had been known to hold a grudge, not usually against me, but there was a distinct possibility that I could be in her bad graces now.

Melba was not at her desk when Diesel and I paused in the office doorway. That was unusual because Melba seldom missed work, but perhaps she had taken the day off to rest after the incredibly stressful events of the weekend. I certainly couldn't blame her if she had.

Feeling relieved, as well as a bit guilty, I continued up the stairs to my office on the second floor. The moment the door was unlocked and open, Diesel ambled through to the window embrasure behind my desk. He leaped up into the broad sill so he could keep an eye on the enemy squirrels and birds who threatened his empire. He chirped a couple of times at a squirrel I spotted in the tree.

I left him to his guard duty while I awakened my computer and started my day by checking email. Other than the occasional request to work in the archive to consult some of the materials it contained, or to consult books in the rare book collection, most of my email was college miscellanea.

One email had been issued by the president's office on the subject of the tragedy at the Farrington House Hotel over the weekend. It was brief, with a minimum of details, but it did say that Wil Threadgill had revised the schedule of his workshops with the music students. His master classes would be delayed by two days, to begin on Wednesday instead of today.

That bit of information didn't surprise me. I figured Wil wasn't in the right frame of mind to work with the students just yet. The sooner Kanesha was able to solve the murder and the attacks on Wil and his band members, the better Wil and his group would be able to concentrate on their purpose for coming to Athena.

I worked on email while Diesel napped in the window. Evidently he had secured the perimeter and now felt like relaxing.

Email done with, I turned to cataloging. I had always enjoyed the process. So many librarians preferred interacting directly with the public, helping them find what they needed for their particular purposes. I liked making resources accessible for those searching in the online catalog. Sometimes I missed the card catalog days, though I really didn't miss having to file all those sets of cards, as I had done in my earliest years as a librarian.

A knock at the door grabbed my attention, and as I laid aside the book I had been examining, I saw Melba in the doorway, arms crossed over her chest, and a scowl on her face. I gazed blandly back at her, leaving her to fire the first salvo.

"In case you were wondering where I was, I had an appointment with my doctor this morning," she said, uncrossing her arms and advancing into the room. She dropped into the chair in front of my desk, and Diesel eased out of the window to let her rub his head. Her scowl faded at the sight of my cat, and I thought maybe she wasn't so annoyed with me after all.

"I hope everything checked out okay," I said.

"Everything except my blood pressure," she said, avoiding my gaze, concentrating on the cat. "Of course, I have *absolutely no idea* why my blood pressure would be so high."

I ignored the sarcasm. "You've been under a lot of stress the past few days, so it's not surprising."

Melba leaned back in her chair, and Diesel settled at her feet, his head against her leg. "It's been a nightmare. I'm not really mad at you, Charlie. I'm just frustrated as hell by the situation. I don't know what to think."

"About anything in particular?" I asked, sensing her hesitation to get to the point.

Melba grimaced. "About Wil. I know this might sound crazy, but I'm worried that he has more to do with all this than you might think."

"How so?" I asked, keeping my tone neutral.

"The letters he wrote were so sweet and so natural-sounding," Melba replied. "In person he's sometimes sweet, but he's also withdrawn, like he's separating himself from everyone, even from me. He told me I was one of his best friends in his last letter before he came here." She looked at me, an appeal in her gaze.

"That reaction, withdrawal, isn't unusual in a situation like this," I said, choosing my words carefully. "John Earl Whitaker's death was a profound shock. He died in a terrible way. Then the attacks on two of his friends. He's probably suffering shell shock to some extent."

Melba nodded. "I understand that, but he's, well, I'm not sure I know how to express it." She frowned and thought for a moment. "It's almost like he's put himself outside it all, that it doesn't really touch him. Am I making sense?"

"Yes, you are. I think it could be a response to the murder and the attacks. He's protecting himself by giving himself time to process everything." I sounded like a pop psychologist, I realized, and I had no degree in psychology. Just based on my experience with many people over the years, I supposed. I also thought Wil's response might have a lot to do with feelings of guilt. Either because he was directly responsible for these terrible events, or simply guilt because they were targeted by their association with him.

"Maybe," Melba replied. "I don't know." She took a deep breath, and after she exhaled, she said in a rush, "Charlie, do you think Wil is behind all this?"

EIGHTEEN

||||||||||||||||||||||||||||||||||||||||||||||||

"I have considered that," I said. "You have to look at every possibility, no matter how painful it can be. If Wil himself is behind all this, what is his motive? Why would he want to kill John Earl Whitaker, a man he hasn't seen in forty years? Why would he want to hurt his band members, especially his close friend Zeb?"

Melba threw up her hands. "That's what I've been asking myself. I can't come up with an answer, unless he's just hard-down wacko."

I was glad Melba wasn't so far gone on Wil that she wasn't able to retain a certain amount of intelligent perspective on the whole mess.

"I mean," she continued, "I haven't seen him in forty years, and all I have to go on is his letters, and it's not like there are dozens and dozens of them. Maybe a dozen total. And in a letter you can keep back all kinds of things, especially if you're smart, and Wil is smart."

"I agree with you." I decided to step out on a metaphorical limb. "Frankly, I'm relieved that you're willing to consider Wil as the culprit."

"Because you thought I was so gaga over him that I'd lost all sense of perspective." Melba's expression turned grim. "I know everybody thinks I'm a fool when it comes to men. I'm not head over heels in love with Wil, Charlie. I do love him, but I'm not in love with him." She shook her head. "That schoolgirl crush faded a long time ago. I've just been excited about seeing an old friend and getting to know him again."

I heard the sincerity in her voice, and I felt suddenly that a weight lifted. "I understand, and I'm happy to hear it," I said.

Melba gave a brief smile. "I knew you and probably everybody else were worried about me, but I do know how to look after myself, and after my heart."

"I'm not going to sugarcoat it and pretend we weren't worried," I said. "I'm glad you're so clear-eyed about this."

"Thank you." She rose from the chair. "And thank you, sweet boy," she said to the cat. "Just having you near me makes me feel better. Now I'd better get downstairs and tackle my email." With one last rub on Diesel's head, she left the room, and moments later I heard her footsteps on the mahogany staircase.

Diesel went back to the window after watching the doorway for about twenty seconds, and I resumed cataloging. When my desk phone rang, I was startled because I average only two or three calls a week, at most.

I picked up the receiver and identified myself.

"Hi, Charlie, Wil Threadgill here."

"Hi, Wil, how are you doing?" I asked, surprised that he'd called me at work. Then I realized he didn't have my cell number.

"Still shaky," Wil said, and I could hear the strain in those two words. "Trying to wrap my head around all this. Crazy stuff."

"It certainly is," I said. "How are Zeb and Mr. Colson doing?" I felt slightly funny calling anyone *Jackrabbit*.

"Oh, Zeb's fine, although his hand's a bit sore. Jackrabbit is all stitched up. Thank the Lord that crazy idiot who stabbed him didn't hit any vital spots."

"I'm so glad to hear that," I said. "Have they released him from the hospital yet?"

"Probably later today," Wil said. "Vance is taking care of all that."

Vance, I remembered, was Wil's manager.

"Look, the reason I'm calling is I would love it if you and Diesel could join me for lunch today. Here in my suite, of course. I can't face the public yet."

I couldn't think of a reason to turn down Wil's invitation, though I knew my family would think I should. My bump of curiosity had swelled.

"Sure," I said. "What time?"

"How about one o'clock?" Wil asked. "I'll have the food here when you and Diesel arrive. Can I get something for him?"

"Maybe a little chicken, unseasoned," I said. "I'm fine as long as it's not seafood. Not a fan, I'm afraid."

"No problem." Wil chuckled. "I'm not a big fish person myself. See y'all at one." He rang off.

I turned toward Diesel. "Looks like we're going out to lunch," I said. "I'd better let Azalea know. I hope she hasn't started cooking yet."

I called the house, and Azalea answered. I explained that I wouldn't be able to come home for lunch today because something had come up.

"That's fine," Azalea replied. "Was just going to be salad and a sandwich and some lemon icebox pie for dessert. The salad and the pie I made will keep for dinner tonight."

I thanked her and rang off.

I pulled out my cell phone and told Melba that Diesel and I were having lunch with Wil at one.

She responded a couple of minutes later to say simply, "Good."

I got back to work and did my best to focus on cataloging, but it was occasionally a struggle. I would be working on a book, assigning appropriate subject headings, and then my brain would dart off on the subject of Wil Threadgill. Perhaps I could get him to open up about the people in his entourage. He ought to be aware of any grudges one of them could have, based on potential past disputes or arguments. At least he could share with me whatever he had told Kanesha.

I would have to caution him not to mention to Kanesha that he had talked with me, of course. If she found out, she would not be happy with me, because she would assume—correctly—that I was involving myself in the case.

I had to focus on my work, because the college wasn't paying me to sit here and gather wool, even interesting wool. I forced my attention back to the book I was cataloging, with moderate success.

Thus it went until a quarter to one, when I set everything aside and got Diesel back in his harness to make the walk back home. We needed the car to drive to the hotel. It was too far to walk, both for me and for Diesel.

We arrived at Wil's suite in the Farrington House promptly at one, and after a few seconds, he answered my knock on the door. He greeted us warmly, and I could see the strain in his expression. His eyes looked tired, and his back slumped a bit. I figured he hadn't been sleeping well.

"Our lunch arrived about three minutes ahead of you," Wil said as he escorted us to the dining area in the suite. Diesel chirped happily because he could no doubt smell the chicken Wil was providing for him, not to mention the other savory odors. I sniffed appreciatively myself.

Wil reached the table slightly ahead of me and Diesel. He began removing covers from the dishes, and I saw green beans with shaved almonds, loaded mashed potatoes, what looked like a corn casserole, and chicken breasts cooked with broccoli, onions, and tomatoes. In a separate dish lay a single chicken breast that appeared to be unseasoned. Cats can't eat anything cooked with onions, and I appreciated Wil's remembering my instructions.

Wil gestured at a chair, and I took my seat. Diesel parked himself right beside me, and I removed the leash from his harness and laid it aside.

"I wasn't sure what you might want to drink, but I figured iced tea would be okay." Wil nodded at a pitcher on the table between us. "It's not sweet tea, though. I prefer it without sugar myself, but there's sugar and other sweeteners here if you need any."

"Thank you," I said. "You've thought of everything. This all looks delicious."

"Go ahead and start helping yourself." He passed the bowl of green beans to me, and I scooped some out with the ladle. We continued in this fashion until my plate was full to overflowing, and I noticed that Wil had also put good-sized helpings on his own plate.

I took the plate of chicken breast provided for Diesel and began tearing it into appropriate-sized pieces. I thought I might as well get the conversation started. "What's on your mind, Wil? What do you want to talk about?"

Diesel, aware of the chicken, prodded at my thigh with one large paw, and to forestall the inevitable meow, I gave him a piece. He immediately gobbled it down, and I gave him another while I waited for Wil to respond.

"You don't waste time getting to the point," Wil said with a chuckle. "I'm still trying to make sense of all this. I've answered so many questions, and multiple times, till my head swims when I try to comprehend it all. This is the first time I've been involved in anything like this."

I forbore saying that I was happy he hadn't been involved in a murder before this. For someone who professed to be such an aficionado of crime fiction, he sounded curiously naïve about the process of investigation. I supposed, however, that reading about it and experiencing it for oneself could be disorienting.

"It can be a bit overwhelming," I said as Diesel poked my thigh again. I handed down more chicken. He had me well trained. "Tell me about John Earl Whitaker. What was he like all those years ago when y'all had the band?"

Wil laid his fork aside and looked pensive. "He was outgoing, for one thing. Never met a stranger, could talk to anyone. Had a pretty good voice, although his range was limited, and he was our singer. Also played a pretty good guitar. I put the band together, but he was our front man, and the one who got us gigs. The band gave him the focus he needed, because as a solo act, he just couldn't pull it together. He tried, but it didn't work." Wil suddenly smiled. "He was my best friend for years. We did everything together from third grade on. We shared everything."

"What happened to your friendship when you left for California?" I ignored the thrusting paw and ate some of my own food before it got cold.

"I wanted him to go with me," Wil said, the smile erased. "I thought we made a good team. Me writing and him playing and singing. He was handsome back then, before he took to drinking so hard." He shook his head. "I almost didn't recognize him the other night. He looked twenty years older than I expected."

"Why wouldn't he go with you?" I asked.

"I'm not completely sure," Wil replied. "A couple of things, I guess. He was in love with Natalie, big time, and didn't want to leave her. I even said Natalie could come, but she wouldn't. So he stayed with her."

I detected a faint tinge of hurt in those last words. "What was the other thing?"

Wil's mouth twisted in anger. "He was wavering, until Natalie told him she was pregnant. That ended it. He was a good guy, and he wasn't going to abandon her and their child." He grunted. "I thought she was lying, and I also thought someone else could be the father. Natalie was a bit wild back then. That was before she started taking her religion so seriously."

"Really? Any idea who?" I asked.

"Yeah," Wil said. "Me."

I almost choked on a bite of chicken. I coughed and laid my fork down. "You were sleeping with her, too?"

Wil nodded. "Back then she was the typical rebellious girl. Her father was incredibly strict with her, and she would sneak out of the house to go to some of our gigs with us. I was the first she latched on to, and we had a bit of fun. I was seventeen and feeling my oats. Looking back, I'm not proud of what I did. I guess I felt suffocated by her wanting all my attention. After a few times together, I told her I was done, and she took up with John Earl right away.

"She was a beautiful girl and John Earl was already a little in love with her," Wil continued. "The way she went after him, he was a goner from the outset."

"Is there any chance you were the father of the child?" I asked.

Wil shrugged. "I doubt it. I used condoms the few times we were together. I did keep in touch with John Earl for a while, and he told me they got married. Also wrote to tell me Natalie'd had a baby."

That was pretty forthright. I wondered if he had shared any of this with Melba, or whether she had found out about it from another source. I would have to think of a diplomatic way to bring it up, despite what she had told me earlier about her feelings for Wil.

A knock sounded at the door of the suite, forestalling any

comment I might have made. Wil thrust back his chair and dropped his napkin by his plate.

"I'm not expecting anyone else," he said. "I'll get rid of whoever it is." He went to the door.

The moment I heard the voice of the unexpected person, I knew I was in for it.

NINETEEN

||||||||||||||||||||||||||||||||||||||||||||||||||

I braced myself for Kanesha Berry's words when she saw me in Wil's suite. Diesel trotted toward the door to greet her, so even if she hadn't seen me from the doorway, she knew I was present.

"Come on in, Deputy Berry," Wil said.

"Thank you, Mr. Threadgill." Kanesha entered the room and approached the table as I rose from my chair.

"Good afternoon," I said.

Kanesha's right eyebrow arched. "Perhaps." She gestured to the table. "Sorry about interrupting your lunch. Please go ahead. I can speak with Mr. Threadgill in another room."

"Sorry, Deputy, but I plan to remain in this room. Charlie and Diesel are my friends, and I don't see any reason we can't talk right here. In fact, if you haven't had lunch, I can send for another place setting. We have more than enough."

"No, thank you," Kanesha said, though I thought I detected a slight hesitation in her manner. She probably hadn't had time to eat since early this morning, I figured.

Wil pulled out a chair at the table for her. I expected her to argue the point with him, but, whatever the reason, she yielded and seated herself. "Very well, Mr. Threadgill, I'll talk to you here." She kept her gaze fixed on Wil, as if I weren't present. She ignored Diesel as well, and he came back to my side for more chicken.

Wil resumed his own seat, placed his napkin back in his lap, and had a few sips of his tea. "What do you want to talk about?"

Kanesha suddenly turned to me. "I'm not happy that you're here, but evidently Mr. Threadgill has made you his confidant. I can't stop him talking to you, so you might as well get this firsthand."

"I understand." I felt slightly embarrassed at this direct approach, and I wasn't sure why. Kanesha rarely made concessions, and for her this was an almost gracious one. "Thank you."

Wil had been calmly eating during this exchange, and when Kanesha turned back to him, he laid his fork aside. After draining his tea glass, he wiped his lips with his napkin. "Ready when you are, Deputy."

Kanesha regarded him for a moment before she spoke. Wil gazed blandly back at her. His attitude seemed respectful, but I thought he was probably weary from all the questioning. I know I certainly would be.

"I want to go over the preparations for your performance at the reception," Kanesha said. "We've gone into this several times already, but I want to make sure there's not anything you've forgotten. Perhaps you might remember some little detail that could help if we go through it one more time."

Wil shrugged. "I'm willing, though I'm not sure it's going to yield anything new." He paused for a moment. "The local sound crew that the hotel hired, along with their own staff, did the original setup with the wiring and the mics, and they erected the platform in the room."

"Yes, and we've gone over all that with them. They insist that everything was thoroughly tested before you and your band came in to make any necessary adjustments and to test the equipment." Kanesha glanced at me. "The mic stand was not hooked up with a live high-voltage wire at that time."

"We got in the room around four-thirty," Wil said. "We got everything hooked up, guitars and so on, and had a run-through of a few songs. We had to tweak the amps and the speakers, because everything was turned up way too loud for such a small space." He smiled briefly. "We're used to playing much larger venues, and our usual settings wouldn't work for that space."

"I've asked you this before, but I'm going to put it to you again," Kanesha said. "Did anyone, for any reason, go under the platform to make any adjustments while you were testing and rehearsing in there?"

"Absolutely not," Wil said in a firm tone. "There was no need to."

Kanesha nodded. "All right. What time did you finish?"

"I think it was around five-forty-five," Wil replied after a moment's reflection. "I was the last one out, and a hotel staff member was waiting at the door to lock it when I came out."

"Did you exit the room immediately after everyone else?" Kanesha asked.

Diesel moved restlessly by my leg and chirped a couple of times.

He was bored, and also disappointed because no more chicken had been forthcoming. I placed a hand on his head to settle him down, and he subsided.

Kanesha had an expression of barely repressed irritation when she flicked a glance my way.

Wil responded in the affirmative. "I didn't have any reason to linger," he said. "I wanted to get back up here to my suite to have a little time to relax, and then shower and get dressed before I had to face the crowd at the reception." He gave a rueful grin. "I'm not fond of being surrounded in such close proximity by so many strangers, you see."

I understood how he felt. Whether Kanesha did was anyone's guess.

"That time frame tallies with the hotel's records," Kanesha said. "The staff member swears that the room was locked behind you when he left. He saw you get in the elevator before he headed downstairs."

"Good," Wil said.

"The catering staff had already started setting up in the other half of the room," Kanesha said. "Anyone who came in would have had to enter the door to that section."

"Was the room separated by the movable wall at that point?" I asked.

"Not completely," Kanesha said. "There was a gap big enough for a person to walk through. They didn't close it until they finished the setup. People were coming and going with food and other necessary items for about forty minutes. No one reports seeing a stranger come into the room while they were working. They were busy, how-ever, and someone might have slipped in without their realizing it."

"Surely that must be what happened," Wil said. "Or else one of them tampered with the mic."

"We're doing checks on all of them, but so far, nothing suspicious has turned up. I'll have a list of names for you soon, and I'd like you to go through it to see if there are any you might recognize," Kane-sha said.

"Sure," Wil said. "But after all this time away, the chances are pretty slim."

"We have to check any and every possibility," Kanesha said.

"What about the person who attacked Jackrabbit?" Wil asked. "Any leads on that?"

"Actually, there is one, pretty slender, though," Kanesha replied. "A witness came forward who claims to have seen the last moments of the attack on Mr. Colson. All she could tell us was that the person was hooded, probably a good foot shorter than their victim, and that the attacker melted into the bushes pretty quickly. She never got a closer look because she was just entering the parking lot from the other side."

"That's something, at least," I said.

"Jackrabbit's about six foot three," Wil said, "so the attacker is pretty short if the witness is right about the difference in height."

"I'm keeping an open mind about that," Kanesha said. "From the location of the wounds that Mr. Colson sustained, I'd say the at-tacker was several inches taller than reported. The cuts all went down into his back and side."

I suppressed a shudder because I visualized the actual attack too easily. It was a mercy that the attacker missed vital organs and Mr. Colson's spine. He was lucky because he could easily have been killed.

"D'you think the attacker intended to kill him and simply struck the wrong place?" Wil asked.

"Yes, I think the assailant was aiming to kill him," Kanesha said.

Wil drew in a sharp breath as she continued. "Mr. Colson says he heard a rustle of sound behind him. Probably the assailant coming through the bushes, and he was in the process of turning around when the knife struck him."

"Turning saved his life," I said. "That put the would-be killer's aim off."

"Yes, it did," Kanesha said. "Otherwise we'd have a second homicide on our hands. One is enough, and I don't want another one." She glared at Wil. "That's why I want you and every member of your group to exercise extreme caution. This person is likely to try again, but I plan to uncover his or her identity before that happens."

"I sure hope you can," Wil said fervently. "This is all happening because of me, and I don't want another death on my conscience."

Kanesha shook her head slightly. "Until we identify Mr. Whitaker's murderer, we don't know for sure this is really aimed at you, Mr. Threadgill. I'll admit that there's a very strong probability that it is, but until we know the motive, we can't be sure."

Wil didn't appear convinced, and I certainly wasn't convinced myself. That hot-wired mic could have had only one target, and that was Wil.

"Pardon me for saying this, Deputy, but that sounds disingenuous coming from a seasoned professional," Wil replied.

"That may be," Kanesha said, not looking in the least disconcerted by Wil's challenge. "But the minute I start making assumptions about anything to do with this case, that's when I can start making mistakes. Mistakes that could cost someone's life, and I can't have that. Do you understand?"

Wil had the grace to appear slightly abashed, and I felt for him. Kanesha hadn't spoken sharply, but conviction rang in her voice. I had to respect her as a consummate professional. This was one of the reasons she was so darn good at her job.

I knew if I commented aloud to that effect, Kanesha would not appreciate it. Although she ought to know me well enough by now to understand that it would be a sincere statement on my part, she would probably still find it on the smarmy side.

A quick glance at my watch gave me a start. Almost ten after two. I should have been on my way back to work fifteen minutes ago. I had a certain leeway with my lunch hour, and the library director was not a micromanager who made us clock in and out. I still tried to be conscientious about my time, however.

"Wil, I've really enjoyed the lunch, and both Diesel and I thank you for it." Almost on cue, Diesel warbled loudly, and Wil smiled.

"But you have to go back to work," Wil said. "I understand. Thank you both for having lunch with me." He stood and came around to shake my hand when I stood up from the table. He also gave Diesel some affectionate pats.

"I'm sure you'll excuse us, Deputy Berry," I said.

Kanesha nodded. "Certainly." She made no move to leave when Diesel and I did. I regretted not being able to witness the rest of their conversation, however long it might be. I took my job seriously, though I admit my curiosity over murder investigations sometimes conflicted with my sense of duty. Like now, in a big way.

"Come on, boy," I said to Diesel after the door of the suite closed behind us. "Back to work we go."

I parked the car in the lot behind the building. There was no time to take it home and then walk back. Diesel and I entered through the back door and headed up the staircase. I didn't take time to see whether Melba was in her office.

Back at my desk with Diesel up in the window ready to nap, I picked up where I had left off earlier. While I worked, I was distracted by the information Kanesha had shared. If I had been able to stay, she might have talked more about the setup for the performance. I wondered when the murderer was able to get into the room to set up the death trap. Had he or she simply walked through the other room while catering staff were busy setting up? Could it possibly have been someone dressed up as a member of the catering staff?

Would the caterers have noticed a strange person in the room? Then an idea struck me. Unless that stranger had said he was with the band and needed to check something. That was a big risk, because the hotel staff would be able to identify him. This simply didn't add up, and I couldn't figure it out.

I frowned. Surely Kanesha would have mentioned this possibility while she was talking with us. I figured she must have considered this idea and then dismissed it. I was sure that, in the questioning of the staff, they were asked if anyone had come into the room for any reason other than the catering.

This issue reminded me of Golden Age detective stories when the detective had to discern the moment when the murderer had the chance to strike or to set up the death. I recalled the ingenious way that Agatha Christie had worked it out in *Hercule Poirot's Christmas*.

The ringtone of my cell phone alerted me that my son was calling. I answered, saying, "Hello, Sean. What's up?"

"Something pretty strange," he said, sounding somewhat amused. "A Mrs. Natalie Whitaker came to see me. In fact, she just left a couple of minutes ago."

John Earl Whitaker's widow? "What did she want?"

"She wants to sue Wil Threadgill for the wrongful death of her husband."

TWENTY

"Can she do that?"

Sean laughed. "She could, but I think the case would be thrown out of court. We would have to prove that Threadgill set it all up with the intent to kill, or at least badly injure, the late Mr. Whitaker."

"Did you tell her all this?" I asked, still incredulous.

"Of course I did, Dad," Sean said. "She got huffy, and when I told her I couldn't take on such a case, she stormed out of my office."

"She sounds slightly off her rocker," I said.

"She's in shock over the sudden death of her husband," Sean replied, a reproving note in his voice. "She's trying to make sense of what happened, and so she's placing the blame on Mr. Threadgill."

"You're right. I shouldn't have said that about her. The poor woman is surely distraught," I said.

"That's the main reason I called you," Sean said. "I don't know her, but if you know anything about her and who her friends are, I think you should get in touch with them and ask them to check on her. She didn't seem stable to me."

Most people wouldn't have bothered with a rather far-fetched lawsuit, but my compassionate son really was worried about Natalie Whitaker. "I don't know her myself, though I met her briefly that night," I said. "Melba does know her, so I'll talk to her about the situation."

"Thanks, Dad," Sean replied. "I have another client coming in shortly, so I'd better go."

I picked up the office phone and punched in Melba's extension. She answered right away. "Hi, Charlie, what's up?"

"I need to talk to you about Natalie Whitaker. Could you come up here? It will be more private."

"Sounds serious," she said. "Let me put you on hold while I check with Andrea."

Andrea Taylor was the library director, and Melba was her administrative assistant. They got on like the proverbial house afire, so I was sure she wouldn't mind letting Melba take a few minutes to come talk to me.

"I'll be right up," Melba said.

Moments later I heard the clack of her heels as she hurried up the stairs. She moved quickly into my office and took her usual chair. Diesel had already jumped down from the window to sit by the chair, and Melba began rubbing his back while shooting me an interrogative glance.

"Natalie Whitaker went to see Sean this morning." I explained what the woman wanted, and Melba frowned, her hand on Diesel's back stilling for a moment.

"I know she blames Wil for John Earl's death," Melba said, resuming her strokes of the cat. "She's obviously more distraught than I thought she'd be. Wil didn't murder John Earl. I think she'll realize that at some point and calm down."

"That may take a while," I said. "Do you know who her close friends are? Someone needs to be looking after her."

Melba shook her head. "Natalie's never been real friendly to anyone. I think it was because of John Earl. She was ashamed of him and didn't want anybody around." She paused. "I know, I'll call her priest and talk to him."

"You know him?" I asked, and I wasn't at all surprised when she confirmed that she did.

"Father Ramon Machado," she said. "Though I don't agree with a lot of his ideas or his advice to Natalie about her marriage, I know he is conscientious. He'll find someone who can look after her."

"I'm relieved to hear it, and I know Sean will be, too. He seemed really concerned about her mental state when we talked."

Diesel meowed loudly, apparently because Melba had paused in her physical attentions to him. She laughed and scratched his head affectionately.

"You're nothing but a big old sponge, soaking up as much attention as you can get." She rose from her seat, and Diesel gave an indignant warble. "Why don't you come downstairs with me, boy, and I'll see if I can't find a treat for you." She looked at me for approval for this suggestion, and I nodded.

"Keep the number of the treats low," I said as she left my office with Diesel right alongside her.

Now that there was a plan of action to get some help for Natalie Whitaker, I found it easier to concentrate on the job I should be doing. The one I received a salary for and not for my kibitzing as an amateur detective.

Within ten minutes, both Melba and Diesel were back in my office, the former frowning mightily.

"Something wrong?" I asked. Diesel moved behind me to crawl into the window.

"Wrong, strange, whatever you want to call it." Melba lowered herself into the chair. "I called the church and spoke to Father Machado. I told him I wanted to speak to him about Natalie Whitaker."

"And?" I prompted when she fell silent.

"He told me he had reached out to her to offer her help. He called her to find a time to come see her, but she put him off, saying she was too upset to talk to anybody. Then she hung up the phone." Melba shook her head. "He's concerned about her, and so am I. I'm going to call her when I get off work and see if she'll let me come over."

"I didn't realize you were a close friend," I said.

"I'm not," Melba replied. "But she needs to talk to someone. If she'll talk to me, I'll try to get her to talk to Father Machado, if nothing else."

"I wish you luck," I said. "The poor woman needs help."

Melba rose. "I'll let you know what happens. I'll call Helen Louise. Maybe she'll go with me to see Natalie."

"That's a good idea," I said. Helen Louise had a kind heart, and she was a sensible person. Given her law background, perhaps she could get through to Natalie Whitaker about her plans to sue Wil

Threadgill for wrongful death. I hoped she could be brought to see that Wil really couldn't be held responsible, especially since he was almost certainly the intended target.

"I'll let you know what, if anything, happens," Melba said.

I thanked her and returned to work when she left. I managed about a quarter hour of concentrated labor when I was roused from my concentration on cataloging by a tentative knock at the door. I looked up to see Alex standing in the doorway.

I rose at once and went to greet her, along with Diesel. "Good afternoon, sweetheart," I said, giving her a hug.

She clung to me for a moment, then released me to rub my cat's head. "Good afternoon," she replied, her voice husky.

I led her to the chair and urged her to sit. Diesel remained by her side, chirping at her while I returned to my chair. She was obviously in an emotional state, and Diesel was anxious about her.

"I'm glad you came to see me," I said, keeping my tone matter-of-fact. "What can I do for you?"

Alex pulled a handkerchief from her purse and dabbed at her eyes. She didn't respond until she put the handkerchief away again.

"I know Sean talked to you about what we've been discussing." She smiled briefly. "Or arguing about, I probably should say."

"He told me that you'd like to stay at home with Rosie and not go back to work," I said. "I don't think that he really has a problem with that."

Alex shrugged. "He says he doesn't, but I know he's worried about our finances. They'll take a big hit if I don't go back to work."

"Seems to me the practice is still doing well. You have another lawyer, and Sean mentioned taking in someone new, perhaps a junior partner," I said. "That should help bring in more money, shouldn't it?"

"Yes, it would, but I still feel guilty, like I'm letting Sean down," Alex said.

"Has he said or done anything to make you think you are?" Sean had not given me any hint that he had done so.

"No, not at all. Sean is incredibly supportive. He's an amazing man, and I love him now more than ever." Alex's tone had turned fierce. "It's all on me. I'm the one who's worried about the farmhouse and how much it's costing. Sean ran full steam into all the renovations. He consulted me, but it was really his decision."

"You're not keen on living in the country, I gather," I said.

Alex shrugged again. "I'm not totally opposed to it. It's just that I've always lived in town, close to friends, work, my favorite stores and restaurants. The idea of living in the country away from all that unnerves me, frankly."

"I can understand that," I said. "I've never lived in the country, either, but one of the reasons I was happy to leave Houston and move back here was the sheer size of Houston. It had become overwhelming. I am much happier here with the slower pace."

"Sean is, too," Alex said. "He told me you suggested that we keep the house in town, and I wanted to thank you for that."

"I think it's a good idea. Once the farmhouse is renovated and livable, you can try it, maybe on the weekends. That will give you a chance to sample living in the country, but you'll still have the house in town during the week. How does that sound?"

"I like that," Alex said. "Sean said the same thing. It would be nice for Rosie to have that experience, don't you think?"

"I agree," I said. "I loved going to that house to visit my grandparents."

Alex stood suddenly and gave me a lovely smile. "Talking to you always makes me feel better," she said. "I know you want what's best for the three of us, and you've helped me see things more clearly. I'll talk to Sean when he comes home tonight."

"That's wonderful." I got up from behind the desk and went to give her a hug. Diesel rubbed against her legs and warbled. She bade us goodbye, and I could see by the way she walked she did feel better.

I thought about calling Sean and sharing my conversation with Alex, but I reconsidered. Alex wanted to tell him, and she should. Otherwise it would be between the two of us. I would wait to hear from my son.

A glance at my watch informed me that it was about seven minutes until three. Quitting time. I sighed. I really hadn't accomplished much today. I should probably work late to make up for it, but I knew I wouldn't be able to concentrate properly. Maybe I would come to work an extra day this week instead.

"It's time to go home, boy," I told Diesel as I started gathering my things. Diesel understood the word *home* and climbed down from the window. We had reached the door when the phone rang, and I went back to answer, hoping that it wasn't a last-minute call from someone on campus who needed something from the archive right away.

"Hi, Charlie," Wil Threadgill said. "I hate to ask this, but can you come back to the hotel after you finish work? I've got something important to tell you."

"I'm leaving work right now, actually," I replied. "Sure, I can come back. What's up?"

"I'm pretty sure I know who's behind everything," Wil said.

TWENTY-ONE

I tried to press Wil for details, but he insisted that he would tell me once I reached his suite. He ended the call, and I decided Diesel and I might as well head out for the Farrington House. My curiosity would have to wait to be appeased a few minutes longer.

When Diesel and I reached Wil's suite, we found a sheriff's deputy at the door. She asked for my name, and when I supplied it, she checked a list on the clipboard she held. Evidently my name was there, and she stood aside for Diesel and me to enter the room. Kanesha was evidently taking no chances that any unauthorized person could access Wil's suite.

We found Wil seated in an armchair sipping a bottle of water. He rose to greet us and gestured for us to sit. I chose a sofa, and Diesel climbed up beside me after greeting Wil briefly. He laid his head against my thigh. His tail flopped up and down.

"I'm burning with curiosity," I said. "What did you find out?"

Wil set his bottle on a coaster on the small table beside his chair. "Let me give you a little background first. About a month ago, I had a feeling something was off with my accounts. I'm incorporated, and I pay myself a salary like I pay everyone else from the same business account. I also have a separate account for the projects I do completely on my own."

I nodded to show that I understood. "So you get paid by your corporation into two accounts separately."

"Exactly," Wil said. "I began to notice that the monies going into my separate account didn't seem to be adding up properly. The amounts appeared lower than I thought they should be, based on the payments I received." He frowned. "Money gets set aside for estimated tax payments each quarter, so at first I thought that must account for it. But then I noted payments being made for expenses that I didn't remember incurring. The more I checked, the more I found, going back about five years."

"What did you do?"

"I had a good idea who was responsible, but to be sure I hired an accountant who billed herself as a forensic accountant to audit my books." He picked up his phone. "I received her report by email about thirty minutes ago, and she confirmed what I suspected. My assistant Chelsea has been embezzling from me to the tune of nearly half a million dollars."

My mouth almost dropped open in shock, but I managed to stop it from happening.

"Have you confronted her yet?"

Wil shook his head. "I want to wait until Deputy Berry can be here. I think this constitutes a good motive for murder, don't you? She must have found out somehow about the audit."

"That's a reasonable guess," I said, "but what could have tipped her off?"

"I don't know. My lawyer in California will have to go into that with the accountant and the police," Wil replied.

"Does Chelsea know enough about the sound equipment and electronics to have rigged that microphone?" I asked.

"She does. She started out as a sound tech with me, and I promoted her to my assistant when I saw how organized she was. She also had studied accounting before she quit school to work in the music industry."

Things weren't looking good for Chelsea Bremmer. She would have access to Wil's suite, naturally, and she could easily have put the slivers of glass in the ice bucket. She also knew that Jackrabbit Colson would go outside for a smoke at some point, where she could attack him. She was average height, and I remembered that the witness claimed the assailant was shorter than Colson.

"Have you called Kanesha Berry yet?" I asked.

"I have," Wil replied. "She's due here in about ten minutes. I'll call Chelsea when the deputy arrives and tell her I need to talk to her. Deputy Berry already knows what I've told you."

The answer to this horrible murder and the attacks evidently boiled down to the greed of a young woman who hadn't been able to resist the temptation to embezzle. Then when she realized she was about to get caught, she struck out at the man who had hired and trusted her.

"I'm sure Miss Bremmer is well paid for her job," I said.

Wil named a figure, and my eyes widened in surprise. The amount seemed pretty generous to me, but I knew living in California was an expensive proposition.

"It's above average, by a good bit," Wil said, "but I believe in paying people well. It encourages them to do a good job." He shook his head. "Evidently Chelsea got greedy, and I think I know why."

"Why?" I asked. "If I'm not being too nosy."

Wil grimaced. "No, I'll tell you. She likes to party, and she has expensive tastes. She also likes to shower gifts on her girlfriend of the month."

"Has she told you all this?"

"Not directly," Wil said, "but I've picked up gossip from various sources in the last few months. That's one reason I was getting suspicious about my accounts. I know how much I was paying her, and all that high living cost more than she was earning from me."

"I'm sorry this has happened," I said, "but if this is the answer to the murder and the two attempts at murder, I'm glad for your sake, particularly, that it will soon be over."

"Amen to that," Wil said. "I'm sorry, I've completely forgotten my duties as host. How about something to drink? And for Diesel?" He stood.

"Some water for Diesel would be good," I replied. "I'll take a diet drink if you have one."

"Absolutely." Wil went to a cabinet to retrieve a bowl, then to the fridge to extract a bottle of water and a diet drink. He handed me my bottle before he bent to place the bowl near the coffee table. He poured water into it, and by the time he was finished, Diesel was there, ready to lap it up. Wil smiled down at him. "I sure do envy you such a beautiful cat, Charlie."

"Thank you," I said.

Wil returned to his chair, and we talked desultorily for a few minutes while we waited for Kanesha to arrive. The knock finally came, and Wil got up to let her in.

Kanesha scowled at the sight of me and my cat, but Wil paid no attention. He gestured for her to take a seat, and she did so in a chair opposite the sofa, near Wil. She nodded to acknowledge my presence but didn't offer a verbal greeting.

"I received the information that you asked the accounting firm to send me," Kanesha said to Wil. "I looked through it, and it's pretty obvious Miss Bremmer has been embezzling for years. She will certainly be charged for this crime in California. What remains to be seen is whether she was attempting to murder you when Mr. Whitaker was killed instead."

"Or whether she attempted two other murders," I said when she paused.

In response to that remark, I received a raised eyebrow.

"It's bad enough she stole from me and violated the trust I placed in her," Wil said. "I hate to think of her as a cold-blooded killer, but I can't see that anyone else has a motive."

"Thus far in the investigation we haven't uncovered another one," Kanesha said. "Still, when we confront her with the embezzlement, I want to hold off on the other crimes at first."

"You'll be in charge, of course," Wil said.

Kanesha cut a sideways glance at me.

"Please let me stay. I won't butt in," I said. "Diesel and I are here simply as moral support for Wil. This is a huge shock to him."

Diesel had finished drinking water, and he sprawled on the floor at the end of the coffee table. He could look at everyone this way, and at the moment, he had his gaze fixed on Kanesha. So far she had completely ignored his presence. Not unusual when she was laser-focused on an upcoming interrogation.

"Why don't you get Miss Bremmer here now?" Kanesha said. I breathed a sigh of relief. She wasn't going to insist that Diesel and I leave the room.

Wil picked up his phone and texted his assistant. She responded within seconds. Wil told us that Chelsea would be here right away. He got up to be at the door when she knocked.

Less than two minutes later, she walked into the room, smiling. She stopped short, however, and the smile vanished when she spotted me, Diesel, and Kanesha. She shot a frown at Wil.

"What's going on here? More questions?" she asked.

"Yes," Wil said. "Take that chair." He pointed to the only empty one around the coffee table, which happened to be next to Kanesha.

Chelsea did as she was bid. Once seated she glanced back and forth between Wil and Kanesha. Chelsea nodded briefly in my direction, and I noted with interest that Diesel made no move to approach her. That was certainly telling, and I thought Wil noticed it, too. He frowned as he glanced first at Diesel, then at Chelsea.

Kanesha nodded at Wil to open the conversation. He took a deep breath before he spoke.

"Chelsea, I want you to know that I've recently had an accounting firm audit my accounts."

I was watching Chelsea to gauge the effect of this statement, and I saw her back stiffen and her eyes widen. "Is that so?" she said in a tone that aimed for nonchalant but didn't quite achieve it.

"I had suspected for some time that something was off, and they have confirmed it," Wil said.

"In both the corporate accounts?" she asked.

"Yes, but particularly in my personal account, reserved for the work I do entirely on my own. The account through which you and band members are paid is fine. They're still looking into it, but they haven't so far discovered any issues with it."

"That's good," Chelsea said. "And your personal account?"

"There is a significant problem there, to the tune of half a million dollars missing over the years." Wil paused, and when he continued, his expression was fierce. "Over the years since you came to work for me, and I gave you access to that account to do the necessary record-keeping and make payments to the IRS for estimated taxes."

"You think I've been stealing money from you?" Chelsea forced a laugh that sounded hollow, probably even to her.

"Yes, I do," Wil said. "That really hurts me, Chelsea, because I've trusted you and relied heavily on you. I don't like betrayal."

"The police here are going to take you into custody," Kanesha said. "You will be transferred to California for the arraignment and any indictment to follow."

"And if I swear to you that I didn't do it?" Chelsea asked, now sounding desperate.

"I would find it extremely hard to believe." Wil shook his head. "I'm thoroughly disappointed in you. I thought I could count on you to do the right thing. I paid you generously, well above what you would have made elsewhere."

"I'm not going down for this alone," Chelsea said angrily. "Get on your phone and tell Vance to get up here right now. And when he gets here, ask him about Verity Trust Investments Company."

TWENTY-TWO

|||||||||||||||||||||||||||||||||||||||||||||||||||||||||||||||||||||||||

I happened to be watching Wil's face when Chelsea mentioned Wil's manager, Vance Tolliver. Wil's expression of shock made me feel bad for him. I wondered what Chelsea's gambit was. Had she really colluded with Tolliver to defraud Wil of half a million dollars? Or even more?

Wil stared hard at Chelsea, and the shock faded from his expression. When he spoke, his tone chilled me. "I don't know what your game is, but I've known and worked with Vance for many years. You'd better have evidence to back up your accusation that he was also stealing from me."

"Call him and get him in here." Chelsea's terse reply and hard look convinced me she wasn't just stalling for time.

Wil pulled out his cell phone and called his manager. "Hey, Vance, can you come to my suite right now? Something's come up we need to discuss." He listened briefly. "No, that can wait. I need you right now." He had kept his tone neutral, but firm. Wil ended the call and set down his phone. "He's on his way. He's at the bookstore here on the square."

"Maybe we should go," I said, looking first at Wil, then at Kanesha. I could tell she was about to tell me we should, but Wil forestalled her.

"No, Charlie, I need an independent witness here, besides Deputy Berry," Wil said.

I didn't have the heart to persist after those words, and whatever protest Kanesha might have uttered remained unexpressed.

We sat in uneasy silence for several minutes while we waited for Tolliver to arrive. The bookstore was only a three-minute walk away, but the time stretched out, feeling far longer than only a few minutes.

When a knock sounded on the door, Wil rose and went to admit his manager.

"What's all this about?" Tolliver asked. "Can I get some water? I'm parched." His advance into the room stalled. He looked at Kanesha, Chelsea, Diesel, and me and frowned. "What's going on here?"

"Have a seat there on the sofa," Wil said, "and I'll get you some water. I'll explain in a moment."

Tolliver shrugged. "Whatever you say, big guy." He took his place at the other end of the sofa from me. Diesel eyed him with curiosity but made no move to approach him. Again, not a good sign.

Tolliver nodded at me and Kanesha, but he stared curiously at Chelsea. It wasn't hard to see that she was in a highly emotional state. He didn't speak, however. When Wil handed him a bottle of water, he twisted off the cap and drained about half of the contents while Wil resumed his place.

"You're here, Vance, because Chelsea seems to think you can help her explain the half-million dollars that is missing from my personal account."

Tolliver nearly dropped the bottle of water on the floor. He uttered a couple of vulgar words and shot first Wil, then Chelsea, an incredulous look.

"What the hell are you talking about?" Tolliver said, his face reddening, whether in anger or agitation, I couldn't tell.

"If you're addressing that question to me," Wil said, his tone even, "I'm talking about the fact that an accounting firm that I hired recently to audit my corporate books has found some serious problems. As I said, they're estimating that half a million dollars has been taken out of my account during the time that Chelsea has worked for me. When I asked Chelsea about it before you arrived, she insisted that you be here. I'll leave it to her to explain why she insisted on your presence."

Chelsea glared at Tolliver. "He knows why he's here. You heard him, Vance. Half a million dollars."

Tolliver shrugged. "Yeah, I heard that, but I don't know nothing about it. I don't do anything with those accounts. His accountant handles most everything, and that's sure as hell not me."

Chelsea laughed, a bitter sound. She looked at Wil. "Remember when I started working for you and you decided to have me deal with the IRS and paying your estimated taxes?"

Will nodded. "Yes, I do."

"Who do you think set up the access I needed to your account in order to handle all that for you?" Chelsea nodded her head toward Tolliver.

"Vance did," Wil said. "I remember that. I had to remind him a couple of times to do it."

Tolliver shifted uneasily on the sofa. "So what? That was years ago. I have no access to those accounts. I turned it over to the accountant and to Chelsea here. If you think I've been draining money from you, you're freaking crazy, big guy."

"What is Verity Trust Investments?" Wil asked suddenly.

Tolliver's head jerked up. "What are you talking about?"

"Just what I said. What is this so-called Verity Trust Investments?" Wil said, an edge to his voice. "Interesting that the name carries your initials, V and T."

"That's my private investment stuff," Tolliver said. "Nobody's business but mine."

"So if my lawyer back in California asked a judge to subpoena the records in the case I'm going to file against Chelsea, and possibly you, you wouldn't be worried about that?"

This was a side of Wil I hadn't realized existed. He generally seemed soft spoken and laid back, but what I witnessed now was the hard-hitting, no-nonsense businessman. Frankly, this side of him made me nervous.

"What would you want to do that for?" Tolliver said. "Look, big guy, Chelsea here is obviously trying to squirm out of responsibility for whatever she's done." He shot a hard glance at the young woman. "I don't know why she's trying to get me involved in these shenanigans, but I'm not having it. It's her responsibility, whatever it is."

Chelsea responded to this with a string of profanity aimed at Tolliver's breeding, background, and morals. When she finished this, she said in conclusion, "I think the police and courts will find out exactly how deeply you were involved in this."

She faced Wil. "I'm not taking responsibility for the whole thing. He got me into it years ago when I asked to borrow some money. I was too embarrassed to ask you." Her mouth twisted in a bitter smile. "I should have got my courage up and done it anyway. Instead I ended up with this viper."

"I think that's enough," Kanesha said, rising. "This will have to be referred to the authorities in California. I'm placing you both under house arrest here in the hotel, and guards will be at your doors twenty-four seven until you leave for California. That won't be until the investigation into the murder and the attacks is satisfactorily concluded, however." She looked at the two of them in turn. "It's clear that embezzling has taken place, based on what I've heard from Mr. Threadgill and the records he's received from the forensic accountants. What remains to be seen is whether the murder and the attempted murders have any relationship to the embezzling. You are both now the prime suspects."

When Kanesha got tough, she was frightening. Even Tolliver, for all his earlier bravado, wilted quickly under the onslaught. Chelsea had begun crying, quietly, thank goodness. I didn't think I could take loud sobbing. My poor cat had been in my lap, curled up against me for the past several minutes because of all the rampant emotion in the room. I decided that I had to get him out of the situation immediately.

I spoke to Wil, but I made sure Kanesha heard me. "Diesel is upset, and he needs to be at home where everything is calm. I'm a little upset myself. I hope you understand why I can't stay."

Wil appeared disappointed, but after a look at Diesel, he nodded. "I understand completely. Go on home."

"You know where to reach me." I put Diesel gently on the floor, and he followed me with alacrity as I made my way to the door. Kanesha made no effort to stop me. I was sure she was happy to see us leave.

I drew a huge sigh of relief when I shut the door to the suite behind me. Holy moly, that had been intense. "Come on, boy, we're going home." I strode rapidly down the hall to the elevator, and Diesel scampered ahead of me.

Once we reached the car and were safely inside, I cranked it and turned up the air conditioner to cool us off before we headed home. I was still a bit shaken by what I had witnessed, and I knew poor Diesel had been even more bothered by it all. I should have taken him out of the situation sooner, but things were happening so quickly I didn't have much time to think. Plus, to be honest, I was fascinated by it all.

I thought Wil was probably correct about who was behind the attacks and the murder, an attempt on his own life. Either Chelsea Bremmer or Vance Tolliver, or perhaps the two of them working in concert. Suddenly I recalled Tolliver's odd warning to me the night John Earl Whitaker died. Had he been afraid that I would somehow find out about the embezzlement? If so, he certainly had overestimated my abilities. I couldn't imagine what else he could have been referring to. Talk about a guilty conscience, though.

After a few deep breaths of the now cool air, I shifted into gear and drove us home. The kitchen was empty when we entered from the garage. Ramses came scampering in within a minute, though, followed by Azalea. Ramses attempted to engage Diesel in play, but big brother wasn't having it. He put a large paw on Ramses's head and forced him away. Ramses followed him into the utility room.

I noticed Azalea gazing at me in a speculative way. "You don't look so good," she said. "Something upsetting you?"

"We've just come from seeing Wil Threadgill at the hotel," I said. "There was a scene during which he confronted two of his people about something, and Kanesha was there as well."

"Things got heated, then." Azalea went to the refrigerator and pulled out a pitcher of sweet tea. She poured me a glass and set it on the table. "You sit down and have that. It'll help you feel better."

I knew better than to argue with Azalea, so I sat and sipped at my tea. By the time I had downed half the glass, I did feel better. Whether it was the sugar or simply the coldness of the drink, I didn't know, but her tonic worked. I drank down the rest of the tea.

"More?" Azalea indicated the pitcher.

"Don't mind if I do," I said.

Azalea refilled my glass and replaced the pitcher in the fridge. I thanked her and started to drink.

"You best leave all this mess to Kanesha," Azalea said in a mild tone. "You got other things to worry about than all that craziness with those California folks."

"You're talking about Alex," I said. "I had a talk with her earlier today, and I think she's feeling better about wanting to stay home with Rosie and giving the house in the country a try."

"Thank the Lord," Azalea said. "I've been praying that she's gonna find the peace she needs."

"I really appreciate that. Looks like all our prayers may be answered," I said.

"I need to be starting dinner for everybody," Azalea said, as Diesel and Ramses returned to the kitchen. Ramses again attempted to inveigle Diesel into play, but my big boy batted him away.

"Now y'all scoot on out of here," Azalea said. "I ain't got time to be stepping all around you while I'm trying to get dinner on."

"Come on, boys." I rose from the table and set my empty glass in the sink. "Let's go to the den and relax."

"Scat." Azalea flapped her apron at Ramses, reluctant to leave the source of his favorite treats.

I scooped him up and carried him to the den. Diesel reached the door ahead of us and pushed it open. I closed it behind us before I let Ramses down.

Once I was comfortable in my recliner, footrest up, Ramses jumped into my lap and stretched out. Diesel was too big for the footrest, and he settled into his usual spot on the floor beside us. I grabbed the remote and turned on the TV. I found a rerun of one of my favorite home renovation shows and settled in to relax.

Sometime later the ringing of my cell phone roused me from my nap. I fumbled to get the phone out of my pants pocket, but the call went to voice mail before I could answer it. I blinked at the time, yawning. Nearly five-thirty. I had slept for a good hour. Peering at the caller ID, I saw that Melba had called. She would be home from the library by now, I reckoned.

I called her phone, and she answered right away. "Hi, Charlie. How come you didn't answer?"

Suppressing another yawn, I said, "I was asleep and couldn't get my phone out in time. But I called you right back. What did you want? Anything happen I should know about?"

"I just got off the phone with Wil. He's really upset about this embezzlement mess," Melba replied. "He trusted both those jerks, and he's hurt."

"I don't blame him. He may discover that he's lost more than a half a million," I said.

"He's not so mad about the money," Melba said shortly, "as he is about being betrayed. Loyalty is important to him. Besides which one of them, or both of them, who knows, might be trying to kill him and other members of the band."

"That's what really bothers me about all this," I said. "That's an extreme solution to covering up the embezzlement."

"I guess so," Melba said doubtfully. "But what other motive is there?"

TWENTY-THREE

|||||||||||||||||||||||||||||||||||||||||||||||||||||||||||||||||||||||||||||

In bed that evening, trying to get to sleep while Diesel and Ramses slept undisturbed, I instead found my mind returning over and over to Melba's question. If the embezzlement wasn't the motive for the murder and the attacks, then what could it be?

Try as I might, the only thing I could come up with was hatred, a desire for revenge for some sin on Wil's part. What could he have done?

He took off for California, leaving his bandmates high and dry. He was evidently the creative force behind the band, no matter how talented the remaining members were. Wil had said John Earl Whitaker made a good front man for the group, but unless they contented themselves with covering the music of other groups, their opportunities were limited. They would have to be really outstanding to have a profitable future simply performing the works of others.

According to the only band member besides Wil with whom I

had spoken, Mickey Lindsay, I got the impression that the group wasn't that good without Wil, the songwriter and most talented musician among them. He had the success in Hollywood to demonstrate that.

I decided eventually that it might prove helpful to delve further into the past. Find out how the band members felt about Wil abandoning them and running off to California. I would have to start with Mickey Lindsay, since the only other band member I knew of was dead. That decision made, I was finally able to relax and drift off to sleep.

Diesel and Ramses were in the kitchen keeping a close eye on Azalea at the stove, her back to me, when I entered the room the next morning. The tantalizing scent of bacon frying on the griddle had their complete attention.

"Now, you boys will just have to wait," Azalea was saying as I reached the table. I greeted her, and she acknowledged it with a wave of her spatula. "Coffee's on the table."

I helped myself and added cream and sugar. The first cup of coffee of the day was bliss on the tongue and much-needed caffeine for my brain. The first sip went down smoothly, and I had another.

"Breakfast's almost ready," Azalea announced. She laid her spatula aside and bent to open the oven door. She pulled out the plate of biscuits she had kept warm and set them on the table. "Scrambled or fried this morning?"

"Fried is fine." I was suddenly ravenous, and I knew I would get the fried eggs sooner than scrambled.

A couple of minutes later, I tucked into my eggs, bacon, and biscuits, while Azalea shared a few bits of bacon with Diesel and Ramses.

When those morsels had been duly grabbed and swallowed—I wasn't sure either cat actually chewed them—Diesel came to me, and the paw landed on my thigh. I pinched off a piece of buttered biscuit for him. Not quite as good as bacon, but he didn't refuse it.

I debated asking Azalea about Mickey Lindsay and the other members of Wil Threadgill's band. On reflection, however, I decided to wait until I saw Melba at work. I knew she would know exactly where each of them was and what they were doing these days. If anyone could round them up for a chat about the old days, Melba could.

Half an hour later, Diesel and I entered the library administration building, and we paused to greet Melba. She was on the phone and only waved at us. She jerked her head in the direction of upstairs and my office, and I knew that meant she would join us as soon as she could get away from her desk for a few minutes.

Diesel and I continued upstairs. I unlocked the door and left it open, as I usually did. My cat and I assumed our usual places, and I started the workday as always by checking email. Luckily I found nothing that needed my immediate attention, so I set to work with cataloging.

Melba didn't make an appearance until nearly an hour later. Diesel climbed down from the window when she entered the room, and they greeted each other with the usual affection. Melba took the chair in front of the desk.

"Any news from Wil?" I asked.

Melba shook her head, and that surprised me.

"I haven't been able to talk to him since last night," she said. "I don't know what's going on."

That was odd. I thought Wil was communicating regularly with her. I wondered what had stopped the flow of information. I said as much.

"I have no idea," Melba replied. "Unless Kanesha has threatened him on pain of death to stop talking to me. And to you."

I could see Kanesha telling Wil that he couldn't involve me any further in the investigation. If Wil obeyed her, however, I would be surprised. He struck me as strong-minded and independent, and I could see him defying the chief deputy. On the other hand, she may have put it to him in a way that discouraged him completely from doing so.

"He could be trying to protect you, and me, too," I said. "He wouldn't want the person behind all this to target us, and if cutting us off would keep us safe, I'm sure he would be willing to do that."

Melba sighed. "I'm sure you're right, but it's still aggravating. I can't stand not knowing what's going on."

"I have an idea that might help you take your mind off that," I said.

She perked up. "What is it? Tell me."

"I kept thinking about your question, about the motive for all this nastiness," I said. "The only thing I could come up with is that someone hates Wil so much they want revenge for whatever they think he did to them."

"That makes sense," Melba said. "You think maybe someone in the band other than John Earl?"

"I think it's possible. Wil left them in the lurch, and years later he's a big noise in Hollywood, rich and successful. One of them might feel that Wil cheated him out of success and wealth."

"He did cut them off completely," Melba said. "None of them has ever made a lot of money. I don't think they could afford to go out to California and track Wil down. I also don't think he made any effort to keep in touch with them." She frowned. "I know John Earl Whitaker was known to say that if he ever saw Wil again, he'd beat the living daylights out of him."

We both knew how that ended, and I grimaced at the mental image of John Earl Whitaker's last moments. Melba's expression reflected my own.

Hastily I said, "I thought it might be helpful to get them all together to talk about the old days. How they all felt when Wil left them. I know Mickey Lindsay said he didn't harbor any ill feelings against Wil, but the others might. Who else is there still around?"

Melba thought for a moment. "Mickey, of course, but he's a sweetheart. I believe him when he says he doesn't have anything against Wil. Jimmy Tatum was the drummer, and he works at that big chain store near downtown. The only other one was Doug Rinehart. He played guitar along with Wil. Was decent at it, but Wil was the best."

"Where is Doug Rinehart now?" I asked.

"He's a cop on the Athena force," Melba said. "He was at the Farrington House the other night when John Earl got electrocuted. I only saw him briefly, though. Didn't get a chance to talk to him afterward, but he looked pretty shook up the last time I spotted him across the room."

"Does Mickey work?" I asked. "He mentioned heart surgery, and he looked like he's had a hard time recently."

"No, he can't work anymore. He's on disability," Melba said.

"His wife still works, though. She's got a good job, so they're doing okay, I guess."

"Do you think they'd be willing to get together and talk about the old days?" I asked.

"I don't see why not," Melba said slowly. "Probably better, though, if I get in touch with them and set it up. Okay to do it at my house instead of yours?"

"That's fine with me," I said. "Should I bring Diesel?"

Hearing his name, my cat warbled loudly.

Melba laughed. "Of course, don't you dare leave my darling boy at home. Besides, you know he's a good icebreaker."

"True," I replied. "Let me know when you have it set up, and I'll make sure I can be there."

"I'll try to set it up for one night this week." Melba rose from her chair. "The sooner the better. Are you free the next few nights?"

"Far as I know. I'll double-check with Helen Louise, though, in case I've forgotten something." I had better call her right away, I reckoned, so that I didn't let it slip my mind. Things seemed to do that more often these days, especially when I got busy.

"I'll start calling them," Melba said. "I don't have their numbers, but I'm sure I can get ahold of them pretty easily." She laughed, giving me an arch smile. "Both Doug and Jimmy are divorced, and I can probably lure them to the house with the promise of a home-cooked meal."

I laughed, too. Melba was a pretty good cook. Not anywhere near Azalea's class, or Helen Louise's, but she had several dishes she made very well.

"Work your wiles on them, then," I said.

Melba left, and I settled back to work. Diesel napped in the window, and I forced myself to focus on cataloging. At some point, a niggling thought intruded. I was supposed to do something. What was it?

"Check with Helen Louise about this week," I said, annoyed with myself for not doing it the minute Melba left, but also glad that I at least remembered it the same day.

I called Helen Louise, and after the preliminary greetings were done, I explained what Melba and I intended to do. "Do we have anything planned in the evenings this week?"

Helen Louise chuckled. "Charlie, love, I'm going to have to start texting you a schedule, and then text you reminders periodically to look at your schedule."

"Am I really that bad?" I asked.

"No, you're not." She chuckled again. "But you do have a habit of getting caught up in things and letting other things slide a bit. Especially when there's a murder to solve."

Guilty as charged, I thought.

"To answer your question, no particular plans this week," Helen Louise said. "I do know Doug and Mickey, though, so why don't I plan to join you and Melba? I can keep an eye on you and keep you from getting into trouble. Besides, I know who Jimmy is, though we're not really acquainted."

"It's fine with me," I said. "Melba's going to offer to cook dinner for Jimmy and Doug. Says they're both divorced."

"She keeps up with those things better than anyone I know," Helen Louise said. "I'll call her and find out what she's planning to serve, and I can bring a dessert or anything else she might want."

"That sounds great," I said. "Your desserts are the best in town, if not in the whole state."

"Flattery will get you everywhere." Helen Louise laughed. "I need to get back to work, love. I'll give Melba a call when I have some slack time."

I bade her goodbye and set aside my phone. Back to work cataloging, now that I had accomplished my task. Diesel continued to nap in the window. Occasionally I heard a genteel snore behind me, and I had to smile.

After our usual break for lunch at home, Diesel and I returned to the office at one o'clock. Work ended at three, and that meant I had two hours to catalog, after another quick check of email.

This time I did find a request from a historian from a Louisiana university who wanted to consult some papers belonging to an early-twentieth-century Mississippi state legislator that we held in the archive. I replied, giving her suggested dates and times, and explained our policies on working with our collections. I was always pleased when scholars wanted to make use of our resources. That lent importance to our collections.

Around two o'clock, Melba entered my office. She appeared to be agitated, and I regarded her with alarm. She collapsed into the chair without saying anything.

"What on earth is the matter?" I asked.

Diesel had climbed down from the window and gone to her. He placed his head on her knee and chirped. She placed a trembling hand on his head.

Her eyes filled with tears. "Mickey Lindsay died earlier today."

TWENTY-FOUR

IIIIIIIIIIIIIIIIIIIIIIIIIIIIIIIIIIIIIIIIIIIIIIIIIIIIIIIIIIIIIIIIIII

I stared at her, dumbfounded. "What happened?"

"It wasn't his heart." Her voice shook.

I grabbed some tissues from the box on my desk and got up to give them to her. She dabbed at her eyes.

"What, then, if it wasn't his heart?" I asked.

"Hit and run." Melba started sobbing.

"Oh my lord," I said.

"His granddaughter found him in the street in front of his house. His wife was at work and asked her to check on Mickey when he didn't answer the phone."

"That poor girl," I said. "And poor Mrs. Lindsay. How horrible." I thought for a moment. "How did you find out?"

"Doug Rinehart. I told you he's a city cop," Melba said, trying to regain control. "When I called him about ten minutes ago, he told me about it. He was really upset, too. He and Mickey were still good friends."

"Has anyone told Wil about this?" I asked.

"I don't know," Melba said. "Why, do you think this has anything to do with him?" She looked even more upset at the thought.

"I honestly don't know," I said slowly. "But it seems like a strange coincidence, don't you think? Two members of Wil's current band attacked, and now another original member of his band is killed, this time by a hit-and-run driver."

Perhaps it *was* a simple coincidence and had nothing to do with Wil Threadgill and the horrible mess currently surrounding him. I had an uneasy feeling, however, that Mickey Lindsay's death was somehow connected to it all.

"If that's the case, and Mickey was killed because of his connection to Wil," Melba said, her voice steadier now, "then the killer is probably someone from Athena. Not from California."

"I'm beginning to think so," I said. "Why would any of the California group target Mickey Lindsay?" I shook my head. "Just doesn't make any sense. What could he possibly have known about any of them that would have been dangerous for them?"

"I don't think he could have," Melba said. "Wil didn't have any direct contact with them after he reached California. At least that's what he told me in one of his recent letters."

"Do you think he's been talking directly to any of them since he's been back in Athena?" I asked.

Melba shrugged. "I don't know that he's had much time, but he could have, I suppose."

"Can you find out? I think we ought to know that."

"I'll call him. I need to get back downstairs." She rose.

"One more thing before you go," I said. "I think it's even more important now to talk to the two remaining members of the band. Especially before something happens to either one of them."

"I think you're right," Melba said. "I'll tell them it's urgent that they come to my house tonight to talk. I think Doug Rinehart is pretty shaken up by this, so unless he's on duty, I'm sure he'll be there. Jimmy I may have to browbeat into it."

I had no doubt that Melba would be successful. She was exceptionally good at browbeating when the occasion demanded it.

About ten minutes after Melba went back to her office, she sent me a text, saying that Wil said he hadn't talked to either Jimmy or Doug. He thought he might have spotted Doug in the hotel the night of John Earl Whitaker's murder, but he never had a chance to talk to him in all the chaos.

I acknowledged her text with a *thanks* and laid my phone aside. I wondered if Mickey Lindsay had been the only one of the three who tried to talk to Wil. If Melba could get the two men to her house tonight, we should be able to find out.

I didn't hear from Melba again until Diesel and I were ready to head home for lunch. She caught us when we came downstairs to exit the building.

"All set for tonight," she said with a triumphant smile. "If you and Helen Louise, and Diesel, of course, can be at my house at six-thirty, we can talk about how we want to do this. The guys are supposed to be there at seven."

"That sounds like a good plan," I said. "I'll let her know. She said she'd bring a dessert. Anything else you need?"

"A bottle or two of wine wouldn't hurt. Some vintage that goes well with chicken casserole. I've got a couple in the freezer I'm going to heat up. Also some green beans and dinner rolls. That should be enough, don't you think?"

"Sounds fine to me," I said. "We'll be there. With wine."

Lunch consisted of roast beef, potato salad, and English peas, accompanied by freshly baked rolls. Diesel and Ramses could have only bites of buttered roll and English peas, because the roast had been cooked with onion. Despite the occasional sniffing at the scent of the roast, they both seemed content with their tidbits.

Azalea had disappeared upstairs while I ate lunch and treated the boys. I thought about Alex and Sean. I hadn't heard from either of them since my conversation with Alex.

I put down my fork and retrieved my cell phone. I hesitated for a moment, but then I called Sean. He answered right away.

"Hi, Dad, what's up?" His voice sounded tired and strained.

"I was just calling to check on you and see how things are going," I said. "Any news?"

Sean sighed into the phone. "We talked about everything last night. I told her I really didn't have a problem with her not coming back to work, and I think I finally convinced her. She told me she talked to you, and I appreciate whatever you told her."

"I'm glad I could help," I said. "What about the farmhouse?"

"She liked the idea of keeping the house in town and starting to spend weekends at the farmhouse when the renovations are done," Sean said. "We still have a few things to work through, but I think we're getting there. Look, I've got a client in the waiting room now. I'll have to let you go."

"Thanks, son. Don't worry," I said, trying to sound as positive as I could.

"I'll try not to." Sean said goodbye and ended the call.

Diesel meowed at me. I knew he sensed my concern—though I certainly felt better after my talk with Sean—and wanted to comfort me. I scratched his head and tried to reassure him. Ramses took advantage of the distraction and jumped into my lap. He stuck his nose in my plate. I had to laugh at that as I removed him and took a scrap of roast beef away from him. "Naughty boy," I said. "That will make you sick." I consoled him with some English peas.

I realized I hadn't yet called Helen Louise about tonight. I picked up the phone and called her. I got her voice mail, and I left her a message. I would pick her up about ten minutes before we were due at Melba's, if that was convenient.

A few minutes later she texted me to say that was fine. She would be ready, wine in hand for the evening.

Diesel and I went back to the archive. I was determined to focus on work, and only on work, for the rest of the afternoon. For the most part I succeeded, with only momentary lapses as thoughts about Alex and Wil and their problems intruded.

I parked my car in front of Helen Louise's house at six-nineteen. Diesel stayed in the car while I went to her door and rang the bell. She opened the door a few seconds later. She greeted me with a kiss before handing me the two wine bottles. She carried the dessert in a covered dish. Once in the car, she greeted Diesel, and we stowed the wine on the seat between us. She placed the covered dish on the floorboard between her feet.

We arrived at Melba's house right on time. She admitted us, and

I sniffed appreciatively at the aromas wafting toward us from the kitchen.

"Smells delicious," I said after greetings had been exchanged. Diesel chirped happily. He recognized the scent of chicken.

Melba laughed. "I have some chicken just for you, handsome boy. No onion anywhere near it, and with a little rice."

The cat chirped again, then meowed loudly.

"Not yet," I told him. "You'll have to wait until everybody eats." He gave me a grumpy look but ceased meowing.

Helen Louise patted him. "I'm hungry, too, but it won't be long now." He purred as she continued to stroke him.

"Give them to me, and I'll put them in the fridge. I have a bottle already open, but I have to tell you, it's not going to be as good as these," Melba said.

"I'm sure it will be fine," Helen Louise said. "I'll come with you and put the dessert in the fridge, too. You boys get comfortable here, and we'll be back soon." She disappeared into the kitchen with Melba, and Diesel and I made ourselves at home on the sofa.

True to her word, Helen Louise returned less than two minutes later with wineglasses in hand. She gave me one before settling into one of Melba's cozy chairs. "Melba will be along in a minute."

I sipped at the wine and discovered that it was good. Melba had made the right choice.

Melba came in with her own glass and took her usual seat. "Now, about tonight," she said. "How do we want to do this?"

"Did you say anything to these men about the purpose of this meeting?" I asked.

"I did," Melba said. "I didn't want them to feel blindsided and get angry and storm out. Jimmy has a temper, from what I've heard. Doug is pretty laid back so I'm not worried about him."

"I think we should wait until we get close to dessert time," Helen Louise said. "They should be fairly mellow by then. I assume they're both wine drinkers."

"I checked, and they are," Melba replied.

"Good," I said. "I hope we brought enough wine."

"I have more if we need it," Melba said. "No worries."

"Do you think Doug Rinehart will be willing to talk to us about the circumstances surrounding Mickey Lindsay's death?" I asked.

"Probably," Melba said.

"It's horrible," Helen Louise said. "Such a nice man, and after all he went through with his heart issues and his surgery. He didn't deserve that."

"I hope they catch the jerk responsible," Melba said, her tone heated. "I'd like to get ahold of him with a whip or a baseball bat."

"Can't say I blame you," I said. Hit-and-run drivers were cowards. Bad enough for the mayhem they caused, but avoiding responsibility for what they'd done was unforgivable. If this had been a deliberate attack, I wondered what Mickey Lindsay had known or possibly done to become the target of a ruthless murderer.

We enjoyed our wine while we chatted by mutual agreement on other subjects until the two guests arrived. Talking about Mickey Lindsay's death was completely dispiriting, and we didn't know much of anything about the circumstances.

Promptly at seven, Melba's doorbell rang, and she went to admit the ringer. Evidently both men had arrived at the same time, because she brought them both into the living room.

They offered a contrast in coloring and size. The taller one stood about six three, had short-cropped gray hair, a dark tan, and the bearing of a policeman. He looked familiar, and I reckoned he must be Doug Rinehart. The second man was about six inches shorter, on the portly side, completely bald, pale, and wearing a scowl. This had to be Jimmy Tatum.

He was talking and gesturing. ". . . craziest thing. Why on earth would some nutcase be following me from work to here?"

TWENTY-FIVE

||||||||||||||||||||||||||||||||||||||||||||||||||||||||||||||||||

Tatum broke off when he realized that Helen Louise and I, along with Diesel, were listening to his remarks. He appeared somewhat taken aback, as if he was unaware Melba had other guests.

"More about that in a minute," Melba told him. "Let me introduce everybody." She proceeded to do so, and I had been correct in my guesses as to which man was which. Doug Rinehart's handshake was firm and dry, while Tatum's was a bit on the flabby side. They both smiled at Helen Louise, but Tatum looked askance at Diesel. Rinehart patted Diesel's head.

"No offense," Tatum said, glancing between me and Helen Louise. "Cats make me uneasy."

Helen Louise offered him a wry smile. "No offense taken."

I wasn't offended, but Tatum's remark did nothing to endear him to me, or to Helen Louise. I could read that easily.

Rinehart shot the other man a cool, appraising glance, shifted his gaze to me, and quirked an eyebrow as if to say *Pay him no mind.*

Melba offered them both wine, and Tatum accepted eagerly. He gulped half of his down in one go, while Rinehart took measured sips.

"Bring your wineglasses, and we'll go into the dining room," Melba said. "Dinner's ready. Just has to be put on the table."

We all followed her, and Tatum kept an eye on Diesel. The cat had made no move toward Tatum. My boy always knew when he was around someone who didn't like cats. He never attempted to make friends with such persons. He was too smart to waste the effort.

Melba had set the table with her best china, silver, and linen tablecloth and napkins. A lovely centerpiece with fresh flowers lent elegance to the whole. Melba indicated where we should sit, me on her right and Helen Louise on her left. Rinehart was next to Helen Louise and Tatum next to me.

"What, no place for the cat?" Tatum guffawed at his quip. I noticed his wineglass was empty.

When no one answered his attempt at humor, his face took on a sulky expression. He pulled out his chair and sat while the rest of us were still pulling out our chairs. Melba disappeared into the kitchen, and Helen Louise followed her to help. Diesel sat between my chair and Melba's. He knew we would be the ones to offer him tidbits.

Melba and Helen Louise soon had the food on the table, and we began the process of serving ourselves. Melba went around replenishing wineglasses, and with that done she took her seat. She raised her glass and said, "Let's enjoy ourselves."

Eating commenced. Rinehart right away offered a comment on how tasty he found the casserole. Tatum appeared to be too busy eating to say anything. Helen Louise and I exchanged amused glances. Melba and I doled out bits of chicken to Diesel, and Rinehart cast an amused glance our way from time to time. Tatum never noticed, as far as I could tell.

Conversation remained desultory until we had finished our dinner, and Helen Louise went back to the kitchen to prepare the dessert. Melba offered coffee, and Rinehart and I accepted.

Over dessert, one of Helen Louise's delicious chocolate cakes, and after compliments from Rinehart, Melba broached the subject of Mickey Lindsay's death.

"Any ideas on the identity of the driver?" she asked.

"Not yet," Rinehart said. "There was a witness, but it happened early this morning before the sun was up." He laid his napkin beside his empty dessert plate and had a sip of coffee before he continued. "Apparently Mickey had gone out to fetch the paper, and it must have been lying in the street. According to the witness, who lives at the far end of the block, she heard an engine rev up and saw the car—no lights on, evidently—head toward Mickey and strike him."

"That means it had to be deliberate," I said.

Rinehart nodded. "Sounds like it to me, but we can't be certain."

"Did the witness give a description of the car?" Helen Louise asked.

"No, it was too dark. A couple of the streetlights were out. We discovered that they had been broken some time ago, and the city hadn't repaired them yet." He shook his head. "Dangerous, but it was the driver's good luck."

"Poor Mickey." Melba dabbed at her eyes with her napkin.

"Never could catch a break, Mickey couldn't." Tatum shook his head. "Had that bad heart, and his son died when his kid was young. Seemed like bad luck followed him around."

"I suppose you could look at it like that," Rinehart said. "Mickey never let it get him down, at least until his heart problems came along. He was a good guy, and he deserved way better than he got."

I felt really bad for the late Mickey Lindsay. It sounded like he'd had some bad breaks in his life, and now he had been deliberately killed by someone. But why?

"Do you think his death is connected in some way with John Earl's death?" Melba asked. "And the attacks on Wil's band members?"

"What are you talking about?" Tatum appeared confused. "John Earl's dead? And who's Wil?"

We all looked at him in astonishment. Tersely, Rinehart explained the events of recent days. Tatum's face drained of color as he listened. "What the hell is going on?"

"That's what we'd all like to know," I said.

"How come I ain't heard about any of this?" Tatum said, indignant. "And what about the nutcase following me?"

"Don't you read the local newspaper?" Helen Louise asked. "Or listen to people talking at work? I can't believe people weren't talking about it."

Tatum shrugged. "I don't pay much attention. I got my work to do, and I do it. Don't come into contact with the customers much working in the back in the stock area like I do." He picked up his wineglass, noticed it was empty again, and looked around for a wine bottle. Melba went to the kitchen to bring out a new bottle. When she returned, she filled his wineglass and he drank half of it.

"Shame about John Earl," Tatum said. "Another guy who couldn't catch a break. Course, the way he put away the booze, he couldn't stay sober long enough to do much." He offered a tipsy grimace.

"Yeah, drinking too much can be a problem." If Tatum caught the note of irony in Rinehart's voice, he didn't acknowledge it.

"Doug, you're a cop, and you know most of the people involved. What do you think about what's going on?" Melba asked.

"Someone's got it in for Fred, or Wil, I guess he goes by now," Rinehart said. "I'm not sure why. Somebody must be bearing a grudge against him."

"Someone here in Athena?" I asked.

Rinehart shrugged. "For over forty years? Don't make much sense to me. I can't think of anybody who'd hate Wil that much to carry it all these years."

Tatum snorted. "Other than John Earl, and he's the one who's dead."

"So John Earl bore a grudge against Wil?" Helen Louise asked.

"Sure did," Tatum said, his eyes slightly unfocused after his third, fourth, or maybe fifth, glass of wine. "John Earl just knew he was going to be the next Elvis, and he blamed Fred, um, Wil, for running off and leaving him in the lurch." He giggled. "Knew he wouldn't get nowhere without his best friend."

"Wil knew how to write to make John Earl sound his best,"

Rinehart explained. "John Earl had a limited vocal range, but he made the most of what he had."

Tatum snickered. "Yeah, he sounded like a strangled cat if he tried to hit high notes." He poked my arm. "No offense, buddy."

"None taken," I said. "What about the rest of you? Were you angry with Wil when he disappeared? Did that break up the band?"

"We tried to hang on for a while, covering tunes from hit bands," Rinehart said. "John Earl couldn't really handle it. We needed a singer with a bigger range, but he wouldn't have it. I quit because I got tired of arguing with him." He shrugged. "Besides, my father was putting pressure on me to either get a real job or get out of the house."

"So you went to the police department," Melba said.

Rinehart grinned. "Yeah, up and joined the Establishment. Made my dad happy." The grin faded. "Best decision I ever made, I got to tell you. Sure, it's got challenges, but I've made it through, and I'm retiring in about fifteen months."

"What about you, Jimmy?" Melba asked. "Were you angry with Wil?"

Tatum nodded. "Yeah, for a while. Long as we were playing, we had girls hanging around. Some of 'em got a real kick sleeping with a guy in a band. That all dried up when the band broke up."

"How charming," Helen Louise murmured with a wicked grin in my direction. Diesel warbled.

Tatum started. "What was that? Some kind of cricket?"

"No, it was my cat," I said. "He makes sounds like that."

"Weird," Tatum said, frowning. "Anyway, other than losing the attention, I guess I wasn't too upset. We weren't hardly making a living anyway, and my mama—she was a widow woman—was pushing me to get a job, too. So that's what I did."

"You're not jealous of Wil's success?" Helen Louise asked.

"Well, yeah," Rinehart said. "I'd love to have that kind of money, but Wil's got the talent, and he worked harder than any of us ever did. He deserves what he's got, and I sure don't resent him for it. Jimmy don't, either, do you?" He stared across the table at his former bandmate.

For a moment, I thought Tatum might disagree, but instead he said, "Nope, me either. Wil's a good guy." Suddenly he giggled. "John Earl sure thought so. Was always mooning around Fred like a puppy."

Rinehart glared at Tatum, and I wondered what made him do that. Had Tatum said something he shouldn't have?

Melba was quick to follow up on Tatum's remark. "What do you mean about mooning around, Jimmy? We already know that Wil was John Earl's best friend."

"Don't pay him no attention," Rinehart said sharply. "He's drunk and doesn't know what he's saying."

Tatum glared at Rinehart this time. "I sure as hell do know what I'm talking about. I was the one caught them fooling around once. I know you saw 'em yourself. You told me you did."

Melba, Helen Louise, and I exchanged startled glances. *Fooling around* meant the same thing to all three of us.

Melba cleared her throat. "What do you mean by *fooling around*?"

Rinehart pushed back his chair and rose. "I'm not listening to any more of this garbage. Thanks for the meal, Melba. Nice to meet you folks, but I've got an early shift tomorrow. I need to get home and in bed. I'll see myself out." He stalked out of the room, and moments later we heard the front door close, none too softly.

Tatum shook his head. "Poor ole Doug. He's what you call one of them homophones." His expression grew puzzled. "Isn't that the word? Anyway, he don't like seeing two men kissing, and that's what Fred and John Earl was doing. Didn't look like nobody was forcing 'em to, either."

TWENTY-SIX

|||||||||||||||||||||||||||||||||||||||||||||||||||||||||||||||||||

I looked at Melba to gauge her reaction to this somewhat shocking revelation, but to my surprise she didn't appear at all fazed by it.

Helen Louise's expression mirrored my own, however. We were both taken aback by the notion that Wil and John Earl might have had an intimate relationship. That in itself was one reason Wil might have wanted to flee Athena. Forty years ago, it would have caused quite an uproar in this town. Even today there were plenty of people who would have a problem with it.

"Jimmy, I think it's time you had some coffee." Melba rose from her chair. "You come on with me into the kitchen. You're in no shape to drive home right now."

"If you say so." Tatum got up unsteadily from his place at the table, and I put out an arm to keep him from stumbling onto me. I got up to help him into the kitchen. Diesel ducked under the table.

Melba was loading the coffeemaker when I managed to steer

Tatum into the kitchen. He wasn't badly drunk, only a little unsteady on his pins. I put him at the table and left him to Melba's tender mercies. She rolled her eyes at me. "I'll be back with y'all as soon as the coffee's ready and I can pour him a big mug of it."

I nodded and returned to the dining room. I resumed my seat and shared a glance with Helen Louise, who had evidently been laughing.

"You're amused?" I asked, my own lips twitching.

"Yes, it's pretty funny, don't you think?" Helen Louise grinned. "I'm not sure he's that tipsy. He had only three glasses of wine. Either he's an easy drunk, or he's putting it on."

"Could be," I said. "But why would he want to do that?"

Helen Louise shrugged. "I haven't a clue. Melba knows him better than we do."

"What do you think about his story about Wil and John Earl Whitaker?" I asked.

"I don't recall ever hearing either one of them was interested in anything but girls," Helen Louise said after a moment's reflection. "That doesn't mean anything, though."

"I don't remember anything like that, either," I said. "Though I doubt I'd have paid much attention if I had."

"It's true, though," Melba said, surprising us both. She had a tray with cups of coffee for each of us, along with cream and sugar. She served us before taking her place once more at the table.

"You knew about it?" Helen Louise asked.

"Not back then when it happened," Melba said after blowing on her coffee. "Later on, Wil told me he had experimented a bit, mostly because John Earl wouldn't leave him alone." She looked down at her coffee. "To tell the truth, I don't think Wil's that interested in either women or men. All he thinks about is music."

"That's not so unusual," I said. "Highly successful and motivated people have that kind of intense focus. Or at least, I read that somewhere."

"That's Wil," Melba said, once again looking up and exchanging glances with us. Diesel had come out from under the table to sit by her chair. She stroked his head almost absent-mindedly.

"Do you think that experimentation has anything to do with what's going on now?" Helen Louise asked.

"I don't know," Melba said. "I think it may explain a lot about John Earl and the way he behaved after Wil left. If he really was in love with Wil and turned to drinking because of it, well, I just don't know." She shook her head.

"But he was obviously involved with Natalie, too," I said. "They got married."

"Because she said she was pregnant with his child," Melba said. "And in love with her, too, according to what Wil said. I didn't know it at the time."

Something in her tone alerted me to the fact that she didn't completely believe the story.

Helen Louise picked up on it, too. "You think Natalie was faking the pregnancy in order to get John Earl to marry her?"

"Maybe," Melba said. "I don't know. Only she knows the truth of it, and I don't expect she'll ever say. But John Earl married her, and they did eventually have a daughter, Shaylene." She thought for a moment. "I'd say she's at least forty or forty-one now."

We sipped our coffee, and conversation lagged briefly. Then we heard Tatum calling for Melba from the kitchen. "I'll be back," she said.

She returned alone. "Poured him another cup of coffee and insisted he drink it. By the time he's done, he ought to be able to drive himself home."

"If not," I said, "we can take him home."

"He should be fine after two cups of strong coffee," Helen Louise said. "I don't think he was all that tipsy."

"I agree," Melba said. "I think he only wanted a bit of Dutch courage in order to tell us what he'd seen." She shook her head. "Doug Rinehart surprised me with the way he acted."

"How so?" I asked.

"I don't think he's really a homophobe," Melba said. "I think it's just that he believes sleeping dogs ought to be let alone. No point in dragging that up now."

"He's probably right," Helen Louise said. "Hard to see how it could have a bearing on the present situation."

"If Whitaker hadn't been killed, it might have," I said. "I wonder what he would have said to the group in that room if he hadn't died right away."

"As drunk as he appeared to be, it might have been anything," Melba said. "He had almost no inhibitions to begin with, and when he was drunk, well, he was liable to say anything to anyone."

That gave me a startling idea. I started to mention it, but then I reconsidered. I should probably think it through more carefully before I broached it to anyone else.

Jimmy Tatum came into the dining room to announce that he felt fine now and was going to drive himself home. Melba got up to check him out. Evidently his condition satisfied her, and she sent him on his way after accepting his thanks for the dinner and the coffee.

"Take some aspirin when you get home." Melba led Tatum out of the dining room and to the front door.

"We'll help Melba clean up," Helen Louise said. "Then home, don't you think?" She rose from her chair.

"Yes, this has been an interesting night." I rose also, and Diesel accompanied us when we carried dishes and silverware into the kitchen.

"Just set them on the counter by the sink," Melba instructed us. "I'll scrape them clean and wash them in the morning."

There were few leftovers to deal with, and we soon had those tidied away, along with the remaining china and cutlery from the table. Melba insisted that we leave the rest to her. Helen Louise demurred for a moment, but Melba finally shooed us out of the kitchen and to the front door. Diesel chirped on and off the whole time, until Melba squatted beside him to give him a hug. That made him warble happily.

Back in the car, I cranked it and got the air-conditioning going. The night around us was muggy, although not all that hot. The car felt stuffy, and I waited until the air was circulating well before I shifted into drive and headed to Helen Louise's house.

"Do you think we learned anything useful tonight?" Helen Louise asked.

"We did," I said. "For one thing, we can be pretty certain that Mickey Lindsay was deliberately killed. But why?"

"For some unknown reason," Helen Louise said.

"And it's possible the same person was following Jimmy Tatum," I said. "Maybe someone has it in for the whole band. And how are we going to find out why?" I said, feeling frustrated. "What could Mickey have known that cost him his life? What could Jimmy Tatum and Doug Rinehart possibly know?"

"Maybe Mickey saw something he shouldn't have, and the killer found out about it," Helen Louise said.

"That's a distinct possibility," I said. "I wonder if he told a member of his family, if he did see something."

"I'm sure the police or Kanesha will be talking to them, if they haven't already," Helen Louise said.

Diesel meowed in agreement from the backseat.

"I hope he did tell them, if he had anything to share with the authorities," I said. "I want whoever killed him to pay for it. The person doing all this is ruthless and completely cold-blooded."

"Yes, you're right." Helen Louise's voice held a strange note. When she spoke again, I understood what it was: fear. "Charlie, finding out that Mickey was deliberately killed scares me. You've been talking to Wil, and you were present when he confronted his assistant and his manager. If either, or both of them, are responsible, they could target you next."

"I don't think so," I said calmly. "There's no need to kill me after the fact. I'm not worried about them, and I'm beginning to think that the embezzlement and the murderous attacks aren't connected."

"I suppose you're right about your knowledge being after the fact, as it were," Helen Louise said, sounding more like her usual cool self. "That still leaves someone else out there who might be responsible and isn't aware of exactly what you might know. I'm sure most everybody knows by now that you've been talking to Wil about all this, and the killer might think you're dangerous."

I turned the car into her street and soon pulled into the driveway. "I understand your concern," I said, "and I have to confess I'm a little worried myself. I will be vigilant, I promise, but I'm not going to cower inside the house behind locked doors until Kanesha solves these crimes."

Helen Louise sighed. "I know. I also know you'll be careful, but this person strikes when people are vulnerable. Don't forget that."

"I won't. I'm not going to put myself in that position if I can at all help it," I said. "I give you my word on that."

"I'll hold you to it." She opened her door and stepped out of the car. I got out to escort her to her front door. Diesel remained in the car.

We shared a quick embrace and a kiss before she unlocked her door and stepped into the house. She paused a moment to regard me in the light spilling out from her entranceway. "Be careful," she said and closed the door.

I walked back to the car thinking about what we had discussed. I could be absent-minded and therefore vulnerable sometimes, but I assured myself that until this case was solved, I would not let myself get distracted like that. I had to keep focused.

I looked carefully before I backed the car out of Helen Louise's driveway. I could see nothing suspicious on her well-lit street. My house stood only a few blocks away, and Diesel and I made it home and into the garage without incident. We entered the kitchen, and Ramses greeted us in his usual excited fashion. He started to climb up my pants leg, but I extracted him before he could cause me or my pants much damage. I realized he was overdue to have his nails clipped.

The kitchen clock informed me that it was nearly ten-thirty. Time for bed. I turned out most of the downstairs lights, leaving only the usual few on in case Haskell, Stewart, or Alissa came in later. The cats scampered up the stairs ahead of me. I followed them slowly, my thoughts occupied by the startling idea that had occurred to me not long before we left Melba's house.

As I prepared for bed, I considered my idea that the embezzlement was not related to the murders and the attacks. The only connection between the two was Wil Threadgill, and I couldn't see Vance Tolliver and Chelsea Bremmer resorting to murder over half a million dollars. Yes, it was a large amount of money, but was it worth prison time for murder? Somehow I just couldn't see that it was.

The two murders and the assaults with intent to harm or kill were different, however. Wil was definitely a target, as were those around him whom he cared about. Hurting them would definitely hurt Wil more than embezzling money from him would. Half a million dollars likely only put a mere ding in his assets.

No, I couldn't shake the feeling that there was something darker and downright evil behind the two murders and the assaults. I thought the truth lay somewhere in Wil's past here in Athena. The question was, how could we dig it out?

TWENTY-SEVEN

I woke with the determination the next morning to talk to Wil Threadgill again, despite what Kanesha Berry might say or do. This time, I decided, I would push him hard on topics that he hadn't really discussed before. I still had the idea in the back of my mind that he might be the killer himself, for reasons yet unknown. I didn't want to believe him guilty of these heinous crimes, because I found him likable. But psychopaths were often likable, I knew. Was Wil Threadgill a psychopath? I didn't think I could broach the subject with Melba, though she was more objective about him that I had thought.

Today was Wednesday and therefore not a workday. I had the leisure to spend some time with Wil Threadgill, if he was available. I remembered, however, that after a delay of two days, he was supposed to start his work with the music students at Athena today. If I could find out his schedule, I might be able to attend one of his sessions, or at least catch him in between. I figured Melba might know what his schedule was. If she didn't, she always knew the right person at Athena College from whom to find out what she needed to know.

I ate my breakfast, being sure to share some of the extra bacon with Diesel and Ramses. Halfway through my meal, Azalea excused herself and headed upstairs. Today was the day she stripped the beds and remade them with fresh linen.

She had still not returned to the kitchen by the time I finished. I put my dishes in the sink. I knew better than to stack them in the dishwasher. I headed to the den with the cats on my heels. I checked the time, and it was now a few minutes after eight. Melba ought to be in her office by now. I settled on the sofa with Ramses in my lap and Diesel stretched out beside me.

Melba picked up right away. "Good morning, library administration. This is Melba Gilley. How can I help you?"

She sounded perky, but then she always did when she answered her work phone.

"Hi, Melba, it's just me," I said.

"Hello, just me. What can I do for you?" she said.

"I want to talk to Wil again," I replied. "I know he's supposed to start working with students today, though. Do you happen to know his schedule?"

"That I do. His embezzling assistant gave it to me a few days ago before she was under house arrest," Melba said with grim satisfaction. "I don't think they've changed much about his first day. In fact,

I think Wil is planning to extend his stay so that he can put in all the time they originally planned for."

"That's really good of him," I said. "Especially with all the stress he's facing right now."

"I'm looking at today's schedule," Melba said. "He's supposed to have lunch with some of the music faculty from noon to one. Then he appears to be free for a couple of hours after that. How about I see if I can pick him up and bring him to your house? It would be easier than trying to talk on campus."

"That would be great. Let me know when you find out if he is willing to do it and is free." I thanked her and ended the call.

I put Ramses gently down on the floor in order to retrieve my laptop from my desk. He squeaked in annoyance before he decided to climb onto the sofa next to Diesel. He stretched out along Diesel's frame, and the resulting picture was sweet, but also amusing. There was so much more of Diesel. He made Ramses look small.

Once again on the sofa, I opened the laptop and powered it up. I knew many people left theirs on all the time, but I didn't do that. I could go days without touching it, and it seemed a waste to let it run that long.

I checked my personal email and quickly deleted the sales messages and other oddities. Once I had done that, I was left with only two new messages. One was from my friend Jack Pemberton, a true crime writer I had met in the course of investigating a cold case not that long ago. Jack emailed occasionally just to check in, giving me updates on his writing and his family. I responded in kind, except that I didn't allude to the murders here in Athena. That would be for another email conversation. I had no doubt this would be a juicy subject for one of Jack's books. He wrote well and did thorough research, and I would be interested in his take on the situation once the killer was identified and arrested.

I didn't recognize the name of the sender of the remaining message. The name was Donna S. Boudreaux, and I didn't think I'd ever met anyone of that name. I would have skimmed it and deleted it, but the subject line had caught my attention: "Talk about W. Threadgill."

Miss Boudreaux didn't tell me anything particularly personal about herself. She simply claimed to be in a position to know certain potentially helpful facts about Wil. She also said she knew about my involvement in previous murder investigations and wanted to consult me before deciding to go to the authorities with what she knew. Could I meet her somewhere to talk?

I was intrigued, naturally, and my first inclination was to try to schedule a meeting with her as soon as possible. Then I wondered how she had gotten my personal email address. Perhaps she knew someone who knew me and thought it would be okay to share it. That wasn't really proper etiquette, though. I would have to find out how she got it and deal with that later. I didn't want my private email address getting out there where anyone could find it. I had managed to stay out of the press, for the most part, the past few years when I was involved in murder investigations. I wanted to keep a low profile.

I texted Melba to ask if she knew anyone named Donna Boudreaux. A few minutes later she responded that she didn't. If Melba didn't know anyone of that name in Athena, then this woman was definitely a stranger.

I had to wait another twenty minutes before Melba called to tell me that the meeting with Wil was on. "I'll pick him up and bring him to your house. Should be there by one-fifteen at the latest."

"Sounds good. See you then." I put my phone down and reread the email message from Donna Boudreaux. It sounded innocuous enough, and I was curious. I responded to her email with an invitation to meet with me in the archive office tomorrow morning at nine, if that was convenient. I would make sure Melba knew about the appointment, since I had never heard of this person before.

Within minutes she responded that she would meet me there. I acknowledged receipt, then closed out my email and set the laptop aside on the broad back of the sofa.

I punched the speed dial for Sean's cell rather than his office phone. I was anxious to talk to him.

Sean answered after three rings. "Hi, Dad, how are you?"

"I'm fine, son. How about you and yours?" I asked, trying to sound nonchalant.

"We're doing pretty good," he said. "I'm in the office, so it's okay to talk freely. I'm sure you're calling about Alex."

"Yes," I said. "I tried to stop myself from bugging you, I really did."

Sean chuckled. "You're not bugging me, Dad. I know you're worried. I've got good news for you. I was going to call you anyway. Alex and I are flying out of Memphis on Friday to spend a few days in Chicago. We need some time away from everything here, and there's an exhibit at the Art Institute we both want to see. And the Field Museum, too."

"That sounds great. You two haven't had a break for a while. Is Rosie going with you?"

"Rosie is going to stay with Laura, Frank, and Charlie. Our nanny will go in and help with her during the day. She and Charlie's nanny are friends, so that makes everything easier."

"That sounds like a good plan," I said, though I was a bit disappointed not to be asked to look after my granddaughter. "How long do you expect to be gone?"

"We're planning to fly home on Tuesday afternoon."

"All right. I'll let you go, but I'm sure I'll talk to you again before you leave," I said.

"I'm sure you will," Sean said, a light touch of humor in his tone. "Bye, Dad."

Now that the immediate worries over Sean and Alex were settled, I focused my thoughts once again on the murders and the attacks. Wil no doubt could tell us more about his time in Athena before he left, and whether he could think of anything that could be tied to the present situation. By now he'd surely had time to think about it. Perhaps he already knew something but was withholding the information for reasons unknown.

I wondered if he'd had any contact with Natalie Whitaker since his return to Athena. Was he aware that she was attempting to sue him for the wrongful death of her husband? Sean had turned her down and advised her to wait for the conclusion of the investigation. Another less scrupulous lawyer—and there were several in Athena— might take her case.

Perhaps I should try to talk to Natalie Whitaker. She obviously had a point of view about Wil and his history with her late husband. I wondered if she knew the truth of John Earl's feelings for Wil. I also wondered whether Wil, after all this time, would own up to anyone besides Melba about what had happened in his youth with his best friend.

Natalie, I felt sure, harbored feelings of resentment against Wil, and not only because of the bizarre circumstances of her husband's death. She might have known about John Earl's feelings for Wil and resented them. I really had no idea, and all this speculation only confused me. I would ask Melba about talking to Natalie. She knew the woman, and perhaps she would agree to set up a meeting with her for the two of us.

I hated spinning my wheels like this. I knew I should leave the whole mess alone. Kanesha would handle the investigation with her accustomed intelligence and thoroughness. She really didn't need me to butt in. I couldn't curb my insatiable curiosity, unfortunately, and I couldn't resist an appeal for help from someone, even if I did suspect that Wil could be behind everything in this horrible case.

My cell phone rang. Melba was calling. "Hi, what's up? A change in plans?"

"Oh my lord, Charlie," Melba said, obviously upset. "Chelsea is dead."

TWENTY-EIGHT

"Dead? How did it happen?" I asked, trying to take it in.

"Suicide, they think. She had an empty bottle of some kind of tranquilizer by her bed. Wil is devastated," Melba replied, her voice a bit stronger now.

"Did she leave a note?" I asked, at once suspicious, given the other happenings.

"Not that I know of. Wil just gave me the barest details when he called," Melba said. "We won't be coming over to your house after all."

"No wonder. I'm really sorry to hear about Chelsea's death. If it is suicide, then I suppose she couldn't face up to what she'd done," I said.

"Poor girl," Melba said. "These people seem cursed. It's like that Agatha Christie book, you know, where they're on an island and people are dying one after the other."

"*And Then There Were None*," I said, automatically supplying the title. "I guess it does seem like that. Three people have died, and two were injured and lucky not to have been killed."

"I don't like it," Melba said. "I read that book when I was about twelve, I guess, and it scared me to death. I've never read it since."

"It scared me, too. I was about the same age," I said. "But I don't think what's going on here will turn out like it did in the book." I reminded Melba of the solution.

"I reckon you're right about that," Melba said. "Still, it's scary."

"I agree with you," I said. "But I do have some good news to share. Sean and Alex are going to Chicago on Friday for a break. They're flying out on Friday and flying back on Tuesday."

"That's great. Some time alone together will be good for them," Melba said.

I bade her goodbye and put my phone aside again. My thoughts went immediately to Chelsea Bremmer. Her death saddened me, whether she committed suicide or whether it was murder. She was too young for her life to come to such an end.

If she had died by someone else's hand, I knew Kanesha would figure it all out. I felt bad for Wil, too. Three people he knew, two of whom had once been close friends, had died. Two others had been assaulted. If Wil hadn't done these things himself, I suspected he might be feeling responsible in some way. All this had probably happened because of him and someone's obsessive hatred. At least, I thought it must be obsessive.

I was convinced that the motivation for all this lay somewhere in the past in Athena. Somewhere in Wil's past. He was the center of all this, so the catalyst had to be his coming back after four decades away.

Forty-odd years ago I was focused on finishing high school and getting ready for entering Athena College. I didn't pay much attention to high school gossip. I didn't care who was dating whom, who made the football or basketball teams, or things like that. I was an academic nerd. I cared more about my grades than what my fellow students might be doing. I wasn't part of the "in crowd," and I frankly hadn't wanted to be. Melba hadn't, either, and that was probably the main reason we remained friends.

Shortly after graduating from Athena College, I married Jackie, and we moved to Texas for graduate school, pursuing our master's degrees in library science. I had lost touch for a while with friends in Athena, like Melba, and my only news about hometown doings came from my parents and my aunt Dottie. Neither my parents nor my aunts cared for scandal, so there was little reason for them to put such things in their letters, or to talk about them during phone calls. Jackie's parents had the same attitude to gossip as mine, so she didn't hear anything, either.

Whatever had happened, though, had been before we graduated high school. I had thought hard about it, but all I could remember was people talking about Wil's disappearance and the reasons for it. He left home to get away from his father's abuse, and everyone agreed he would be heading for California. Nashville was closer, but Wil hadn't been interested in country music.

Melba was more in tune with the local gossip than Jackie and I ever were. People told her things. She was the type of person people confided in, both girls and boys. Whatever had happened over forty years ago hadn't involved Melba, or she would have remembered it by now. The fact that she didn't know was actually disturbing. It must be something pretty bad. Wil knew whatever lay behind this, I was sure, but would he be willing to tell anyone?

With my overly active imagination, I could come up with numerous scenarios that might cause someone to harbor a grudge that had festered over four decades. It had erupted into rage, I was willing to bet, when Wil's imminent return to Athena became public knowledge. Wil would be within easy reach for the first time in over forty years. The temptation had obviously been too much for the grudge-bearer. I couldn't quite understand the level of hate it must take to kill and harm people the way this person had.

I felt at loose ends now that Melba and Wil wouldn't be coming to my house to talk about the case. I pushed thoughts of Chelsea Bremmer's death away. I didn't want to contemplate that until I knew more about it, whether it was truly suicide or another murder.

For once, when I had some time to myself, I didn't feel like reading, though I usually had a number of books waiting in the to-be-read stack. I decided on impulse that I'd head downtown to the square to Helen Louise's bistro. I could tell her the news about Alex and Sean going to Chicago. The fact that the Athenaeum, Athena's only independent bookstore, was also on the square might also have been on my mind. I hadn't dropped in there in at least a week, and I knew that Jordan Thompson, the owner, probably had at least a couple of books set aside for me.

"Come on, Diesel, we're going to visit Helen Louise and Jordan."

Hearing those names, Diesel immediately raised his head and warbled. He slid off the sofa, nudging a sleepy Ramses out of the way. "Come along, boys," I said.

After a stretch and a yawn, Ramses hopped onto the floor and followed Diesel and me to the kitchen. We found Azalea there, and I told her that Diesel and I were going to run a couple of errands. Before we departed, though, I told her about Sean and Alex's getaway trip, and she smiled.

"That's a great idea. They need some time, just the two of them," she said. "Don't worry, I'll look after that little scamp there." She indicated Ramses with a quick nod.

I fetched Diesel's harness and put it on. He was always well behaved, and I knew he wouldn't dart away from me. The leash and harness were simply precautions, and he had adapted to them quickly as a kitten.

There was an open parking slot in front of the bistro, and I pulled the car into it. Diesel climbed out when I opened the back door and waited for me to take hold of the leash. He pushed against the bistro door, making the bell jangle as we entered.

The lunchtime rush hadn't started, and customers occupied only a few tables. Helen Louise looked up from the cash register, and her expression turned from serious to happily welcoming. Some customers had complained in the past about the presence of a cat in the bistro, but Helen Louise never backed down from allowing him. Most people by now knew Diesel and seemed perfectly comfortable having him in the restaurant. We always occupied a corner table near the register, so he was never in close contact with their food and drink.

Helen Louise finished the transaction at the register and thanked the departing couple. She met us at our usual table and gave me a quick kiss. Diesel got a greeting, too, and he meowed in response.

"What a pleasant surprise." Helen Louise took the chair I held for her. "I wasn't expecting you today."

As I took my seat and Diesel sat between us, I replied, "I hadn't actually planned it, but I have some news to share with you."

I told her about my conversation with Sean, and she smiled. "That's great. Now, how about lunch? Or are you planning to go back home for it?"

"Lunch would be great." I smiled. "I'd much rather have some of your French onion soup and a salad."

"Perhaps a bit of chicken breast as well, for Monsieur le Chat?" Helen Louise arched an eyebrow as she glanced down at Diesel.

Even though he didn't know any French, Diesel knew the word *chicken*, and thus he warbled. Helen Louise and I laughed, and my heart felt lighter. This had been the right thing to do.

"You're lucky that French onion soup is on the menu today." Helen Louise rose. "I'll be back soon with everything. Iced tea to drink?"

"Yes, thanks."

Now that Henry was a joint owner of the bistro, Helen Louise had cut back her hours, working mornings until the lunch rush ended around one. Henry had proved capable, not only as a manager but also talented as a chef, rivaling Helen Louise's skill, even though he had not studied at the famed Le Cordon Bleu in Paris as she had.

Helen Louise returned with our food. She had chosen salad and quiche for her own lunch, while one of her assistants took over the cash register. I tackled my salad first in order to let the French onion soup cool. I had more than once burned my tongue on it by sipping it too soon.

"Anything new with the murder investigation?" Helen Louise asked after a few bites of salad.

I set my fork down. "Sadly, yes." I told her about Chelsea Bremmer's death. Her eyes widened in shock.

"How terrible," she said, laying her own fork aside and picking up her glass of tea.

Diesel tapped my thigh to indicate that another bite of chicken breast should be delivered, and I obliged.

"It's awful," I said. "I'm wondering, though, if it was suicide. Given everything else that happened, I'm suspicious."

"I would be, too," Helen Louise said. "I'm sure Kanesha will be considering both possibilities. Surely it wasn't accidental."

"I'm willing to bet it wasn't," I said. "If I see Haskell tonight, I'll try finding out what the official line is. Or maybe Melba will find out from Wil."

"If you find out anything definite, please let me know," Helen Louise said. "That poor young woman. What a tragic ending for her."

After a moment we both resumed eating. Suddenly the sound of a throat being cleared caught our attention.

I looked up to see a shabbily dressed woman standing a few feet away from the table. She looked familiar, but I couldn't remember where I'd seen her before.

About the time I remembered, Helen Louise spoke.

"Hello, Natalie, won't you please join us?"

Natalie Whitaker, the widow of the murder victim.

TWENTY-NINE

||||||||||||||||||||||||||||||||||||||||||||||||||||||||||||||||||||||

I stood quickly and pulled out a chair for Natalie Whitaker.

She demurred. "I don't want to interrupt y'all's lunch," she said in a soft drawl.

"Not at all," I said. "Please sit down. Would you like anything to drink? Have you had lunch?"

"A glass of tea would be nice," she said, casting a glance at Helen Louise.

"Right away." Helen Louise pushed back from the table and went behind the corner to get the requested drink.

"I'm really sorry for your loss, Mrs. Whitaker. I can only imagine how difficult all this has been for you."

"Thank you, Mr. Harris, that's mighty kind of you," she said, her eyes downcast. "John Earl was a trial to me, but he was my husband, and I loved him."

I nodded and resisted the urge to reach out and pat her hand where it rested on the table. I noticed that both her hands were work roughened, and I remembered being told she was the breadwinner for her family. I figured she was only a year or two older than Helen Louise and me, but she looked at least a decade older. Life had not treated her well.

Helen Louise returned with the tea and placed it before Natalie Whitaker. "Are you sure you wouldn't like anything to eat? Perhaps some soup or a slice of quiche?"

"No, really, I'm fine," Mrs. Whitaker responded. "I apologize for coming in here like this. I stopped by your house, Mr. Harris, and Miss Azalea kindly told me where you would be. I hope you don't mind."

"Not at all," I said. "Is there something I can do for you, Mrs. Whitaker?"

She glanced at Helen Louise, then back at me.

"You can talk about it with both of us," I said. "Helen Louise and I are engaged, you know."

A pained expression flitted by, and I realized that had not been the most tactful thing to say to a bereaved widow. She simply nodded, and I choked back an apology that I realized would have added insult to injury.

"I know we all went to school all those years ago, but I was a couple years ahead of y'all," she said. "I didn't know you back then, but I've heard a lot about both of you, especially you, Mr. Harris, and how you and your cat solve murders."

I glanced down at Diesel. He hadn't stirred from his position, not even to approach Natalie Whitaker. Usually he wasn't hesitant to greet strangers, unless they made him nervous. He didn't appear upset, but I think the woman's demeanor and rather downtrodden appearance had put him off.

"Yes, we've had some experience," I said cautiously. "But it's really Chief Deputy Berry who is the investigator."

Natalie Whitaker shrugged. "I hear you're pretty good at figuring things out."

"So what is it you think I can do?" I asked.

"I want you to prove that Wil Threadgill murdered John Earl," she said. "I talked to your son because I heard he was the best lawyer in town." She sniffed. "He told me I didn't really have a case. Said I'd have to wait until the investigation was over." She shook her head. "Not what I wanted to hear, but two other lawyers told me the same thing."

"My son and the other lawyers were right, I'm afraid," I said. "Why do you believe that Wil Threadgill caused your husband's death?"

"Nobody else would want him dead, that's why," she said heatedly. "Wil was always jealous of John Earl and all the talent he had. He was a great singer, and all Wil could do was write a few songs. They never sounded like much to me, but what did I know, just a hick girl from the back of nowhere."

The bitterness in her tone shocked me, and I saw that shock reflected in Helen Louise's expression. Here was someone who obviously hated Wil Threadgill, but how could she have contrived to set up the murder attempt? She wouldn't have had access to the room and the equipment. If she had been spotted there, someone would have reported it to Kanesha by now, surely.

"Both Wil and John Earl were talented," Helen Louise said in a calming tone. "They had different gifts, though."

"Maybe so," Natalie said. "I don't know much about music. Can't carry a tune in a bucket. I don't even sing in the choir at church." She smiled briefly. "Choir director wouldn't have me."

"That's too bad," Helen Louise said.

Natalie Whitaker shrugged. "No big deal. Well, Mr. Harris? Will you do it? I can't pay much, at least not until John Earl's insurance comes through."

"I would never think of taking money from you, Mrs. Whitaker," I said, taken aback. "I'm not a professional, and as such, I certainly can't charge anyone."

"That's a relief," she said. "I'm going to need what little bit of insurance money comes in. Got a leaking roof and a car about to give up the ghost. But you haven't said whether you'd help me."

Helen Louise and I exchanged glances. Mrs. Whitaker came across as utterly pathetic. From the way she dressed and her manner with us, I reckoned she had felt defeated for years, if not decades. Marriage to an unrepentant alcoholic, especially one who couldn't, or wouldn't, hold down a job, was a soul-destroying exercise. I felt immense pity for her, but I couldn't promise her to do what she wanted. I had to try to explain it to her.

"I'm interested in what really happened," I said gently. "At this point I don't know who is behind it all. I believe that Wil was the intended target of the, well, of the incident that killed your husband. Wil was meant to die, not Mr. Whitaker."

"I agree, Natalie," Helen Louise said. "Wil didn't have any idea that John Earl would show up, let alone that John Earl would grab that microphone away from him. John Earl was killed by accident."

"So y'all are telling me it's not Wil's fault." Natalie Whitaker looked disgruntled. "It's always the same. Wil gets everybody on his side, and they just spit on John Earl." She rose suddenly. "Thanks for nothing." She scurried away, leaving us too taken aback to respond.

Helen Louise shook her head. "I think she's still too distraught to listen to reason. Given time, maybe she'll understand."

"Before anyone can get her to see things differently, Kanesha's going to have to figure out who is behind all this," I said. "I think only the truth will get through to her, whatever it is."

Helen Louise frowned. "Charlie, have you considered the possibility that Wil might actually be the one behind all of this?"

I nodded. "I have, though it pains me to do so. Everyone is a suspect, even Wil. I haven't really come up with a convincing motive for him, unless he's the one seeking revenge for something that happened all those years ago. The problem is, neither of us really knew Wil all that well back in high school."

"No, we didn't," Helen Louise said. "Melba knew him better than we did, but so far she hasn't said anything that could explain why Wil would hate any of these people enough to murder and attack them." She shook her head. "I really don't think Wil is the killer."

"I agree, but I think he's the catalyst," I said.

"I think you're right." Helen Louise sighed. "What on earth could he have done that would cause this much hate and rage against him? And against the people around him?"

"I think Wil may be the only person besides the killer who has the answers."

"Do you think he knows who it is?" Helen Louise asked.

"Possibly," I said. "And if he does, why is he shielding that person?"

"Guilt, maybe?" Helen Louise replied.

"That makes as much sense as anything else," I said.

Helen Louise looked at the uneaten portions of our meal. My onion soup had grown cold. "How about I warm that up for you?"

"Thanks. I'd appreciate it." Natalie Whitaker hadn't affected my appetite, though I did feel for her distress.

"Back in a minute or two." Helen Louise picked up the bowl and disappeared into the kitchen. Diesel took this opportunity to let me know that he could use more chicken breast before he expired right there in the restaurant. Luckily for my malnourished cat, there were several bits of the chicken left, and I gave him one.

Helen Louise soon returned with my soup, and we resumed our meal. After I had consumed about half the contents of the bowl, I set my spoon aside. "I really want to talk to Wil," I said. "But with this latest development I don't know if I'll be able to get to him."

"I imagine Kanesha won't want you anywhere near him right now," Helen Louise said.

"I'm sure she won't," I replied. "But I've got that itchy feeling, the one that bugs me until I can scratch it and make it go away. I think talking to Wil is the only thing that will get rid of it. I'm sure he knows something that will make all this make sense, if I can only get it out of him."

Helen Louise shot me a look of sympathy. "I know, my love. I've seen you go through this before. But this time you may have to stay itchy and let Kanesha do her job. Wil at this point might not want to talk to anyone."

"True," I said, picking up my spoon again. "But I'm going to talk to Melba and see if she has any suggestions. Maybe he is still communicating with her. Kanesha can't stop him from calling people, surely."

"If she told *me* not to talk to people, I'd certainly do what she said," Helen Louise replied. "I'd never want to get on her bad side."

"I've been there," I said wryly, "and while it wasn't fun, I got through it."

"Don't forget you've got a wedding to go to in February," Helen Louise said with a mischievous grin. "I'm expecting you to show up, so don't do anything rash."

"I promise I won't," I said, though I figured I ought to be crossing my fingers under the table. I always had the best intentions, but sometimes things simply got away from my control.

Diesel chirped to inquire whether there was any chicken left, but I had to disappoint him. I finished my onion soup and the last of my tea, and it was time to move on. Diesel and I went to the register to pay for our lunch, but Helen Louise simply shook her head. "Call me later," she said as I put my wallet away.

"Will do," I said. "Come on, boy."

We left the car parked where it was and walked to the bookstore, only a minute or so away from the bistro. Jordan Thompson looked up as we entered, and she gave us a broad smile. Diesel pulled at the leash to get to her so she could tell him how handsome he was, and also to get a couple of treats.

I shook my head at Jordan and mouthed the words *no treats*, and she nodded in understanding. She made a great fuss over Diesel, and if he was truly disappointed over the lack of treats, he didn't show it.

"I have a few things set aside for you, Charlie." Jordan pulled a stack of five books from behind the counter and set them down for me to examine.

Two were by authors new to me, and the other three were old favorites. I had several large stacks of unread books at home, but I couldn't pass these up.

"I'll take them," I said. "You do know that my family call you my dealer, don't you, with books being my drug of choice."

"I've been called worse," Jordan said with a huge smile. "I get that from quite a few customers, actually. I love my bibliophiles, otherwise I couldn't stay in business."

"I'm happy to contribute," I said. "Every town should have a thriving independent bookstore."

I handed over my card, and Jordan rang me up. Once the books were bagged, Diesel and I bade Jordan goodbye. Back in the car, I told Diesel we were going to see Melba, and he meowed happily.

The drive to campus took only a few minutes, and after parking, Diesel and I entered the administration building through the back entrance. When we reached Melba's office, I could hear her talking from out in the hallway. She sounded upset.

As we drew closer to her open door, I heard her say, "And they're sure she was murdered?"

THIRTY

Diesel uttered a loud warble, and Melba looked toward her door. She motioned us in while she listened to whoever was on the other end of the call.

"That's really horrible. Does Kanesha have any idea why she was killed?" Melba pointed to a chair, and I took it. Diesel sat by my side.

She must be talking to Wil, I figured, and about Chelsea Bremmer's death. So it wasn't suicide after all. I couldn't say I was surprised. Given everything else that had happened, suicide seemed a bit too coincidental.

Who would have wanted Chelsea dead? My thoughts went immediately to Vance Tolliver. Though he had disclaimed any part in the embezzlement scheme, I hadn't found his denials convincing. He probably had the best motive for getting Chelsea out of the way.

With her dead, he could insist that Chelsea was the sole person behind the embezzlement of Wil's money.

Kanesha would sort him out pretty quickly, I thought. He probably thought he was dealing with a hick cop from Mississippi, but he would underestimate Kanesha to his own detriment. She would nail his hide to the wall if he was guilty of murder.

Did Vance murder the others? John Earl Whitaker had died by accident, with Wil as the actual target. In that case, Tolliver might have wanted Wil out of the way to cover up the embezzlement. It might be more extensive than the accounting firm had realized.

I couldn't see that Tolliver had any reason to attack two members of the band and run Mickey Lindsay down in the street, however. Did that mean there were two murderers? That was possible, but how probable was it? Tolliver might be Chelsea Bremmer's killer, but the other deaths and the two attacks seemed more connected, to my way of thinking. I would love to know what Kanesha's thoughts on these incidents were.

So lost in my own reverie as I was, I hadn't realized Melba had finished her call and was saying my name. "Charlie, back to earth."

"Sorry, I was thinking about what I overheard. It was about Chelsea Bremmer, I gather."

"Yes, it was. They've concluded it was murder," Melba said. "That was Wil I was talking to. He told me they didn't find any clear fingerprints on the pill bottle, only smudged ones. Isn't that stupid?"

"If the murderer tried to wipe the bottle clean, then yes, it's incredibly stupid. It takes away the possibility of suicide," I said. "Who would be that stupid, though?"

"Wil doesn't know, but he suspects his manager," Melba said.

"But how did he get to Chelsea's room in the first place? He's had a guard at his door, and there was one at her door, too."

"They didn't have adjoining rooms, did they?" I asked.

Melba shook her head. "Wil didn't say, but I doubt they did."

I had forgotten about the guards. Kanesha had put both Vance Tolliver and Chelsea Bremmer under house arrest. Melba was right. It would have been difficult, if not impossible, for Tolliver to get to the other room, and with Chelsea present, how could he have done all he would have needed to do?

"I don't think Wil has many of the details," Melba said. "Kanesha wouldn't confide everything to him, because that's not how she works. I think all she told him is that she's pretty sure it was murder, and not suicide."

"I'm sure they'll be going over every person who went into her room from the time she was put there under guard until her body was discovered," I said. "Somebody managed to get in there, unless Chelsea tried to wipe the bottle herself after she took the pills. But why would she do that? Did they find a note of any kind?"

Melba frowned. "Wil didn't say, but surely he would have mentioned it if Kanesha had told him."

"Maybe we'll hear more about it later," I said. "Look, the reason I came by is to talk to you about Wil."

"What about Wil?" Melba asked, her eyes narrowing.

"I'd really like to talk to him again," I said. "I think he's the only one who can shed light on the person who hates him enough to be doing all this." Then I told her about Natalie Whitaker's surprise visit to the bistro during lunch. "She seems determined to blame Wil for her husband's death."

"That's ridiculous," Melba said, "when Wil was the one who was supposed to get electrocuted. I think she's gone off her rocker over John Earl's death." She sighed. "Knowing Wil, however, I'd be willing to bet he'll fork over a lot of money to her anyway, whether she takes him to court or not."

"I think you're probably right." I wondered privately whether Wil would do it out of generosity or out of feelings of guilt from his abandonment of his friends all those years ago. What would John Earl Whitaker's life have been like if Wil hadn't gone away? Based on what Jimmy Tatum had told us, I suspected that John Earl's feelings for Wil might have been more than simple friendship or brotherly love.

"Is Wil able to leave the hotel?" I asked.

"He is, but mostly to go back and forth between the campus and the hotel," Melba said.

"Do you think I could get in to see him at the hotel?"

"I don't see why not," Melba said. "I don't think Kanesha is keeping him isolated when he's at the hotel. There's a guard on the door, but surely he wouldn't stop you from entering Wil's room."

"I'll give it a try," I said. "I'll tell the guard Wil wants to see Diesel and me. Can you ask Wil if it's okay, and if it is, what time should I come?"

"Sure," Melba said. "I'll text him and let you know what he says."

I rose from the chair. "Then I guess we'll head back home."

Melba gave Diesel her usual affectionate goodbye, and then my cat and I headed for the car.

We entered an empty kitchen, and I headed immediately to the den with my stack of books. Diesel turned up a couple of minutes later, Ramses chasing after him. Ramses, no matter where he was in the house, always seemed to know when Diesel and I returned. He leaped into my lap the moment I sat in the recliner, and I had to give him head scratches and belly rubs for several minutes before he would finally settle down. I picked up my book when he did. Diesel had already fallen asleep on the sofa.

I settled in for some quiet time. I was thoroughly immersed in my book, one of the new ones I picked up earlier from Jordan, a new book by Anne Lee Huber, when my cell phone buzzed at me. That meant a text message. I laid my book aside and eagerly pulled out my phone.

As I anticipated, the message was from Melba. I was disappointed, though, when I read it. Wil couldn't meet with me today. He would be busy the rest of the afternoon, plus he had an evening session with some of the senior music students. By the time he finished, he'd be too tired to talk to anyone.

The good news was that he invited me to have breakfast with him in his suite tomorrow morning at seven. I texted Melba back immediately to tell her that I was happy to accept Wil's invitation. She would convey that to him.

"We have a date for breakfast tomorrow morning, Diesel," I said.

Diesel yawned and looked vaguely interested before putting his head back down and going back to sleep. I had to grin. If ever I were reincarnated, I hoped I would come back as someone's pampered and indulged house cat. What a life my boys had.

I settled once again to reading and was mostly able to focus on the book. When thoughts of the murders tried to intrude, I pushed them away, but eventually they were too persistent for me to ignore. I sighed and put my book away.

I picked up my phone and texted Stewart. If he was in the house, I wanted to talk to him. Maybe Haskell had told him something. Usually when Haskell did talk to Stewart about the investigations he was working on, he told him things that were okay to share with me. If I was somehow involved, that is. Any other investigations Stewart wasn't allowed to tell me about.

My luck, he was home. Stewart was about to let Dante out in the backyard for a run. I said I would meet him on the screened-in back porch. I left Diesel and Ramses in the den. I actually had to shut the door to keep Ramses from following me. I heard plaintive mewing and a few scratches at the door as I walked away down the hall.

I made it to the porch about thirty seconds before Stewart came in with the poodle. Dante pranced around me, happy to see me, and I picked him up and hugged him. I told him what a handsome boy he was, and he licked my face. Laughing, I put him down, and Stewart let him out in the backyard.

We took chairs side by side, facing out into the yard, so Stewart could keep an eye on Dante.

"So what's up, Charlie?" Stewart asked, one eyebrow arched. "Are you fishing for information?"

"You know I always appreciate your company," I said with a grin.

"Of course," Stewart said. "I am by far your wittiest and most entertaining friend. But somehow I suspect it's not my wit you're wanting. Feel free to prove me wrong, however."

I had to laugh. Stewart could talk piffle very well. He reminded me of Lord Peter Wimsey trying to cheer up Harriet Vane when he met with her in prison.

"Your wit is always welcome," I said. "But you're right. I'm actually fishing for information. Has Haskell told you anything about the investigation into the murders connected with Wil Threadgill? That you're allowed to share with me, that is."

Stewart threw back his head and laughed. "You are a hoot. You know Kanesha probably has nightmares about you getting involved in any of her investigations."

"I seriously doubt any such thing," I said. "Nightmares are probably terrified of her."

Stewart laughed again. "I'll have to share that with Haskell."

"Be my guest," I said. "Now, how about answering my question?"

"All right." Stewart gave a heavy, theatrical sigh. "I'll spill all the beans I have, but there aren't many. I'm not sure what it is you want to know, so why don't you ask me questions. That'll make it easier."

"If that's what it takes." It was my turn with the theatrical sigh. "Has he said anything to you about Chelsea Bremmer's death?"

Stewart looked startled. "No, he hasn't. I haven't talked to him since early this morning. He left around five because Kanesha called him. What happened?"

I told him what I knew about the woman's death. "It first looked like suicide, though apparently there was no note. Then they discovered that the tranquilizer bottle had no prints on it."

"Not even hers?"

"No, not even hers," I said.

"That's suspicious," Stewart said. "Do you think she was killed by the same person as the others?"

"It's possible," I said. "I think it's also possible she was killed by Wil's manager, Vance Tolliver, because of the alleged embezzlement. Do you know about that?"

Stewart nodded.

"Both of them were under house arrest with guards at their doors, so I can't figure out how Tolliver could have left his room without anyone knowing, much less get into her room. She would surely have kicked up a fuss if he managed to get in there."

"I agree. I don't see how he could have done it," Stewart said. "This is like one of those locked-room puzzle mysteries you've told me about. An impossible crime."

"The other possibility is that she wiped the bottle herself," I said.

"You think she was trying to point a finger to Tolliver?"

"Maybe," I said. "I'll be interested in what Haskell may have to tell you when you see him next."

"I'll see what I can get out of him." Stewart grinned. "I have my ways."

"I'm sure you do," I said in my wryest tone.

"What other questions do you have?" Stewart asked.

"Has Haskell said whether they have any solid leads on any of the attacks? Especially the hit-and-run death of Mickey Lindsay?"

"No, he hasn't. That's so sad about Lindsay. I've heard his grand-daughter sing, and she's really talented." Stewart shook his head. "I know the family must be devastated."

"Has Haskell said anything about what Wil has had to say about all this? I'm pretty sure that the motive behind all this is rooted in the past—with the possible exception of Chelsea Bremmer's death— and I believe Wil has the key to it. If only he will tell us. Something bad must have happened all those years ago before he left, and one of his friends has carried a grudge ever since."

"That makes sense, I suppose," Stewart said. "But it sounds to me like whoever it is must be off his rocker. Or hers. Carrying that burden for forty years, it's just a little bit insane, don't you think?"

"Depends on your point of view, I guess. If Wil did something truly awful, I can see whatever happened has been festering all this time. With Wil finally back in reach, the wound broke open, and the killer decided to strike."

"Getting back to your question," Stewart said. "Haskell let on that Wil isn't being all that forthcoming. He apparently keeps insisting that he has no idea what's behind all this."

"Then he's lying."

THIRTY-ONE

||||||||||||||||||||||||||||||||||||||||||||||||||||||||||||||||||||

"I know it's a harsh thing to say about Wil," I said. "Especially when I barely know the man, but I'm right. I know I am. He's hiding something, or trying to shield someone. Maybe it's himself. Maybe he doesn't want to acknowledge responsibility."

"That makes a lot of sense," Stewart said. "I'm sure Kanesha has put the pressure on him, but so far he hasn't yielded. Unless something happened today. Maybe this Chelsea Bremmer's death will be the catalyst to his confessing whatever he knows."

"It ought to be." I realized I had started to dislike Wil Threadgill. "As long as he holds out, the killer may continue to strike. How many deaths does he want on his conscience?"

"Good question. Maybe you should put it to him," Stewart said.

"I plan to," I said. "I'm having breakfast with him tomorrow morning." A memory surfaced. "I have another meeting tomorrow as well. With a woman named Donna Boudreaux. She claims to have important information about all this. Do you know who she is?"

"Donna Boudreaux?" Stewart shook his head. "I don't think so."

"Melba didn't recognize the name, either," I said. "I'm a little suspicious about Miss Boudreaux because of that. What can she possibly know?"

"Maybe that's not her real name," Stewart said. "Maybe she doesn't want you to know who she really is."

I felt like an idiot and said so to Stewart. "I never even considered that. I wonder if you're right."

"Don't sound so surprised," Stewart said. "I'm useful, not merely decorative."

I laughed. "You're both extremely useful and terribly decorative."

"Terribly?" Stewart asked. "Well, really."

"You know what I mean," I said in mock exasperation.

He grinned and then glanced out into the yard. "Looks like I'd better go out there and pick up Dante's little presents." He waggled a plastic bag that he drew from his pocket. "Back in a minute." He went into the yard to scoop up the poop. He and Dante returned moments later. Dante danced around as if he hadn't seen me a few minutes ago, and I picked him up once again to give him the attention he wanted.

"Come along, Dante," Stewart said. "I need to deposit your poopies in the garbage."

I released the dog, and he hopped down to follow Stewart from the porch. I got up and went along behind them. I stopped in the kitchen, however, while Stewart went into the utility room to use the garbage can there.

They came back, and Stewart went to the sink to wash his hands. "I have no idea what time Haskell will get home tonight, but if it's after you've gone to bed, I'll talk to him about the case. He might have some new tidbits to tell me, and I'll give them to you tomorrow."

"Thanks, I appreciate it," I said. "I'm going to let the cats out of the den. I'll see you later."

Ramses was indignant when I released him, and I heard loud complaints from him. Diesel had a few to share as well. "Now, both of you stop that. It couldn't have been that bad."

Ramses meowed loudly. Diesel chirped in a minatory manner.

I figured Diesel had probably tried to sleep while Ramses was making noise and scratching at the door. Diesel stalked away from both of us toward the kitchen. Ramses ran after him when he realized Diesel was leaving him behind.

Stewart and Dante were no longer in the kitchen, so I presumed they had gone back up to their third-floor suite. I grabbed a can of diet drink from the fridge and went back to the den to read. Ramses and Diesel appeared a few minutes later and assumed their previous positions. I held my book up over Ramses while he got himself situated in my lap. He must have been tired because he settled after only four gyrations around.

The boys and I remained in the den until nearly five-thirty. Azalea came to the door to inform me that supper was ready. "I'll be there in a couple of minutes." I brandished my book. "I have about three pages left."

Azalea nodded and turned away, but I called her back because I remembered to tell her I wouldn't be having breakfast at home in the morning.

"That's fine," she said. "Supper is on the stove. I'll see you to-morrow."

"Thanks. Have a good evening." I turned back to the book and read the remaining few pages. I put it aside with great satisfaction. I gently urged Ramses off my lap, and the three of us went to the kitchen where my meal awaited me, with probably a few treats for the cats.

After a briefly restless night, I woke the next morning eager to meet Wil Threadgill in his suite at the hotel. I hoped there would be no problems gaining access. Surely Kanesha Berry had not given any orders to keep me from talking to Wil. After showering, shaving, and getting dressed, I headed down to the kitchen for coffee. The usual scents of frying bacon and baking biscuits were absent, and Ramses and Diesel glared at me accusingly. Or at least, that was how it seemed. They missed the scent of bacon, too.

"Sorry, boys," I said. "Azalea hasn't cooked breakfast. Maybe she'll give you some treats later." I poured myself a mug of coffee, added the cream and sugar, and took my place at the table. While I drank my coffee, I checked my email on my phone but found noth-ing of interest.

At six-forty-five I was ready to leave the house with Diesel. We drove to the hotel and parked. I had already put Diesel in his har-ness, and we went into the hotel and up to Wil's suite. There was a young police officer on duty outside the door. I greeted him, and he acknowledged me. He made no move to stop me, or even ask my name, when I knocked on the door. Moments later Wil opened it and beckoned us inside.

"Good morning, Charlie, Diesel," Wil said. "I hope you'll approve my selection of items for your breakfast." He smiled. "I figured you would be happy with a fairly traditional breakfast."

"That will be fine," I said as we followed him to the table.

"Just help yourself." Wil poured coffee for me while I removed covers from the dishes on the table. I helped myself to scrambled eggs, bacon, buttered grits, and biscuits. Breakfast was my favorite meal.

Diesel meowed loudly, having scented the bacon. Wil laughed. "He's hungry, too."

"He loves bacon," I said. "As much as I do, if not more."

"There's plenty for all three of us." Wil fixed his own plate, but I noticed his quantities of the various foods were smaller than mine. I decided not to think about that and enjoy my meal.

"How are you doing?" I asked. "This latest death must have been particularly awful for you."

"Chelsea, you mean?" Wil said. "It was a great shock. Chelsea was emotionally high-strung, and suicide wouldn't have surprised me, frankly. But murder is entirely different, if they determine that's what it was." He shook his head.

"I can't figure out how it was done, if it was murder. Suicide seems more likely to me," I said between bites of scrambled eggs and bacon. "How someone got into her room, past the guard. Surely if someone had gone in there, the guard would know."

"You're right. As far as I know, none of us went in her room,"

Wil said. "Frankly, I think she really did commit suicide. I think she tried to wipe her fingerprints off the bottle to confuse everyone." He shrugged. "Maybe she wanted us to think she was murdered. I doubt she was in her right mind at the time."

"Who was she hoping might get accused of her murder?" I asked.

"Vance, no doubt," Wil said. "They had a screaming match after you left, and it took Deputy Berry and two police officers to drag them apart."

"That's awful," I said. "I'm glad we weren't present. Diesel doesn't like it when that kind of thing happens. He's too sensitive." I gave the cat a couple of small bites of bacon.

"I didn't like it, either," Wil said. "I can't handle that level of crazy emotion. I'm a hermit most of the time, and I don't like spending time around a lot of people, especially when they're worked up like that."

"I don't, either." I decided it was time to start asking my questions. I prefaced them by saying, "The reason I wanted to see you again, Wil, is to ask you some questions."

Wil's eyebrows rose as he regarded me, looking wary. "What questions? And why?"

"Leaving the question of Chelsea's death aside," I said, "I think everything else is linked to something in the past. Your past here. I can't explain those threatening letters you got in Los Angeles, warning you not to come here. The police will have to figure that out." I paused for a sip of coffee. "Everything else points to your past here and what happened before you left Athena."

"I've told you what happened," Wil said with a frown. "I don't know what else there is to say."

"I've heard from someone who knew you well back then," I said, "that John Earl Whitaker was more than a friend, in some ways."

Wil looked taken aback. "What do you mean, more than a friend?"

"That you and he were lovers," I said bluntly.

Wil laughed. "I'll bet Jimmy Tatum told you that."

"He did, actually," I said. "Is there any truth to it?"

"Jimmy was always jealous because John Earl and I were best friends," Wil said. "I'll admit that John Earl and I would fool around a little, but only when were stoned or drunk off our behinds. There was nothing more to it than that."

"It didn't mean anything to you?"

"No, just experimentation," Wil said. "It convinced me that I wasn't interested in guys sexually, if that's what you want to know."

"What if John Earl felt differently?" I asked.

"You mean what if he was in love with me?" Wil sounded incredulous. Then his expression changed, and he looked thoughtful. After a moment, he said, "I never really thought about it before, but there could be something in that."

"What have you remembered?" I asked.

Wil shifted uneasily in his chair and had some coffee before he responded. "John Earl would give me notes, occasionally. And he wrote me a couple of letters after I left Athena that were, well, kind of odd. Talked about how much he missed me. He didn't come right out and say he loved me, but he let me know he felt abandoned."

"Maybe that was his way of telling you he loved you," I said, feeling bad for the late John Earl Whitaker.

"Then why did he marry Natalie? She was pregnant, sure, but if he was into guys, he shouldn't have married her," Wil said.

"It wasn't so simple back then," I said. "We don't know for sure that he was gay, but it's not unusual for a gay man to marry a woman in order to show everyone around him that he's straight."

"Can't argue that," Wil said. "You've certainly given me something to think about. Maybe I ought to talk to Jimmy."

"And Doug Rinehart," I said. "He might know more about it. He wasn't willing to talk about it to me and Melba, though."

"So Melba's in on all this?" Wil asked.

I nodded. "We, along with Helen Louise, had dinner with both Jimmy and Doug. We wanted to find out what they might know about anyone who has a grudge against you."

Wil laughed, a bitter sound. "Heck, I can tell you that. Natalie hates my guts. I've heard she's even trying to sue me for wrongful death because John Earl got electrocuted instead of me."

"She is," I said. "She even approached Helen Louise and me yesterday during lunch at the bistro to talk to me about it. I tried to tell her it wasn't your fault and that she would have to wait for the outcome of the investigation. She really didn't want to hear it."

"I'm sure she didn't," Wil said. "I'm sure she's blamed me for everything that went wrong in her life. I don't think she realized how much John Earl used to drink in high school. Back then he made an effort to not let it show, but later on it got out of control." He shrugged. "I don't think my staying here would have changed that."

"Have you seen or spoken to Natalie since you've been back?" I pinched off more bacon for my impatient cat and had a couple of bites myself.

"No, I haven't," Wil said. "I did catch a glimpse of her that night, but I didn't approach her. I'm not sure if she saw me, though."

"I don't know," I said.

"I really don't want to talk to her," Wil said. "I don't think there's anything I could say to make her feel better. I hate what happened to John Earl, but I can't change things. I'm sure she'd rather I was the one who got electrocuted."

"Here's a question for you. Would Natalie have been able to set it up?" I asked. "I'm not sure how she could have gotten into that room to do it, but if she could have gained access, well, did she have the knowledge to hook up that live wire?"

"Yes," Wil said. "She went around with the band and helped set things up. Her dad was an electrician."

THIRTY-TWO

||||||||||||||||||||||||||||||||||||||||||||||||||||||||||||||

"I did find out something interesting about Natalie Whitaker," I told
Melba in response to her query about breakfast with Wil. "Did you
know her father was an electrician?"

Melba shrugged. "Not that I remember." Her eyes widened. "Oh
my lord. You think Natalie knew how to rig up that microphone
stand to electrocute Wil."

"I think it's entirely possible." I glanced at my watch. I had maybe
ten minutes before I needed to be upstairs in order to meet Donna
Boudreaux. I was anxious to find out who she was and whether she
really had anything worthwhile to tell me.

"She worked at the Farrington House off and on for quite a few
years," Melba said. "But I think it's a while since she did. I don't see
how she could have gotten into that room to do it."

"I don't, either," I said. "But I texted Kanesha to tell her about

Natalie's father, in case she didn't know. She hasn't responded. She will have to be the one to find out whether Natalie can be placed at the scene during the time that the mic was actually rigged. She'll also be the one who has to find proof that Natalie has the knowledge and the skills to do it."

"I guess you're right," Melba said. "I've thought all along that Natalie was the most likely person to want revenge on Wil. She used to talk about Wil ruining John Earl's life. And hers, to some extent, because of John Earl becoming a hard-core drunk."

"I don't think it's really fair to blame Wil," I said. "Nobody forced John Earl to drink like that."

"I agree," Melba said. "It's not fair, but that doesn't stop people from doing it." She paused a moment. "You know, I think John Earl had an uncle, his daddy's baby brother, who was an alcoholic."

"That's sad," I said. "What happened to the uncle?"

"He got religion and gave up drinking," Melba said. "Moved to Tennessee and got involved with one of those crazy snake-handling cults. Got bit and died." She shook her head. "Talk about lunatics."

"That's horrible. I don't know what those people think they're doing." I checked my watch again. "I'd better get upstairs, because my visitor should be here soon. Would you mind keeping Diesel down here with you?"

"Not at all," Melba said. "Come here, sweet boy, and sit by Auntie Melba." Diesel warbled and approached her chair. He went under her desk and sprawled on the carpet. "He'll be fine here."

"Thanks. Be good, Diesel."

Upstairs I unlocked my office and turned on the lights. I sat at my desk and awakened my computer. I was checking emails when I heard a tap at the door. I looked up to see a tall woman with the blackest hair I'd ever seen standing there. She appeared to be in her early forties, and she was dressed neatly in dark slacks, dark jacket, and white blouse.

"Good morning. I'm Donna Boudreaux," she said.

I was already on my feet and moving around the desk. She walked toward me and offered a hand. We shook, and I indicated the chair in front of my desk. "Please, take a seat."

As she did so, I went back to my own chair. I studied her as covertly as I could, now that she was closer and under the overhead lights. Her makeup was heavy, which surprised me for some reason. I supposed it was because of her conservative attire. She wore heavy blue eye shadow, and her mascara was thick. Her lipstick exaggerated the size of her lips, making them look nearly cartoonish.

"Thank you for agreeing to talk with me," Miss Boudreaux said. "I'm sure you're a busy man." She flashed a quick smile.

"On occasion I am," I said. "But I certainly have time to talk to you about the recent murders and the attacks on Wil Threadgill and his bandmates."

"Yes, well, I do have a few things to tell you," Miss Boudreaux said. "I'm sure you've been wondering how a stranger would know anything about the situation."

"Frankly, yes," I said. "Before we go any further, let me ask you whether you'd like something to drink. I have some bottled water, or I could get you some coffee from the lounge downstairs."

"No, thank you, I'm fine." She indicated the large purse in her lap. "I always carry a bottle of water with me."

I nodded. "In that case, can you tell me your connection with the people involved in all this?"

"Certainly. I've known the Whitaker family since I was a child. Shaylene Whitaker and I were almost like twins, you might say." She gave me a coy smile. "We were in and out of each other's houses all the time." Her expression grew serious. "It wasn't long before we played at my house most of the time. Mr. Whitaker was a heavy drinker, and he wasn't very nice when he was drunk."

"That's really sad," I said. "Such a waste."

"He used to hit Shaylene," Miss Boudreaux said, the color rising in her face. "He was horrible. I think he hit Mrs. Whitaker, too, but she was careful to hide it."

"That's really bad," I said. "This is the first time I've heard that he was an abuser."

"Well, you can take it from me that he was." Miss Boudreaux's mouth set in a hard line. "Shaylene tried to run away from home all the time, but Mrs. Whitaker always dragged her back." She sounded bitter. "When she was sixteen, she did run away. I was the only person who knew where she'd gone."

"It's good that she had a friend she could trust," I said.

Miss Boudreaux nodded. "If she hadn't gotten out of that house, who knows what might have happened? He had beaten her pretty badly a couple of weeks before she disappeared. I begged her to go to the hospital, but she refused." She wiped away a sudden tear. "She said it was because of her mother, but frankly I didn't think she owed her mother any loyalty. Natalie, Mrs. Whitaker, never stood up to her bastard of a husband to protect Shaylene."

I felt sick at my stomach. John Earl Whitaker deserved to rot in hell. I had no pity for men who abused women or children. There was no excuse whatsoever for that kind of behavior.

Miss Boudreaux must have read my thoughts from my expression. "I think you understand why Shaylene came to hate both her parents. And I believe Natalie came to hate her husband, too."

"I can see that," I said. "I'm sorry they had such a troubled family life. I wish they could all have gotten help."

"I believe Natalie tried a time or two," Miss Boudreaux said. "She went to her priest, asking for help, but he was worse than useless. He *counseled* Mr. Whitaker, whatever that meant, but it never did any good. After a while, I think Natalie gave up on going to her church for help. The priest insisted she couldn't divorce her husband. I hold the priest responsible for what happened to poor Shaylene as much as I do her parents."

I could understand her anger. The church should be a refuge from the pain and vicissitudes of life, not a rejection of comfort and succor. There should have been a better solution to the problem, and frankly that divorce should have taken place.

"It was a horrible situation, and I agree that the priest should have done more," I said. "What I'm not sure I understand is the relevance to the murders and the attacks."

"I heard Natalie more than once talking to Mr. Whitaker about Wil Threadgill," Miss Boudreaux replied. "Only she always called him Fred. Anyway, she would yell at Mr. Whitaker about mooning over Fred. She would say he ought to've gone to California if Fred meant that much to him. That's when he would hit her, because he stayed drunk most of the time."

"You believe Natalie Whitaker was blaming Wil Threadgill for her husband's behavior?"

"I do," Miss Boudreaux said. "From what I heard—and Shaylene heard it, too, when they would argue about it—was that Fred owed them money and had never repaid it. I think Mr. Whitaker had stolen it from Natalie's father, or something like that, to give it to Fred. Anyway, it caused a big stink with the father-in-law, and he refused to ever help them again. Shaylene never saw her grandparents after that."

"That's really sad," I said. "I'm horrified to hear that Wil borrowed money and never repaid it."

Miss Boudreaux laughed, but with no mirth in the sound. "And he's worth millions, they say. He could have paid it back, with interest, but he wouldn't have anything to do with his old friends. Shaylene blamed him as much as she did her parents."

"Do you think it was Natalie Whitaker who tried to kill Wil by rigging the microphone to electrocute him?" I asked.

She nodded vigorously. "I'm sure she did. She used to help her father. She was an only child, and he treated her like a son, getting her involved in his business. She would know how to do it."

"Do you still keep in touch with Shaylene Whitaker?" I asked. "Has she ever come back to Athena?"

"Haven't talked to her in years. I'm not even sure where she is now," Miss Boudreaux said, sounding uninterested in her friend's whereabouts.

That struck me as odd, but I knew there were many reasons that friendships ended. The friendships of childhood didn't always last, and since the two had parted at a young age, it perhaps wasn't surprising that they had eventually lost touch.

The other thing that struck me as odd was why Miss Boudreaux had felt compelled to share all this with me. What was her purpose? Had she come to hate Shaylene's parents almost as much as her friend had? Why did she want to make such a strong case for Mrs. Whitaker as a killer?

"I can see that Natalie Whitaker might hate Wil Threadgill," I said. "Why would she attack other members of his band, including killing one of them in a hit-and-run?"

"She was probably angry that her husband got killed instead of Threadgill," Miss Boudreaux said promptly. "He should have died, and that probably made her even angrier, so she might have decided to get at him that way. Make him feel responsible for all the bad things happening to his friends."

That seemed logical, in a perverse way, I supposed. But was Natalie Whitaker really that twisted? I simply had no idea.

I decided to put the question to Miss Boudreaux, who apparently knew far more about Natalie Whitaker than I did, or ever would. "Do you really think Mrs. Whitaker is capable of that?"

"I do," Miss Boudreaux replied immediately. "I think she has been full of rage for years. I think it happens to people who live with alcoholics for as long as she did. I mean, it must have built up over so many years. Forty, at least." She paused for a beat. "If she'd done the smart thing, for both herself and poor Shaylene, she would have thrown him out and gotten a divorce when Shaylene was a girl.

Instead, she did nothing, and Shaylene suffered horribly. I'm sure Natalie did, too, but she was the adult and the one who could have done something about it. But she didn't."

"And now her husband's death has unleashed her rage. Is that what you think?" I asked.

Miss Boudreaux nodded in a determined fashion. "I do, and I think the police need to know about it, if they don't already."

"Would you be willing to make a statement?"

She looked alarmed at my question. "Oh, no, I couldn't do that. If Natalie ever found out, she might try to kill me. No, I can't, I just can't." Her breathing became shallower, and I could see panic in her expression.

"No one is going to make you do it," I said. "I'm certainly not going to. I can relate your information to the person in charge of the case, Chief Deputy Kanesha Berry. She will probably press me for my source, but all I will tell her is that it came from a friend of the family."

At those words, Miss Boudreaux appeared to relax. "I guess that's all right. I haven't lived in Athena for a long time, and I married, so I doubt they'd find me. I'm going to get in my car and drive straight home." She rose. "Thank you for talking with me, Mr. Harris. I appreciate it, I really do."

"I'm glad I could hear your story," I said. "I wish you well. Drive safely back to wherever your home may be."

"Thank you, I will." She picked up her purse and headed for the door. I stood there and listened to her low heels clicking on the stairs. I waited a moment before I went downstairs. I wondered whether Melba had caught a glimpse of her. If she had, she might have recognized her as a former denizen of Athena.

When I reached the first floor, however, I saw that Melba's door was shut. That wasn't usual, and I wondered why she had closed it. I knocked on the door, and a moment later I heard Melba calling for me to enter.

When I walked into the office, the first person I spotted was Kanesha Berry, and she did not look happy. She looked even less happy when she saw me.

THIRTY-THREE

I started to excuse myself and back out of the room, but Kanesha stopped me.

"Come in. I want to talk to you," she said, and I did as she bade me. "Pull up a chair."

Once I was seated, she said, "I heard you had breakfast with Wil Threadgill this morning. What was the purpose?"

Kanesha cut straight to the bone, of course. She knew I hadn't gone to see Wil merely for a social interaction.

"I wanted to talk to him about the past," I said. "I'm convinced that the root of everything that has happened is the result of some event from around the time he left Athena forty years ago."

"Even the death of Chelsea Bremmer?" Kanesha asked.

Diesel had come to sit by my chair, and I stroked his head. Kanesha's no-nonsense tone was making him uneasy.

"Possibly," I said, "but I think that could be unrelated. I have no idea how it was accomplished. I thought it possible that she really did commit suicide and then tried to wipe the bottle clean because she wanted everyone to think that Vance Tolliver killed her."

"We're considering that possibility," Kanesha said. "We're still working on those smudged prints."

"I knew you would be," I replied.

Kanesha gazed at me blandly. "Did you learn anything from Mr. Threadgill that gave you any insight into how the past may be connected?"

"Not really," I said. "He doesn't seem to want to point the finger at anyone." I paused, thinking back on our conversation. "I'd say the only exception would be Natalie Whitaker. Wil knows she has no love for him. In fact she is blaming him for her husband's death."

Kanesha nodded. "I've heard that from Mrs. Whitaker herself several times already."

Melba had been silent until now. "That's absolutely crazy. How could Wil have known that John Earl would grab the mic before he could himself? Wil was the one who was supposed to die."

"Are you absolutely sure about that?" Kanesha said. "Based on conversations I've had with various persons who knew both Mr. Whitaker and Mr. Threadgill forty years ago, Mr. Whitaker liked being seen as the front man for the group. It would have been totally in character for him to seize the mic like that, they said."

Melba looked deflated. I didn't have the heart to tell her that I had considered this idea myself.

"Why would Wil want to kill John Earl?" Melba said. "And why would he want to kill Mickey Lindsay or anybody else? It doesn't make sense to me."

"That is what we're still trying to figure out," Kanesha said. "Mr. Threadgill had the means and the opportunity to set up the live wire, but so far we haven't been able to prove that he had access to do it at the appropriate time."

"You won't ever be able to prove it," Melba said. "I'd bet my life on it. Natalie's father was an electrician, and she probably knew how to do it herself."

"I appreciate your faith in your friend Wil," Kanesha said. "I have to consider everyone a suspect, however, and that includes Mrs. Whitaker, too. And, yes, I did know about her father. I will continue to look carefully at everyone involved until I have the evidence I need to make an arrest."

"I think we both understand that," I said with a warning glance at Melba. She glared at me and crossed her arms. She had said she wasn't in love with Wil Threadgill, but I thought maybe she didn't realize that her feelings were stronger than simple fondness. I hoped fervently that she wasn't going to be badly hurt by how all this turned out.

Kanesha turned her attention back to me. "Miss Gilley told me that you had a meeting with a woman who claimed to have information pertinent to the murders. Is that true?"

I wished Melba had kept her mouth shut. I knew that I wouldn't be able to keep Miss Boudreaux's name from Kanesha now. I had little choice but to acknowledge the meeting.

"Yes, I did. She left only a few minutes ago," I said.

"Miss Gilley mentioned a name, Boudreaux. Is that correct?" Kanesha asked.

I nodded. "Yes, though I promised her I would not share her name with the police."

"She must be real naïve," Melba said. "How could you not tell Deputy Berry her name, especially if she had information about the case?"

I wasn't going to lose sleep over the violation of this confidence. I regretted that Kanesha knew the name, but since Melba had already spilled the beans, I could argue that I was off the hook now.

"That's as may be," I said. "She did have interesting things to tell me." I proceeded to give them a précis of Miss Boudreaux's information about the Whitaker family. Kanesha's expression never changed from one of intense concentration, but I could see that Melba was shocked to hear about the abuse meted out by John Earl Whitaker on his wife and daughter.

When I concluded, Kanesha asked, "What was your impression of the reason she had come to tell you all this?"

"Frankly, I thought she was pointing the finger at Natalie Whitaker," I said. "I think she could very well be right. She has the knowledge, and she could have rigged that live wire. She could have run down Mickey Lindsay for reasons unknown. I'm not sure how, or why, she would murder Chelsea Bremmer."

"Plus try to kill Wil or Zeb with that broken glass, or stab Jackrabbit Colson in the back," Melba added.

"What do you think?" Kanesha addressed the question to Melba. "I believe you know Mrs. Whitaker better than I do."

Melba sighed. "I hate to say it, but now that I've heard about all the abuse she suffered, I can see where she thought this was a perfect opportunity to get rid of John Earl. Especially since everybody would think that Wil was the actual target. It probably wouldn't have bothered her if she killed Wil instead."

"And she committed the assaults and the other murder, or murders, to keep up that idea. Like a plot from an Agatha Christie novel." I named the book, and Melba nodded.

"Yeah, you're right. It's a lot like that," she said. "Only I think Natalie, if she is the killer, went way overboard."

"She's had forty years for the rage to build," I said, "and perhaps she saw a way out. Killing her husband wasn't enough to get rid of her rage, I guess."

"I have no proof that Mrs. Whitaker did any of this," Kanesha said. "I'll have to take a harder look at her."

"Did the catering staff notice anyone going into the other room?" I asked. "Surely they would have spotted someone going in there."

"If they did, no one has admitted it, but I'm going to question them again," Kanesha said. "One of them must have seen something, but is hiding it for some reason."

"I hope you get them to tell the truth," Melba said. "Though I feel real bad for Natalie. If she'd stopped with John Earl, people might've understood."

"The killer, whoever it is, wasn't satisfied with that one death," Kanesha said. "And I can't ignore the fact that Mr. Threadgill was the intended target all along. There's still a key piece missing, and I have to find it." She looked hard at me. "And I mean I have to find it, not you, Mr. Harris. Or you, Miss Gilley. I want you both to keep out of this. The killer is ruthless and won't think twice about killing either of you if he or she thinks it's necessary. Are we clear on this?"

I felt sick to my stomach. Kanesha was right. I glanced at Melba and could tell that she was also shaken. We had not been thinking in these terms, and I should have known better. I had a tendency to ignore reality sometimes, and this was perhaps the worst incidence of it. I knew what Sean and Laura, not to mention Helen Louise, would be saying to me right about now.

"You're right, of course. I am certainly clear on it," I said. "If you're through with me, I think Diesel and I will go home now." I stood, and Diesel rubbed against my legs.

"We're done." Kanesha also rose. "Miss Gilley, please take to heart what I've said."

"I will," Melba said.

Kanesha preceded Diesel and me out of the office. She headed for the front door without looking back. I watched her leave, then I led Diesel to the back door to the parking lot. I drove the short distance home in thoughtful silence. I was determined to keep my nose clean and not have anything else to do with the case.

We had barely entered the kitchen when I received a text from Melba. She wanted to know Miss Boudreaux's given name. I sighed and texted back that it was Donna, middle initial *S*. She thanked me and said she was going to send it to Kanesha.

I was relieved to hear it and hoped that was the extent of her involvement in all this mess. I was tempted to text and tell her she shouldn't see Wil again until the case was resolved. I figured it wouldn't do any good, knowing her as I did. She believed so strongly in Wil that she wouldn't listen to anyone, despite the fact that at one point she said she had considered he might be guilty.

I wondered if Kanesha knew anything about Donna Boudreaux.

She hadn't given any indication during our meeting that the surname was familiar. The fact that she wanted her given name told me that she meant to run a check on her. I'd give a lot to know what she would find out, but I knew there was no way Kanesha would share any of what she found out with me. Unless it served some purpose of her own. If she thought I might know something, then she would share a tidbit in order to get me to tell her what else I might know. In this case, however, I couldn't think of anything else I knew that she hadn't already learned.

Ramses found Diesel and me in the kitchen. He tried to initiate play with Diesel, but my big boy wasn't interested. He trotted off into the utility room, and Ramses went along with him. I could hear the faint strains of Azalea's voice coming from somewhere upstairs. She liked to sing gospel music while she worked, and she had a beautiful rich contralto voice. I loved hearing her. I remembered how she had sung at Sean and Alex's wedding. What a blessing that had been. Now I thought about my children, set to depart on Friday morning on a getaway to Chicago. I hoped that their time alone together would help bring them even closer.

I decided I would call Sean tomorrow and offer to drive him and Alex to the airport in Memphis, and I would also pick them up upon their return on Tuesday. That way he wouldn't have to worry about leaving his car in the parking lot. Helen Louise might go with me, as well as Diesel. I decided I would ask Sean first, and if he agreed, then I would check with Helen Louise. She might be busy Friday morning, but I hoped she could come with me.

According to my watch and my stomach, it was time for lunch. There should be leftovers in the fridge that I could warm up for a meal. I opened the door and peered inside. I found half of a casserole of chicken, cheese, broccoli, and rice and decided that would do. I scooped half of it onto a plate and stuck it into the microwave. While it heated, I poured a glass of sweet tea. When the microwave beeped, I pulled the plate out, stuck a finger in the center of the casserole I'd dished out and decided it was warm enough. I didn't like food that would scald the inside of my mouth.

I had some cooked, unseasoned chicken to dole out to my boys, and they were delighted with it. While the three of us enjoyed our meal, I found my thoughts focusing on Sean and Alex. I thought it would be good for her to stay home with Rosie rather than go back to work. Alex had been dedicated to her law career, following in the footsteps of her father, who was practically legendary. I thought that she had perhaps put too much pressure on herself to live up to his standards while trying to be a mother as well.

The issue of living in the country was a different matter. I was somewhat less sanguine that Alex would adapt to living in the old Harris homestead. I understood Sean's passion for it. In Houston, we had had only shallow roots, but here in Athena, those roots went back for generations. I believed Sean, and Laura as well, felt the pull of that history. The farmhouse and the land were the physical embodiment of all that history of the Harrises. They provided that connection with the past that helped ground us as a family.

Alex's roots were different, of course, but I hoped that she would come to love the farmhouse. Sean would have to be patient and allow Alex time to experience life in the country. The farmhouse was only a few minutes from town, after all, and I thought that Alex would eventually adjust. I didn't want to think about the possibility that she would hate living there. I wanted to keep the house in the family.

My phone rang while I was scraping my plate over the garbage disposal. I set it aside and picked up the phone.

"Hi, Sean," I said. "How are you?"

"Doing fine, Dad." His tone told me he was in a good mood. "I've booked our flights and a hotel room in Chicago, so we're all set. Our flight leaves at ten-thirty Friday morning. Alex is really looking forward to this, and so am I."

"That's great," I said with matching enthusiasm. "How about letting me and Helen Louise drive you two to the airport? We can pick you up on Tuesday, also. That way you won't have to leave your car at the airport."

"Thanks, Dad," Sean said. "We'll take you up on that. It will give us time to talk."

It certainly would, and Helen Louise and I could share the news about the impending wedding. I wanted Sean to be my best man. Helen Louise was going to ask Laura to be her matron of honor, and Alex of course would have a part in the wedding, too.

"You're welcome. What about Rosie? Is she excited to be staying with her cousin?"

"You know how she loves Charlie."

I chuckled. "She certainly does. I hope he never gets too big to play with her."

"She won't let him," Sean said. "My baby girl is stubborn when she wants something."

"I wonder where she got that from." Sean had been a stubborn child, so it came as no surprise that Rosie was that much like her father.

"You, of course," Sean said, laughing. "And you passed it down to me. And now to my daughter."

I couldn't argue that point.

"We'll pick you and Alex up at eight on Friday morning," I said. "That will give us plenty of time to get to the airport for your flight."

"Sounds good. Thanks. I'd better get back to work now." Sean and I bade each other goodbye, and I set the phone aside and went back to cleaning up from lunch.

THIRTY-FOUR

I took advantage of the quiet house that afternoon. I read in the den for a couple of hours, then decided I would take a nap. Reading had helped keep my brain occupied, and I hadn't thought about the situation surrounding Wil Threadgill at all. I hoped Kanesha was closing in on a solution to the case. The killer had to be stopped before he or she struck again. I couldn't help thinking about Chelsea Bremmer's death. I was leaning more toward the idea that she had committed suicide. I couldn't see how the killer of John Earl Whitaker and Mickey Lindsay could have killed Chelsea as well. Logistically, it would have been really difficult to accomplish. The more I looked at it, the more likely it seemed it had to be suicide.

What a terrible waste, I thought. Then I made an effort to push all thoughts of the investigation aside so that I could relax enough to go to sleep. Diesel lay stretched out beside me on the bed, his head on the pillow, while Ramses nestled against my side. I concentrated on keeping my mind clear, and eventually it worked. I drifted off to sleep.

When I woke I discovered that I had slept for nearly ninety minutes. Ramses was gone, but Diesel still lay beside me. I reached over and rubbed his side. "Time to get up, sleepyhead."

He chirped at me and turned on his back to stretch.

Downstairs we found Ramses in the kitchen with Stewart. I realized with a start that it was dinnertime.

"I was just about to call you," Stewart said, turning away from the stove. "Dinner's ready. Azalea left about ten minutes ago. I'm about to serve myself. Are you ready to eat?"

I sniffed appreciatively. Azalea had baked a ham, and I saw mashed potatoes and green beans amandine on the stove.

"I think I could force myself," I said.

Stewart laughed. "There's also lemon icebox pie for dessert."

My favorite, and Azalea's pies were always amazing.

Over dinner, I brought Stewart up to date on things, starting with Alex and Sean.

"That's great." Stewart sighed. "I wish I could get Haskell away somewhere for a long weekend. He really needs a break."

"Maybe once this murder investigation is finished, he can get away for a few days," I said.

"I may have to knock him over the head, shove him in the trunk, and kidnap him," Stewart said. "But I'm hoping that won't be necessary."

"I hope not, too," I said with a grin. "Any idea where Alissa is?"

Stewart's expression turned enigmatic. "Alissa has a date."

"Really? That's good," I said. "I've been hoping she'd find some friends her age."

"She has. I don't know much about her date, but he's in one of her classes, and she really seems to like him," Stewart said.

"Good," I said. "I just hope he's a nice kid and treats her well."

"Me, too, but knowing Alissa, she won't put up with any shenanigans." He laughed.

Remembering how Alissa had saved my life not that long ago, I had to chuckle. "She can handle him, I'm sure."

Later, after Stewart and I had cleaned up the kitchen, I headed back upstairs with Diesel and Ramses. They'd had enough bites of ham to fill them up, and they went to sleep right away. I changed into my nighttime attire. It was early for bed, but I was determined to relax.

I looked through the books on the bedside nightstand and chose the latest Mma Ramotswe book by Alexander McCall Smith. These mostly gentle tales of mystery and murder were always a tonic for when I was worried. Mma Ramotswe always worked things out, and I wished she were here to help in the current situation. My Huber book was downstairs, and I didn't feel like going down to get it.

I had been reading for over an hour when my cell phone rang. Melba was calling, and I noted that it was after eight p.m. Dusk had fallen outside.

"Charlie, I hate to bother you this late in the day," Melba said after we exchanged greetings. She sounded agitated. "My car is dead as a doornail, and I need to get to the Farrington House right away. Wil called and said he has something he needs to tell me. He says he has to tell me in person. Can you come get me and take me there?"

"Sure," I said. "I just need to throw on some clothes, and I'll head right over."

She thanked me, and I got out of bed to get dressed. I felt a twinge of excitement. Was Wil finally willing to come clean and reveal something important? I hoped so.

Diesel followed me downstairs and out the kitchen door into the garage. I didn't see any reason not to take him. Melba would be glad to see him, and he could help calm her down.

Melba was waiting for us on the sidewalk in front of the administration building. I pulled up to the curb. She opened the door and climbed in. She turned to greet Diesel and rub his head as she talked. "I really appreciate this," she said as she clipped the seat belt into place. "I think I need a new starter for my car. It's been acting funny the last couple of days. I should have taken it to the shop, but I was too busy."

"I'm happy to help you," I said. "I know you'd do the same for me, so forget about it. Did Wil give you any indication what he wants to talk about?"

"No, he didn't," Melba said. "He sounded a little excited, though, so maybe he has information he's held back and wants to tell me about it." She paused. "The odd thing, though, is that he asked me to meet him at the back door into the parking lot."

"That's strange," I said. "Maybe he wants you to take him somewhere. In that case, he might not be happy to see me and Diesel with you."

"Well, he'll have to like it because I needed to get here quickly. I hate those do-it-yourself cabs, and I hate taxis in general."

"I understand," I said. We drove the rest of the way in silence, and when we reached the hotel, I pulled around the back into the parking lot. I stopped next to the door, and Melba got out. "Hang on a minute, okay?" She shut the door.

I glanced at the doorway and could see Wil standing with the door open. He appeared puzzled because Melba had left the car by the passenger side.

They conversed briefly, then both came out to the car. I rolled down my window as Wil bent to talk to me. "Hi, Charlie," he said. "I was hoping Melba would drive me somewhere. Do you have time to do it instead?"

I hesitated a moment, because I didn't think Kanesha would want Wil leaving the hotel without a police guard.

Wil said, "Frankly I'm glad you're with Melba." He glanced into the backseat. "Diesel, too. Having two witnesses will be even better."

Thoroughly intrigued now, I told Wil to join me up front, and Melba climbed in beside Diesel. Once Wil had adjusted the seat and put on his seat belt, I asked him where we were going. The first chance I got, I decided I was going to text Kanesha and tell her where we were. I could already hear the voices of my children and my fiancée in unison telling me I shouldn't do this, and I felt uneasy about it. Curiosity, my besetting sin, urged me on. I would feel better once I texted Kanesha.

"Where are we going?" I asked.

"To the house where I grew up," Wil said. "I still own it, though it's pretty dilapidated from what I hear. It's been empty for about five years now."

"Who was living in it?" Melba asked. "Were you renting it, or were there squatters in it?"

"Squatters," Wil said. "I didn't really care. I paid the back taxes on it and kept on paying." He shrugged. "I'm not sure why. I don't have many good memories of the place, especially after my mother died."

I couldn't think what to say to that, and evidently Melba couldn't, either. Wil covered the awkward pause by giving me directions. He and his family had lived on a small farm in the rural part of the county, about ten miles from town. The sky was dark by the time we arrived at the driveway to the house.

My headlights illuminated a rutted dirt road with trees lining both sides when I turned the car in. "The house is about two hundred yards farther on," Wil said. "I either need to sell this place, or get a crew out here to tame this landscape. The lights should still be on, because I've been paying the utility bills."

"That's good," Melba said. "This is real creepy."

I drove slowly up the road, wincing at each bump and jerk of the car when I hit a rut too large to miss.

When the headlights hit the house, I could see that it looked in pretty bad shape. The wooden steps up the porch sagged, and the porch itself looked ragged. The house, a single-story wood frame farmhouse, had not been painted in years. The headlights picked up the occasional bit of white paint, but the house was mostly dark and weathered.

"Pull around to the back," Wil said in a bland tone. "We can go in through the kitchen."

I thought that was odd, but I did as he suggested. The dirt road did continue around one side of the house, but any parking area behind the house had grown over with grass and weeds a long time ago.

When I halted the car, Wil unbuckled himself and opened the door. "Let me go in and check on the lights before y'all get out of the car."

He climbed the two stairs to the back door gingerly and opened it. He stepped inside, and moments later the lights in the kitchen came on.

"I guess we get out now," I said. "You go ahead. I'll be along in a minute."

Melba didn't argue and did as I bade her. Diesel remained in the backseat. I pulled out my phone and called up my messaging app. I hoped there would be a tower near enough that I could get a signal and get the text to go through. Connections out in the rural areas here were sketchy. I really should have done it before we left Athena, and I probably could have made up an excuse for texting one of my children. For some reason, I didn't want Wil to know that I was contacting Kanesha.

I composed the text, giving Kanesha the directions, and suggested she should come with at least another deputy or two. I hit the send icon and waited. It hesitated for a moment, but then it looked like it went through. I said a quick prayer.

"Okay, boy, let's go in the house and find out what Wil is up to." Diesel climbed into the front seat and crawled down when I was out. I stepped carefully on the stairs. I was heavier than either Wil or Melba, and I didn't want my leg to go through them if they were rotted enough. They held, however, and Diesel followed me into the kitchen.

The room was empty, but I could see that Wil had turned on lights in other parts of the house. I followed the sound of voices and discovered Wil and Melba in the parlor at the front of the house. The furniture—a ratty sofa, two broken-down chairs, and a couple of badly scarred tables—was thick with dust, and I had to suppress the urge to sneeze.

"Sorry it's in such bad shape," Wil said. "I really should have just had the whole thing razed and sold the property years ago. I am going to arrange for that before I go back home."

"I can find you someone reliable to take care of it for you," Melba said. "They'll clean away all the debris, too."

"Thanks. I'd appreciate that," Wil replied as he slipped an arm around Melba's shoulder and hugged her to his side. "You're the best."

Melba didn't look as happy as I thought she would with this physical affection from Wil. Something was bothering her. She pulled away from him and turned to look into his face.

"Okay, Wil, what's really going on here? Why did you want to come to this place at this time of night?"

Wil sighed. "I guess I owe you both that much. I want witnesses when I confront the murderer tonight."

THIRTY-FIVE

||||||||||||||||||||||||||||||||||||||||||||||||||||||||||||||

What had Melba and I gotten ourselves into? I was tempted to grab Melba and get her and Diesel back in the car and drive back to town. Wil could find his own way back.

And, as my mother used to say, if I had the sense God gave a goose, I would have done exactly that.

Before I could say anything, however, Melba said, "Have you known all along who the killer is, Wil?"

He shrugged. "I've been pretty sure, but I couldn't prove it. I talked about it with Deputy Berry. She insisted she would find the proof, but it's taking too long. My people are in danger, and so am I. It's time to get this over with."

"So who's coming here to meet you?" I asked.

"Natalie Whitaker," Wil said simply. "She's hated me since we broke up. It got even worse when she found out that John Earl and I had fooled around a little. She found out my address," he said. "I got several nasty letters from her. I think someone else sent the other letters."

"She didn't get your address from me," Melba said quickly.

"No, I know you wouldn't have given it to her," Wil said. "I did write to John Earl a couple of times, and I figure she found the letters."

"Did she threaten you?" I asked.

"She did. Swore she'd kill me if I ever came near John Earl again," Wil said. "Frankly, I didn't believe her. I threw the letters away. After she sent me the fourth letter—and I never responded to any of them, by the way—she stopped. Or maybe John Earl found out about it and made her stop." He shook his head. "I know I should have told you all this. I did tell Deputy Berry, though."

"Did you ask John Earl to come out to California?" I asked.

Wil nodded. "At first, I did, but it wasn't long before he was married to Natalie. I even suggested they both come, but I guess Natalie wouldn't hear of it. She was pregnant and didn't want to uproot herself. After that I just let it go. I felt bad for John Earl, but it was up to him. In a way, I was glad they didn't come. It was better not to encourage John Earl if he really wanted more from me than I could give him. I hoped he'd get over it."

"I think maybe he never did," Melba said. "I think that's why he drank so much."

"I hate that," Wil said, looking sad. "Looking back, I know I was completely selfish, but I had to get out of this place." He waved an arm around to indicate the room. "This house became like a torture chamber." He shuddered. "The beatings got more and more brutal. I was tempted to kill my father to make him stop, but I decided to get the hell out of Athena instead. I was really screwed up, and I wasn't much good to anyone the way I was. It took years of therapy, once I could finally afford it, to put some of this in perspective." He paused. "I'm not proud of myself, or the way I treated John Earl and Natalie. I had no idea what their lives turned into after I left. I probably should have come back years ago and dealt with it all, but I thought they'd be better off if I just left everything, and everyone, alone."

I couldn't think of any response to that, so I asked a question. "Did your father know you were going to leave?"

"You think I'd tell him?" Wil sounded incredulous. "If I'd even mentioned the possibility, he would have broken my legs and arms so badly I'd never have been able to walk or play music again."

"Oh, Wil, I never realized it was that bad," Melba said as she moved to embrace him.

"I'm so sorry," I said, knowing how inadequate it sounded.

Wil hugged Melba tightly, and when he lifted his head and looked at me, I could see tears. He released Melba and brushed the tears away. Diesel had gone to him and was rubbing against Wil's legs. Wil reached down and scratched Diesel's head, uttering soft words of thanks.

"Sorry," he said. "I didn't realize how much this place would trigger me. And it's not even where most of the beatings occurred."

I decided it was time to change the subject back to the purpose of this visit to his old home.

"What time are you expecting Natalie?" I asked.

"Nine o'clock," Wil replied. "I told her I was tied up until at least eight-thirty."

I checked my watch, and it was almost eight o'clock now. "About an hour from now," I said.

"I don't think we should let Natalie see us with you," Melba said.

"No, you're right. If you stay in the kitchen with the lights out, she shouldn't suspect anything," Wil said.

"How are you going to explain the fact that there's no car in front of the house?" I asked.

"I'll tell her I took a cab and sent it back to town. Asked the driver to come back at ten o'clock," Wil said promptly. "I haven't driven a car in like twenty-five years, and now wouldn't have been the time to start again."

"I guess not," I said. "Do you have any idea how Natalie got into that room to set up the live wire to the microphone?"

"I'm not sure, but I think she probably disguised herself as a hotel employee and slipped in when nobody was watching," Wil said.

"Natalie used to work at the hotel," Melba said slowly. "If any of the catering staff questioned her, she probably would have said she'd been hired on as extra help. They probably wouldn't think anything about it. Catering staff at the hotel come and go all the time."

"That sounds possible," I said. "Do you have any idea why she would run down Mickey Lindsay? I don't understand the need for that."

"He might have seen her that night at the party," Wil said. "From what Deputy Berry told me, Natalie claimed to arrive there a good half hour after John Earl was killed. I spoke only briefly to Mickey, but I think he was there for at least an hour before it happened."

"Yes, we talked to him early on," I said. "Not long after your speech. Melba introduced him to Helen Louise and me."

"She had to be somewhere close by to turn on that live wire remotely," Melba said. "Don't you think so?"

"Probably," Wil said. "I doubt she'd have the money for anything really sophisticated that had a longer range. Deputy Berry will know for sure. I haven't heard what kind of device it was."

"She could probably have gotten into your suite with an ice bucket with the glass slivers in it," Melba said slowly. "She probably didn't know you were sharing the suite with Zeb."

"No, there's no reason she should have," Wil smiled sadly. "Jackrabbit and I look a lot alike. We're about the same height, and from the back, Natalie could easily have mistaken him for me."

"But you don't smoke, and Jackrabbit does," I said slowly. "Natalie probably didn't know that, either. She just assumed he was you."

"How is Jackrabbit doing?" Melba asked.

"He's okay, and healing well," Wil said. "I feel so bad about that. And about Mickey, too."

"How about Chelsea Bremmer?" I asked.

Wil shrugged. "That I don't know. Either Natalie used her hotel employee gig to get in to do it, or else Chelsea did commit suicide and tried to wipe the prints off to cause trouble. She would be spiteful like that, and after you left that day, Charlie, she swore she'd get even with Vance for trying to shift the complete blame on her."

I glanced out one of the front windows. I thought I'd seen a flash of light. "I think we'd better get into the kitchen," I said. "I think somebody is coming up the driveway."

"Let's go," Melba said. "Be careful with her."

"I will. I'm a lot bigger and stronger than she is, plus I have some martial arts skills she probably won't be expecting." He smiled grimly. "Maybe I should have called Deputy Berry, but I'm pretty sure I can handle Natalie."

"I sure hope so," Melba said as the three of us hurried out of the room and into the kitchen. I found the switch and doused the lights. Melba pulled out her phone and turned on the flashlight app. I closed the door to within about an inch and watched while Melba rooted as quietly as possible through the drawers. Diesel sat by my feet and watched Melba, too.

"What are you doing?" I whispered.

"Looking for weapons," she said. "Look, here's an old ice pick and several knives. What do you want?"

I didn't want any one of them, but I understood the potential need for them. I prayed that Natalie didn't have a gun. If she did, we'd be in terrible danger.

I checked my silenced phone to see if Kanesha had responded to my text. I hadn't heard my phone buzz, and I was afraid she hadn't received the message. To my great relief, I saw she had. All the message said was *on the way.*

I texted to tell her not to come up to the house with the lights on or the sirens wailing and whom we expected. She responded almost immediately with *ok.*

"We have backup," I told Melba softly. "Kanesha's on the way."

"That's what you were doing in the car after I came in," Melba whispered back. "Thank the Lord you did that. I'm terrified that Natalie will show up with a gun."

"Me, too," I said.

We each now held rusty, but still functional, butcher knives. I opened the door a couple more inches, and after I did, we could hear Wil speaking in the parlor to someone. When she responded, her voice was low and indistinct, but it had to be Natalie.

If she didn't speak up, Melba and I wouldn't be able to hear what she had to say. I considered the layout of the rooms. There was a hallway from the kitchen to the parlor, and there were a couple of bedrooms on either side of the hallway, as well as a bathroom. I looked straight down the hallway but couldn't see either Wil or Natalie.

I motioned for Melba to come closer. I whispered into her ear that I thought we should get closer. "I'll go first," I said. She nodded but indicated Diesel.

In the tenseness of the moment, I had forgotten about him. I thought about putting him in the car, but that might alert Natalie that someone else was present. I bent down and told him that he had to stay here in the kitchen. He looked at me and started to make a sound, but I tapped his nose, and he fell silent. I had trained him to do that when he was a kitten, and I was never more thankful than tonight that I'd done that. I didn't often have to shush him, but tonight our lives might depend on his being quiet and remaining here in the kitchen.

I moved quietly through the opening and hugged the wall to the left, hoping that I had chosen correctly. I didn't know which side of the parlor Wil and Natalie stood in, but thankfully I chose correctly. I made it to the bedroom on the left without spotting either one of them. Now that I was closer, I could tell by their voices that they were on the left side of the parlor, near the door.

Melba joined me, moving softly. She had pushed the kitchen door almost closed. Diesel remained quiet behind it.

We both stood as close to the doorway into the hall as we dared, the better to hear what Wil and Natalie were saying to each other.

"I really don't understand this," Wil was saying.

"You don't have to," a voice responded.

Before I could marshall my thoughts, Melba hissed in my ear, "That's not Natalie."

THIRTY-SIX

I recognized the voice, however. "That's the woman who came to see me," I said softly. "Donna Boudreaux."

"That's crazy," Melba said. "What's she doing here?"

"I don't know. Listen."

Wil spoke again, sounding frustrated. "Who the hell are you? Where is Natalie?"

"She's at home, sleeping the sleep of the just," Donna Boudreaux said, obviously amused.

"Oh my lord," Melba whispered.

I already had my phone out, texting Kanesha to send an ambulance ASAP to the Whitaker house. I included the fact that Natalie wasn't here but at home, probably drugged. Then I added a single word, *Boudreaux*.

"Then I repeat," Wil said heatedly, "who the hell are you?"

"Just call me Shaylene," Donna Boudreaux said coolly.

I turned a puzzled face to Melba. "Natalie and John Earl's daughter," she whispered.

So Shaylene Whitaker had come to talk to me in the guise of another person named Donna S. Boudreaux.

"What's her full name?" I asked.

"Donna Shaylene Whitaker," Melba responded. She held up a finger as Shaylene spoke again.

"What have you done to your mother?" Wil asked. It sounded to me like he was close to losing his temper.

"Don't worry about her," Shaylene said. "She's going to get everything she deserves."

"What does she deserve?" Wil asked, obviously trying to clamp down on his temper. His words came out in a nonchalant tone.

"She deserves to roast in hell," Shaylene said, sounding a little heated herself for the first time. "My sainted mother put up with John Earl's crap, letting him get drunk and come home and beat the hell out of both of us. He didn't start in on me until I was about eight, but I saw what he did to my mother."

Wil now sounded shaken. "I had no idea John Earl was so abusive."

"He blamed her for you leaving him behind when you ran off to California," Shaylene said. "She did nothing to stop him from beating me, and I hated her after that, too. If she doesn't die tonight, she's going to go to prison for murder. I've done everything I can to make it look like she's guilty."

I heard footsteps suddenly, and Shaylene appeared in the doorway to the hall. Melba and I shrunk back.

"Come on out, I know you're there." She laughed. "You need to learn how to whisper softly. I couldn't hear what you said, but I knew you were there. Come on out now." The last words were uttered in a peremptory tone.

Melba and I exchanged glances. She whispered, "You go get Diesel and get in the car. I'll go and try to talk to her."

"I'm not going to let you go in there without me." I took her hand, and we walked out of the bedroom into the hall. We both still held our weapons.

Shaylene, now sans the heavy makeup she had worn to visit me as Donna Boudreaux, laughed when she saw the butcher knives. "Now, what do you think you're going to do with those?" She pulled a gun from behind her back. It must have been tucked into the jeans she wore.

Over her shoulder I saw Wil tensing for an attack, but she must have sensed the movement behind her. She immediately stepped aside and turned her back against the hallway wall. She could now watch all three of us. She motioned with the gun to get us into the parlor.

I walked slowly toward her, hoping I'd get a chance to knock the gun out of her hand. She anticipated me and stepped back into the parlor and farther back, the gun still on me. "You're not as clever as you think, Mr. Harris."

She pointed the gun at Melba's head. "If either of you makes a move of any kind, I'm going to blow her head off." She sounded as matter-of-fact as if she had just announced that it was dark outside.

I tried to keep my breathing even. I didn't want to let her think she had scared me, though I could hardly keep my legs from trembling. Melba beside me remained deadly calm.

"Drop those knives," Shaylene directed. "Now."

"You must be insane if you think you're going to get away with killing all three of us," Wil said, his tone cool. "Deputy Berry knows where I am, and when she finds your mother dead, she'll know something's wrong."

Shaylene didn't appear to be fazed at all by his words. "I'll be long gone, and she'll never know I was here," she said. "No one will be alive to tell her. As far as anyone knows, I'm still in New Orleans being the widow Boudreaux." She laughed.

I started to speak and tell her that Kanesha Berry knew her name, even if she hadn't connected her with Shaylene Whitaker yet. It wouldn't take Kanesha long to find out, though. Sadly, however, it might be too late to help Melba, Wil, and me out of this situation. Also my poor sweet cat hiding in the kitchen. If the worst did happen, I prayed that someone found him right away and took him home.

I also prayed that Kanesha and her officers would show up right this minute and put an end to this. My nerves were about shot, and I was afraid I might lose my head and do something foolish. I had never wanted to bash someone over the head more than I wanted to do it to Shaylene Whitaker.

I calmed myself by starting to question her. "So it was you who rigged the mic with the live wire, and not your mother, correct?"

She smiled. "Well, you are clever after all. How did you figure that out?"

I ignored the sneering tone. "Now that I can see you without all the cheap, garish makeup, I recognize you. I saw you that night in the reception room. You were one of the catering staff." This was a complete shot in the dark, but I figured I had nothing to lose at this point.

That surprised her. I had obviously scored a hit.

"I remember seeing you, too," Melba said.

"And if they remember that, other people will," Wil said.

"They'll remember Donna Boudreaux who'd only been working there a couple of days," Shaylene said smugly. "They'll never find me and connect me with it."

"Your mother knew, though, didn't she?" I asked.

"Probably, but she knew how much I hated my so-called father," she said. "This was too good an opportunity to pass up to get rid of him. Here was Mr. Big Hollywood Celebrity back in Athena, and I knew if I worked it properly, I could get John Earl to get to the mic first. A little sizzle, and he'd be dead. Everyone would think Mr. Big was the target, and nobody would be the wiser."

"Possibly," I said. "Why did you attack the other people? And why did you run down Mickey Lindsay?"

"He saw me," she said, "and I couldn't take a risk. He knew me when I was a teenager, before I left Athena." She laughed. "The other things were just for fun. Too bad they both survived. I'm only sorry I couldn't get to that stupid woman who offed herself. Saved me the trouble. By then there were too many guards around, so I had to give up."

"Were you planning to kill everybody?" Melba asked.

"Why not?" Shaylene pointed the gun at Wil but kept her eyes on us. "I wanted him to suffer, knowing that it was because of him that people were dying." She looked at Wil. "If you hadn't been such a bastard and run off and left John Earl behind, then my mother and

I could have had a decent life without the abuse and the drunkenness. You have no idea the hell we lived with." She finished on a savage note. "That's why I'm going to enjoy killing these two and making you watch before you get your own bullet."

"Why do you hate me so much?" Wil asked. "So I didn't take John Earl with me. It's not my fault that he became an abusive drunk."

"Because I got so damn sick and tired of him talking about you all the time. He blamed you, so my mother and I did, too. You were the root of it all, and I'm going to kill the root once and for all."

She pointed the gun at Melba's head again, but before she could pull the trigger, the door burst open. Haskell, Kanesha, and another officer ran in, their guns pointed straight at Shaylene.

"Drop it. Now," Kanesha said. "Otherwise we'll take you out in the next two seconds."

Shaylene gaped at them, but I thought I could see her fingers tensing on the trigger. I knocked Melba sideways and dropped on top of her. Wil also dropped, and then we heard a shot. I lay there trembling with Melba under me. I was afraid to move.

"It's okay, you can get up," Kanesha said. "She didn't hit anyone."

When I got to my feet and helped Melba up, we turned to see Shaylene in custody between Haskell and the other officer. Wil got slowly to his feet.

"An ambulance should have arrived by now at Mrs. Whitaker's place," Kanesha said. "I'm waiting to get an update on her condition."

We all looked at Shaylene. The rage and hate in her expression made me want to step backward, but I held my position.

Wil moved closer to her and said gently, "I'm really sorry that you had to endure all that. If I'd only known, I might have been able to help. I'm sorry."

Shaylene gazed at him, her expression unchanged. Then suddenly she laughed. "You know what's so funny about all this? John Earl wasn't even my father. You are."

Haskell and the other deputy took her out on Kanesha's order, and Melba, Wil, and I stared at one another, utterly aghast.

THIRTY-SEVEN

||||||||||||||||||||||||||||||||||||||||||||||||||||||||||||||||||||||||||

"I'll need statements from all of you," Kanesha said. "I think I heard most of it, but I want to have a record of everything. Statements can wait until tomorrow."

"Thank you," we said in a chorus. I went immediately to let Diesel out of the kitchen. Wil sank onto the filthy sofa, his head in his hands. Sobs began to wrack him, and the moment my cat reached the parlor, he went straight to Wil.

Melba lowered herself gently on the sofa and slipped an arm around Wil. I felt devastated for him. To discover that he had a daughter he'd never known in such a brutal fashion was horrible. Shaylene could be lying about that, of course, and I wouldn't have put it past her. Wil had said he always used protection, but it could have failed, I guess.

I wanted to put an arm around him, too, but I left the comforting to Melba and Diesel. Wil turned and laid his head on Melba's shoulder, and Diesel climbed into his lap. Wil wrapped his arms around my big boy and pulled him close.

"I really screwed everything up, didn't I?" Wil's tear-stained face as he looked in Melba's eyes would haunt me for some time, I knew. "Running away made everything worse for the friends I left behind. Because of me, two people are dead, and we all could have been killed."

"Hush, now," Melba said softly. "You can't take on the blame for what Shaylene did."

Wil sobbed again and buried his head in Melba's shoulder.

"I don't believe for a minute she's your daughter, Wil," Melba said. "She said that to hurt you. She's the spitting image of John Earl, so don't you pay any attention to what she said."

I prayed that Melba was right about this.

Kanesha motioned me aside. "What were you all doing here? Didn't you realize you were dealing with a ruthless killer?"

I didn't think there was much point in trying to explain it, but I gave it a shot. "Melba's car died, and she asked me to come pick her up from work and take her to the hotel. Wil wanted to talk to her. When we got to the hotel, Wil was waiting at the back entrance. I don't know how he got away from the guard, but he climbed in the car and said he wanted to have a look around his family home." I paused for a breath. "I didn't find out that he was expecting Natalie to show up until after we were in the house. Melba wanted to stay in case something happened, and I couldn't go off and leave her and Wil to face a killer."

Kanesha shook her head. "You are either the bravest, most loyal person I've ever known, besides my mother, or you're the absolute craziest."

"Tonight I feel like both, and also the luckiest," I said.

Kanesha shocked me by putting a hand on my shoulder and squeezing it. "You're a good man, Charlie Harris." Then she flashed a brief smile. "But don't ever tell anybody I said that." She turned and walked out of the house.

I let Melba and Wil cling to each other and to Diesel a few more minutes, but then I decided it was time we all went home. I was exhausted, mentally and emotionally, and I craved a hot shower, a glass of wine, and my bed, in that order. I thought Melba and Wil could probably do with the same, and I wanted to get Diesel home to the peace and quiet, away from all the drama.

I got them into the car without much fuss, and I drove us as fast as was safe down the rutted drive. I never wanted to see the place again. It ought to be razed, as Wil said he would do.

When we reached the hotel, Wil asked me to pull around back. He didn't want anyone to see him, grimy and red-eyed, and I understood. Melba got out of the car with him, and I was prepared to wait to let her say good night. Instead she stuck her head in my window and told me to go home. "I think Wil is going to need to talk a while before he can get any rest. I'll stay here until he's done."

"You're a good friend," I said.

She gave me a sad, weary smile. "I'll be okay. Don't worry." She turned and walked back to join Wil, and they entered the hotel.

By the time I reached the house it was only ten-fifteen. It seemed like I had been in that old wreck of a house for hours, but that was only stress that made it feel that way.

Diesel scurried away when we reached the kitchen, and I poured myself a glass of wine to drink while I soaked in the tub. There was no sign of Ramses, but I figured he was probably with Stewart and Dante, his second-best friend after Diesel. Stewart would probably realize I was home again and let him out.

Sure enough, I found Ramses on the bed, and Diesel joined him while I was stripping out of my clothes and running the bathwater. I enjoyed a leisurely soak and my wine, and by the time I was done with both, I felt much more relaxed. I had hopes of sleeping well, too. I debated calling Helen Louise to say good night, but I wanted to be face-to-face with her when I told her what had happened tonight.

It wasn't unusual for us to text each other good night, so that was what I did. She texted back a few minutes later, wishing me a good night, along with an endearment. The boys and I settled down in our usual places in the bed. I turned out the light and was asleep before I had time to think about the events of the last few hours.

Friday morning dawned cold and clear. Azalea had breakfast ready for everyone earlier than usual. As I fed bits of bacon to Ramses and Diesel, I told her what had happened the night before. She put her hand on my shoulder and squeezed it, hard. "The Lord was looking after you."

"Yes, He was." I wondered how Wil was doing this morning. He had been hit by a tidal wave of guilt and regret, though he really couldn't be held responsible for what Shaylene had done. Nor could he be responsible for the way John Earl behaved after Wil left for

California. John Earl made his own choices, and Wil didn't force any of them on him. I would pray for Wil and hope that he could find the healing he needed.

I decided to leave Diesel home today. I knew Azalea would keep a close watch over both my boys, and I thanked her for it before I left.

I arrived at Helen Louise's house at a quarter to eight, and she had obviously been watching for my car. She came out of the house, pulled her door firmly shut, and climbed into the car beside me. We exchanged a quick kiss, and I pointed the car toward the neighborhood where Sean and Alex lived. I pulled into their driveway, and I got out. Helen Louise remained in the car.

Sean answered my knock at the door promptly, and he was smiling at me. "We're good to go," he said softly. He turned his head and called out to Alex, "Dad's here, honey. I'll get things loaded, and we'll be ready to go."

Alex called out, "Be there in a couple of minutes."

"She's saying goodbye to Rosie. Laura will be over soon to pick up her and her nanny," Sean said.

I followed him into the house to assist with the luggage, and we soon had it stored in my capacious trunk. Sean went back to wait for Alex, while I stood beside Helen Louise's open window.

Moments later Sean escorted Alex out of the house, making sure the door shut firmly and locked behind them. I stepped forward to kiss Alex on the cheek. "Would you like to ride up front with me?"

She smiled. "Thanks, but I'd rather be with Sean in the backseat."

"As you wish," I said.

I got back in the car while Sean opened the door for Alex. Once she was comfortably inside, he went around to the other door and climbed in. "Ready, Dad, and thanks again for driving us. You, too, Helen Louise."

I slowed down at the stop sign at the end of the street and said softly to Helen Louise, "Shall we tell them?" She knew immediately what I meant, and she smiled.

"Of course," she said. "It's time to share the news."

"What news?" Sean asked. "Don't tell me you two have finally set the date and figured out where you're going to live."

"That's wonderful," Alex said, sounding excited and pleased. "I'm so happy for you."

"So give with the details," Sean said imperatively. "You've kept us all waiting for far too long as it is."

"First Saturday in February," I said. "You'd better be free."

"We will be," Alex said joyfully.

"And I'm going to move in with Charlie," Helen Louise said. "Laura and Frank are going to sell their house and move into mine."

"That's great," Sean said.

"They'll need the room," Alex said.

"We haven't worked out the rest of the details yet," I said. "We'll let you know when we have."

"Message received," Sean said. "Now that that's settled, let's get on to other breaking news. I heard that someone has been arrested for the murders and the attacks on Threadgill's band members."

"Yes, someone has." I didn't want to be pressed for details. I planned to save those for the drive back from Memphis to share with Helen Louise. I didn't want Sean and Alex going off knowing that I had been in such danger last night. They deserved to enjoy their getaway without worrying about my activities. Time enough to face that when they were home again.

"Okay, here's what happened, according to the story I was told," I said.

ACKNOWLEDGMENTS

My fervent thanks to my amazing editor, Michelle Vega, during a very difficult period. The support was unfailing and appreciated deeply. The same goes for the inimitable Nancy Yost, my agent, whose brisk common sense and unwavering support are bedrock to my career. The teams at both Berkley and the Nancy Yost Literary Agency who do their best to promote and support my books are amazing, and I couldn't do it without them.

I apologize to my readers who have had to wait an extra year for this book, but sometimes life throws you curves (look, I made a sports analogy!). It took me a while to regroup and get my creative mojo back, and I hope readers will enjoy this latest effort. Your eager questions about the next book spurred me on. I appreciate you all enormously.